CW00592132

SOMETIME ... NEVER

Daniel moved out of the shadows and, taking Anna by her shoulders, turned her to face the light. 'You're crying,' he said, bewildered.

'What if I am?' said Anna angrily, trying to wipe away her tears.

'Why?'

There seemed little point in not telling him the truth, since quite clearly there could be nothing between them now. 'Because, like you, the other evening meant something special to me.'

They stared at one another in silence. Carefully, gently, he pulled her to him until her head rested on his shoulder, and her arms slid round his waist. In an instant, the raw emotions of the moment before were replaced by a feeling of warm comfort. They relaxed against each other. Anna's body felt soft and inviting against his own and Daniel longed to kiss her, but he knew the moment was wrong.

Sometime . . . Never

DEBORAH FOWLER

SPHERE BOOKS LIMITED

A *Sphere* Book

First published in Great Britain by Sphere Books Ltd 1986
Reprinted 1988
This edition first published by Sphere Books 1994

Copyright © Shepherd's Keep Studio Ltd, 1986

All rights reserved.
No part of this publication may be reproduced,
stored in a retrieval system, or transmitted, in any
form or by any means without the prior
permission in writing of the publisher, nor be
otherwise circulated in any form of binding or
cover other than that in which it is published and
without a similar condition including this
condition being imposed on the subsequent purchaser.

Printed in England by Clays Ltd, St Ives plc

Sphere Books
A Division of
Macdonald & Co (Publishers)
Brettenham House
Lancaster Place
London WC2E 7EN

To Red Hands

With love and thanks
D.C.

Acknowledgements

I have been lucky enough to receive great encouragement and help from a number of people during the writing of this book. I would like to thank

Elliott Cooper
Alan Fowler
Shirley King
Viola Niness
Hilary Ryan

and particularly Adam Norton – for sharing with me his knowledge and experience of the theatre.

Chapter One

The man sat alone in the book-lined study behind an old mahogany desk. He cradled his head in his hands, his shoulders hunched. He was tense, so tense that his very posture seemed to suggest he was waiting for some form of assault.

Gradually, however, his body began to relax and when, at last, he raised his head from his hands, his expression was calm and self-assured. He opened the right-hand drawer of the desk, removed a small revolver and four bullets and placed them, with infinite care, on the blotter in front of him.

Slowly, he began inserting the bullets into the chamber of the gun. His voice, strong now, had a deep, melodious quality. 'This year, next year, sometime . . . never.' The words of the old nursery rhyme rang out into the stillness as he counted the bullets into the gun. He gave a deep sigh of apparent satisfaction. Then, raising the gun to his head, he squeezed the trigger . . .

After the sound of the explosion had died away, there was a breathtaking silence. Then, from somewhere in the inky blackness of the auditorium, there came the sound of spontaneous applause. Anna, standing in the wings, had watched the scene more times than she could possibly count, and yet, as always, unshed tears collected in the corners of her eyes. Gerald's performance never failed to move her.

'Well done, Gerald,' said a voice from the stalls.

'Never mind "Well done Gerald",' came the reply. Gerald Kingdom rose from the desk and strode purposefully across the stage. 'Never mind "well done", where's my bloody whisky?'

The spell was broken.

Experience during the last few months had taught Anna that

this remark was aimed at her. Running ahead of Gerald down the narrow passage behind the stage, she opened his dressing-room door. She had prepared a bucket of ice a few moments before and as the sound of his footsteps advanced down the passageway towards her, she mixed his whisky with all the speed and dexterity born of considerable practice. He walked into the dressing room, slammed the door and collapsed in the chair, facing his make-up mirror. He reached out for the glass without even looking at Anna and she placed it carefully in his outstretched hand. He took a gulp.

'God dammit, girl, what the bloody hell are you playing at? I asked for a whisky, not a glass of coloured water.'

'I'm sorry Mr Kingdom,' Anna said carefully, 'but Martin has insisted that I make your drinks weaker. You're on in just under an hour, you know. It's well after half past six.'

Gerald swung his chair round to face her, his handsome face contorted with rage. 'I know what bloody time it is.'

She tried to meet his eyes. They were blue, a startling bright blue highlighted by his sudden anger, and they seemed to be boring into hers. Everything about Gerald Kingdom was formidable and intimidating. How could Martin seriously expect her to stand up to him – particularly where his drinking was concerned?

'It's just that tonight is so important . . .' she began.

'Good God, girl, how long have you been in the theatre? Just because this is a first night, it doesn't make it any more important than any other. Every night's important, surely you've learnt that, if nothing else.'

'But all the critics . . .' she began.

'Sod the critics, sod Martin and sod you too.' He paused dramatically – just to see what sort of effect he was having, Anna thought angrily. She could feel tears prick her eyelids and she knew she was blushing.

'Tell me, Miss Wetherby,' Gerald continued, making no attempt to disguise the contempt in his voice, 'whose bloody whisky is this?'

'Yours,' she answered.

'Whose bloody dressing room?'

'Yours.'

2

'And who's bloody well holding this sodding play together?'

'You are.'

'I'm also forty-nine years old,' he continued, glancing in the mirror, as if seeking reassurance, 'and I am in the unique position of being the only person to have lived with me for that length of time. I know precisely when I've had enough whisky, when I've had too much, and when I haven't had quite enough. At the moment, I haven't had quite enough. Fill it up.'

'I can't,' said Anna. 'Martin will kill me.'

'And I'll bloody well kill you if you don't.'

This time he'd pushed her too far.

'If you want some more, fill it up yourself,' she said, her eyes blazing with sudden anger. No one ever spoke to Gerald Kingdom like this, but she was past caring. 'After all,' she continued, 'it's your career that's at stake, not mine. It's you who will be a laughing stock if you go on stage drunk – not me. I've been your nursemaid long enough. If you want to go and ruin everything after all these weeks of work, then that's up to you.'

She wrenched open the door of the dressing room and was starting to leave, when another thought struck her. 'And incidentally,' she said, turning to face Gerald, who was watching her, one eyebrow slightly raised, 'you're nothing but a hypocrite. How can you possibly say that every performance matters, when you're drunk as a skunk during most of yours?' She slammed the door behind her, making the walls shudder.

Anna hesitated, already appalled at what she had just done. Then lifting her chin, she walked hurriedly down the corridor, looking considerably more confident than she felt.

She found Martin Peters, the director, on stage in earnest discussion with the stage manager. A tall, thin, sandy-haired man, Martin always gave the impression of being on the verge of a nervous breakdown. His jerky uncoordinated movements seemed to suggest enormous inner tension and he wore a permanently worried frown. Yet, everybody agreed that he was brilliant, his reputation was substantial.

In normal circumstances, Martin was also kind and caring

3

with a natural intuitive flair for understanding his fellow human beings. But the circumstances were not normal and if Martin's pending nervous breakdown was ever to show itself, undoubtedly it would do so while directing Gerald Kingdom in *Sometime . . . Never*. Helping a movie star to make a comeback in the theatre was hard enough. Directing a play where success hangs entirely on the performance of one man is always a terrible risk. The complications didn't end there, though. The company was too small. A cast of three allowed for no leeway when it came to squabbles and feuds. It certainly didn't help, either, that the leading lady, Celia Compton, was also the producer's wife, questionably competent and loathed by Gerald. Into this cauldron, one only had to add a drink problem in order to serve up every director's nightmare.

Anna walked across the stage.

'Martin, I must speak to you,' she said, firmly.

'Later, later,' said Martin, with a dismissive wave of his arms.

'Now, Martin,' said Anna.

Martin looked up quickly. Anna Wetherby was not normally so assertive. He noted her flushed face, her angry eyes. 'Gerald?' he asked.

Anna nodded.

'Don't tell me he's still drinking!' Martin ran a hand through his hair, his face creased with concern.

'It's worse than that,' said Anna, 'I'm afraid I shouted at him. Martin, I'm sorry, but I simply can't act as a go-between any more. You're furious with me if Gerald drinks, and Gerald's furious with me if he doesn't. I've really had enough.'

'*You've* had enough,' Martin thundered, 'what about me?' If *Sometime . . . Never* and Gerald Kingdom go down tonight, so, by God, do I. But *you*, no one will ever remember you were a part of this mess. The least you can do, the very least, is to help us shorten the odds against failure.'

'I'm sorry, Martin, but you're the director, not me. It's your job to stop Gerald drinking, not mine.'

'You really pick your moments, love, don't you?' said

4

Martin. 'For the whole of the six-week tour, you managed to send Gerald on stage relatively sober each night. Then tonight, our "big night", the opening performance of *Sometime . . . Never* in London's West End, you blow it. What are you trying to do, Anna, sabotage the production?'

'Of course I'm not, how can you suggest such a thing. I care about this play quite as much as you do.'

'Then you've a bloody funny way of showing it,' said Martin. 'Get out of my sight. I've got enough problems without assistant stage managers playing the prima donna.' He turned away from her and for a moment she stood staring at him. With all her heart she wanted to tell him she was quitting there and then . . . but she couldn't. It wasn't just that she needed the money, though goodness knows how she'd manage without it. It was because after all they'd been through together, she was wedded to *Sometime . . . Never* – for better or worse, she had to see it through. Her pride in tatters, she stumbled off the stage.

With all the props carefully checked, and doubled checked, there was little else for Anna to do before the performance began. Finding a stacking chair in a dark corner of the wings, she collapsed, and finally gave in to the tears that had been building up all day.

To the casual observer, the theatre might seem rather a strange career for Anna to have chosen. Hers was an academic background – her father was an Oxford don, her mother a lecturer. Anna had attended Oxford High School for Girls, where it was considered that a place at the University was well within her reach. But Anna had other plans. She was lucky with her looks. Her hair was red-gold, the colour of autumn leaves, her eyes enormous – deep brown, set in a fragile face with high cheekbones and creamy skin. She was not a classic beauty, her mouth was too large, too full, her features were too irregular. Well above average in height, she was, however, a striking figure, and her features had that mobile quality so valuable to an actress. She could look beautiful or plain, seventeen or seventy.

Anna had her own very special reasons for adopting a stubborn single-mindedness when it came to her career. Her parents disapproved, but were eventually forced to accept her decision. She knew they considered her ambitions to be romantic rather than practical, and her talent questionable. Certainly, she could not look to them for moral support when things were rough. 'I told you so' would always hang in the air between them. There was too much hurt, too much misunderstanding.

The only encouragement she regularly received was from Sally, her childhood friend, who envied her choice of career enormously and considered it to be the most glamorous in the world. How wrong Sally was. Anna had joined a repertory company straight from school, at seventeen, initially as an assistant stage manager. Eventually she had been allowed to act occasionally – her first appearance on stage had been as a chambermaid in a Victorian drama, when the first, and only, words she'd spoken were 'Yes Madam'.

During the next five years, Anna advanced a little. She joined a bigger company, and now, at last, she had made it to Shaftesbury Avenue – not only as assistant stage manager, but also as understudy to Celia Compton. Yes, it was progress, of a sort . . . but hardly Sally's idea of glamour.

Sitting alone in her dark corner, Anna thought of all the dreary digs in which she'd stayed, of the sleazy little hotels, the half-empty cold theatres and the loneliness – above all, the loneliness. Was it worth it? Was her persistence fuelled by faith in her own talent, or perhaps some latent desire for self-destruction? It seemed to her at that moment that the latter was infinitely more likely.

She was disturbed from her reverie by the persistent shaking of her shoulder.

'How about a coffee in my dressing room, dear, just to wish me luck.'

Anna started and looked up into the face of Richard Manning. His expression, as always, was kind and smiling, and Anna couldn't help but smile back.

'I'd love to, Richard, thank you.'

She watched him as he poured out two steaming mugs of coffee. Richard Manning was one of those actors whose face

6

the general public always recognise, but to whom few can ever put a name. He'd begun working regularly immediately after the war, indeed war films had been his speciality. He usually played the commanding officer, sitting safely behind a desk while the hero took all the risks. The theatre, however, was his first love, and in later life, he'd been relegated, almost exclusively, to the role of butler, a part he played with enormous relish, and which he was repeating yet again in *Sometime . . . Never*. He'd never been a star, but then he'd probably never wanted to be, Anna thought – the true professional, always even-tempered, always on time, always word perfect.

'There you are, my dear, coffee is excellent for calming the emotions. It'll do you good.'

Anna looked up at him in surprise. 'Heavens, Richard, has someone told you already about the scene I made?' she asked.

'I didn't have to be told, dear. We could hear your scene all over the theatre. I thought the short, sharp lecture you handed out to Gerald rather splendid, and certainly apt. He'd had it coming for years, of course.'

'Good grief!' said Anna, in horror, 'I had no idea everyone could hear. Do you think I'll get the sack?'

Richard considered the question seriously for a moment. 'No dear, I don't think so. If Gerald insists, it might make things rather awkward, but it's not logical. Now at least we've made it to the West End, there's no time to rehearse a new understudy for Celia.' He smiled at her, a sweet gentle smile. 'I'd play a low profile for the next few days, though. The Great Man can be awfully unpleasant when he's conducting a vendetta.'

Anna shuddered. 'I wish I was like you, Richard. You just get on quietly with your job and all this washes over you.'

'It hasn't always been that way, Anna dear. Even *I* was young once, you know. Just like all you young things, I thought I'd be a star, and accordingly, I threw the required number of tantrums to prove I had the right temperament. Then, one day, a well-meaning veteran thespian told me I'd never make the big time, and so from then on, I concentrated on being a very professional supporting man. Frankly, dear, it was the best thing that could have happened to me. I've been married to the same woman for over twenty years, and I don't need to drink the best part of a bottle of whisky in order to go on stage.' He sighed and shook his head, pensive for a moment. Then he brightened. 'How old are you?'

'Twenty-two,' Anna replied.

'Yes,' Richard mused, 'twenty-two is too young.'

'Too young for what?' Anna asked.

'Any real sense of compassion. You shouldn't feel angry with Gerald, you know, you should feel sorry for him. Right now, he's a very frightened, lonely, old man.'

'Frightened, lonely and old aren't the sort of adjectives I'd apply to Gerald,' Anna said, scornfully. The scene in his dressing room was still painfully fresh.

'Then, with respect, dear, you'd be wrong. Take age first, because it's the most obvious. You and I, Uncle Tom Cobbley, the World and his wife, all suspect Gerald Kingdom isn't forty-nine. I've worked with him many times over the years and I happen to know he's in his late fifties. That's no age, I agree, but it is terribly old for an actor who is still trying to be a heart throb.'

'OK,' said Anna, 'point taken, but what about "frightened", I can't accept that?'

'If he wasn't frightened he wouldn't drink. The days of the glittering Hollywood star are over. He's too old to play the male lead any more and he's back in England in a desperate attempt to regain his crown as King of the British stage. The critics are determined he's past it, the public suspect he's past it, and Gerald is terified in case they're all right.'

'And what do you think?' Anna asked.

'I think actors like Gerald Kingdom are a very rare breed indeed. His talent is immense. The question is whether it's big enough to save the man from himself.'

'And lonely?' Anna asked. 'How can you possibly say he's lonely? There can't be a housewife on either side of the Atlantic who doesn't swoon at the mention of his name. The beautiful women in his life have been legion.'

Richard smiled at her sadly. 'Even at twenty-two you must have learnt the difference between being alone and being lonely. Four marriages hardly smack of emotional stability, do they, and then there's the children.'

'I didn't know he had children,' said Anna.

'He had a son, Christopher. He would have been your sort of age, I think, but he died of a drug overdose when he was eighteen.'

'How awful,' said Anna, 'was Christopher his only child?'

'No, there are two more, girls I think, though I'm not certain. They're by his second wife, but she, if you remember, is Australian, and I think he sees them rarely. Certainly, they all live in Australia now.'

'But he has consolations,' Anna suggested.

'I don't think his relationships with women are particularly consoling,' said Richard. 'Actors have such fragile egos to protect . . .' He saw the query in Anna's eyes, '. . . yes, even me,' he said, with a smile. 'Gerald needs a beautiful woman in his life. It doesn't particularly matter who she is, and true love certainly isn't the relevant feature. It's more a question of retaining a self-image.' Richard looked hard at Anna for a moment. 'And talking of self-images, you weren't frightfully good for Gerald's just now, were you?'

'No, I suppose I wasn't,' Anna admitted, trying to ignore the growing feeling of remorse.

Just then there was a thud on the door. 'Ten minutes,' shouted a voice.

'Oh dear,' Richard said, suddenly in a fluster, 'talking to you has made me late.'

'Can I do anything to help?' Anna asked.

'Yes, there is something you can do, dear,' said Richard, with a shy smile. 'After all these years of playing a gentleman's gentleman, do you know, I still have difficulty fixing my tie, particularly when I'm nervous.'

On leaving Richard's dressing room, and with several minutes still to go until the final call, Anna crept out of the stage door and walked round to the front of the theatre. She knew she should not go front of house so close to curtain up, but the rising tension backstage was claustrophobic, besides which, she wanted to take a look at the audience. She was rewarded by seeing the foyer absolutely packed and there were plenty of faces she recognised. It was certainly a night for celebrities. Richard's words still echoed in her head. What if Gerald had been drinking steadily since she left? What if her show of temper had seriously damaged his already fragile ego? Tonight could ruin his career, a glittering career that had spanned over thirty years. And *if* he failed tonight, there would be grounds for saying it was her fault. Unable to stand the suspense any longer, Anna ran back to the stage door. Freddy, the doorman, was on duty, his face grim. 'Where have you been, Miss? You shouldn't be front of house now, particularly with all that's going on.'

'Why Freddy, is something wrong?' Anna asked.

'It's Mr Kingdom,' said Freddy. 'He won't come out of his dressing room. He won't let anyone in, not even his dresser, and he won't come out either.'

'You mean he's refusing to go on stage?' said Anna in horror.

'No, he's going on stage, but no one knows what sort of state he's in, if you take my meaning, Miss.'

Anna nodded and rushed through to the dressing rooms. Martin was standing white-faced outside Gerald's door.

'What's happening?' whispered Anna. 'Is he all right?'

'How should I know?' Martin said, his voice hoarse with tension. 'He won't even speak to me. This is your fault, Anna, and if Gerald can't go on tonight. . .' His words hung in the air, but the innuendo was obvious.

'Beginners please,' came the call. 'Beginners please, Miss Compton, Mr Kingdom.'

Instantly on the call, Gerald opened his door and stepped out into the passage in front of them. He looked splendid in a plum-coloured smoking jacket – his dark hair shone, his blue eyes sparkled, his handsome face appeared relaxed and untroubled.

'He's either drunk, mad, or perfectly all right.' Martin muttered, under his breath.

Gerald strode past Anna and Martin without a glance. He climbed the steps and took his place centre stage, standing alone in the dark, waiting for his audience.

To Anna, those last few minutes before curtain up seemed

the longest of her life. The tension backstage was unbearable. Even Richard, standing beside her, had lost his usual affable expression. They all watched the stage and the brooding figure standing there, motionless and utterly unapproachable. At last the houselights dimmed, the audience babble died away, and after a moment's breathtaking silence, the curtain rose.

In his beautiful measured tones, Gerald Kingdom began to speak. He wasn't drunk, he wasn't mad – he was magnificent.

After the tensions of the day, it seemed impossible that a performance could go so well. Right from the first moment, the enthusiasm of the audience was evident. Aware of their delight, Gerald blossomed, his performance more sure, more able than it had ever been before. By the time he spoke those final poignant words, the audience would have done anything for him. As the curtain fell and the sound of the pistol shot died away, it seemed to Anna that the thunderous applause shook the theatre to its very foundations. She glanced at Martin, who stood silently beside her. Tears were streaming down his face, and she realized that she too was crying. It was a night none of them would ever forget.

'Thank God,' she murmured to herself.

Martin turned and slipped an arm round her as they watched Gerald take the final curtain call.

'No, thank *you*,' he said.

Anna stared at him. 'What do you mean?'

'Gerald Kingdom has just given the performance of his life,' said Martin. 'He did it because he was sober and he was sober because of you. I take back everything I said, darling. It was a dangerous gamble but it paid off. Well done.' He gave her a squeeze.

'I just hope Gerald thinks the same way,' said Anna, ruefully, remembering Richard's warning.

The first night party lasted until dawn. Gerald, Anna noticed, drank hardly at all, and accepted, with his usual grace and charm, the many congratulations that poured in. Anna could have slipped away unnoticed, but Martin's words had made her feel part of the triumph in some small way. She wanted to be there.

It must have been after three when Gerald caught her eye over the top of the admiring crowd milling about him. She was sitting in a corner alone, sipping a glass of champagne. Parting the crowd, Gerald walked over and stood in front of her, his face solemn and, she fancied, menacing.

'So, Miss Wetherby, whilst you preach temperance in others, you're not averse to a little tipple yourself?'

Anna felt her heart beating unnaturally fast. She knew her answer would make or break her future with the company. She smiled at him, trying to keep her voice light and steady. 'I know it's a poor excuse,' she said, 'but I've had rather a difficult day at work. You see, my boss doesn't understand me.'

Gerald stared at her for a long moment. Then, the trace of a smile spread across his face.

'That is very remiss of him. Still, you never know – he might prove a trifle more understanding tomorrow.' Without another word, he turned on his heel and once more joined his admirers.

Anna let out a deep breath and took a gulp of champagne. I've survived, she thought, it's a miracle.

It was indeed a miracle – for, unknown to Anna, no woman had ever criticised Gerald Kingdom before, and been forgiven.

Chapter Two

'You wanted to see me . . .?'

The sentence hung in the air. There was an unfinished quality about it because Daniel never quite knew what to call his father, even after thirty-one years. Walter B Chase sat, small and somewhat corpulent, behind his enormous desk. He was completely bald, his head as smooth as an egg. It was impossible to call him Father, the name didn't suit his image. As for Dad or Pop, the words seemed far too comfortable a way of describing one of Broadway's most ruthless producers. Walter eyed his son over the top of his pince-nez.

'Yeah, sit down, I want to talk to you. I think you've gone nuts.'

The New York offices of Chase Productions' President were luxurious to the point of obscenity. Walter liked everything to look good, or so he said. What he meant was he liked everything to look expensive. He had no taste whatsoever and Daniel all but flinched as he cast his eye around for a suitable chair. Walter B Chase had the reputation of screwing the last five dollars out of a business deal, but when it came to showing the world tangible proof of his success, no expense was spared. Daniel chose a hideously ornate gilt chair, with a pink crushed velvet seat. Its advantage was that it stood a fair distance from his father.

'What brought on this sudden show of filial affection?' Daniel asked.

'Fancy college talk doesn't impress me,' Walter replied. 'Nor indeed does it appear to impress the little scrubbers you knock around with.' He stabbed his pen into a pile of papers on his desk, among which Daniel recognised his expenses.

13

'First, you have to stuff them full of food and wine, in order to get them laid . . . at my expense too.'

Daniel shifted his position on the uncomfortable little chair. He could feel himself growing tense and irritable. It was always the same in his father's presence.

'My expenses are always within the agreed limit, as you well know. Frankly if that's the reason you've dragged me all the way up here, I don't see there's any point in prolonging the conversation. I have a lot to do this afternoon.' Daniel stood up and started to leave.

'Sit down,' Walter commanded.

Daniel kept walking. It had been a long, hard week and he'd had more than enough of his father.

'I said sit down, that is if you wish to discuss your latest fantastic scheme.' Walter's voice was edged with sarcasm, but Daniel stopped in his tracks and turned, his face suddenly alive with interest.

'You mean *Sometime . . . Never?*'

Walter nodded curtly. 'If that's what you call that crap.'

'Didn't you like it – you must have done. You saw the synopsis of the script I prepared and you saw the reviews. You *must* have seen the reviews – weren't they great?'

Daniel's enthusiasm was evident, but Walter chose to ignore it. 'You want to know what I think?' he said, 'I think it stinks. I think the whole goddam play stinks. Who wants to spend an evening watching some old guy blow his brains out? When people go to the theatre they want to be entertained, not ground into the deck. They want to leave the theatre happier than when they arrived. This,' he gestured at the newspaper cuttings, 'this is a crock of shit.'

Daniel had anticipated opposition, but not to this degree.

'OK, OK,' he said, 'so you don't like the play, but you can't ignore the profit potential. It's a relatively low budget production because there are only three characters and one set, yet it's packing the theatre night after night in London. It's got everything – classy theatre and high profits.'

Walter shrugged dismissively. 'It's a cult. You can con the goddam English into a cult, but on Broadway, they want value for money.'

14

'And don't you think Gerald Kingdom is value for money?' Daniel asked.

'Twenty years ago, yeah. Now he's finished, all washed up, just another drunken old bum.'

'A drunken old bum who's filling the theatre night after night. Look, I've just got a feeling about this play.' Daniel groped for words. 'It has a sort of smell about it.'

Walter looked at his son reflectively for a moment. He trusted instinct. Tight budgets, good marketing, carefully balanced books were all very well in their way, but long ago Walter had learnt that real success lay with intuition. He wasn't going to make it easy though.

'OK,' he said, 'if you want to spend your expense allowance this month on a flight to London, that's up to you. Take the trip, see the play, then come back and convince me we should go with it. Do the sums, negotiate the deal, bring me the total package.'

'I hardly think it's fair . . .' Daniel began.

'Take it or leave it,' said Walter, with a dismissive wave of the hand.

Daniel didn't hesitate. 'I'll take it.'

'At least it'll keep you away from the goddam broads for a while anyway,' said Walter. 'Too much of it doesn't do you any good, you know.'

Daniel felt himself flush with anger. It was time to leave before he said something which might jeopardise the decision. 'It keeps me occupied,' he said lightly.

'Yeah, I'm sure it does.'

Walter watched his son leave the office, with a hint of regret in his eyes. Daniel was so very different from his father – tall, slim, with a shock of corn-coloured hair, permanently bleached by the sun. A good-looking man by anyone's standards, with clear pale blue eyes and strong chiselled features. He was a son to be proud of, yet . . . Walter shook his head and, as he would do many times during the day, he looked at the photograph on his desk of a beautiful young woman – his wife, Daniel's mother.

Perhaps, Walter reflected, if he'd looked more like me and less like his mother, there might not have been such a gulf

15

between us. He knew he was kidding himself.

He'd met Elizabeth at a party, given by one of his backers. She was nineteen, an English girl, staying with an American aunt for Christmas. Walter had been thirty-seven and already well-established on Broadway. She'd seen one of his plays the night before and raved about it. In a moment of extreme optimism, Walter had asked her out to dinner, never thinking for one moment she would accept. She had, and to his constant amazement and delight, despite the difference in their ages, their heights, and the fact that she was beautiful and he ugly, a relationship had developed – a bond so strong that it was quite unthinkable that they should not marry. They'd been happy, deliriously happy until Elizabeth had died, giving birth to their son.

No, Walter knew where the fault lay in his relationship with Daniel. He could never forgive the boy for killing Elizabeth, for killing the only woman he'd ever loved.

Back in his office Daniel shut the door, leaning back against it with a great sigh of relief. There was a discreet knock on the door at the far side of his office which adjoined his secretary's room.

'Come in, Mattie,' he called.

Matilda Jackson was no beauty, and the wrong side of thirty. Her thin, nondescript hair was cropped close and her face was infinitely forgettable. Only when she smiled, did anyone notice her – one could not ignore the warmth and friendship she so unconsciously displayed. She'd been Daniel's secretary from the day he first arrived at Chase Productions, straight from college – a raw, gawky boy, full of hope for the future. She'd watched him grow and mature. She'd also watched the dull look come into his eye. She'd seen hope turn to bitterness and enthusiasm to disillusionment. People who thought they knew her well believed her devotion to Daniel was the reason she was a spinster. They were wrong. She was devoted to Daniel, but as a mother might love her child. Matilda Jackson had never married because she'd never been asked.

'How'd it go?' she asked.

Daniel smiled, 'Well he bawled me out over my expenses

... *again*, but then we wouldn't have expected anything different, would we, Mattie?'

'To hell with that,' said Matilda, impatiently, 'quit kidding around, Dan. What did he say about the play?'

'Well ...' Daniel smiled at her.

'Come on.'

'Well, he says it stinks, but he's willing for me to gamble my expense account on a round trip to London.' He shrugged his shoulders. 'He says I'm to negotiate the rights and put in a full proposal for his consideration.'

'Wow!' said Matilda.

'Hey, come on,' said Daniel, 'he hasn't said he'll do it.'

'Nope,' Mattie agreed, 'but it's one step on the ladder. When do you want to leave for London?'

'Book me on Concorde for early next week.'

'Concorde?' Mattie queried.

'Hell, why not, I don't want to waste time. Book me a good house seat in the stalls two nights running, and make sure you tie the whole thing up for early in the week. I don't want to see them perform with the benefit of Saturday night fever, I want to see them on an off day.'

'Do you want me to let them know you're coming?'

Daniel shook his head. 'Emphatically no,' he said. 'This play's one hell of a gamble. I want to see it first, warts and all.'

'Yes sir,' said Mattie with a grin. 'Now what do you want – the good news or the bad?'

Daniel ran a hand wearily through his hair and wandered over to his desk. 'Jesus, Mattie, I think I'll take the good news and can you make the bad news good as well?'

'I'll try,' she said with a smile. 'The *Emma* casting – you had two more to see this afternoon. Well, the good news is that one has cried off. Maths being your strong point, you'll appreciate that leaves you just one to see. That's good news, right?'

'Right,' he agreed.

'The bad news is she's here waiting for you right now. She's obviously an enthusiast, she's already been hanging around for half an hour.' Daniel groaned. 'I can make it sound better by telling you she's pretty.'

17

'Very pretty?' Daniel queried.

'Very pretty,' Mattie confirmed.

'OK,' said Daniel, 'give me five minutes to get myself together and then I'll see her.

After Mattie had gone Daniel sat down at his desk and looked around his office with evident satisfaction. It could not have contrasted more with his father's suite. Everything in Daniel's office was white – the walls, the carpet, the blinds, the desk, the couch – even the telephones and the computer. There were only three spots of colour in the room. One corner was given over to a profusion of green plants, which were Mattie's pride and joy. On the wall hung an original Picasso, which had been painted during his blue period, and in the centre of the office there was a deep sapphire blue rug which perfectly matched the painting.

Daniel lay back in his chair, hands clasped behind his head, feet on the desk. He was looking forward to his trip to London. He loved England, his mother's country. Instinctively he felt more at home there than in the States, or was it just the antagonism with his father that made him feel that way? His face clouded. He hated casting, the job made no sense to him. The kind of bit parts he was asked to audition should have been handled by the director. However, Walter's insistence that every single member of the cast of his plays had to be chosen personally by Chase Productions, was now part of theatrical history. Walter selected the leads, sometimes with reference to his director, sometimes not, and it fell to Daniel to interview the rest.

His father's latest production, *Emma*, was a musical based on the life of Lady Hamilton, mistress to Lord Nelson. It would be a box office success, of course, all the ingredients were there, but Daniel hated the production. It was just an excuse for Walter to stage another of his great spectaculars for which he was so famous, but they'd had their day, Daniel was sure of it. He was currently auditioning the part of Lady Hamilton's maid and confidante. He'd seen over twenty girls so far and had been satisfied with none of them.

Again the discreet knock.

'Come in,' he called.

18

Mattie opened the door with a flourish. 'Miss Rosie Blake,' she announced, with a smile.

Daniel stood up and held out his hand. 'How do you do, Miss Blake,' he said. He noted the tight, dark curls, the pale, almost translucent skin and deep blue eyes. A tiny waist and good boobs, he thought, ideal for period costume. He remembered seeing her photograph now – he'd been impressed with that, but she looked a lot better in the flesh.

'Come and sit down,' he said, with a slow lazy smile, 'and tell me all about yourself.'

It took Daniel just fifteen minutes to decide Rosie was the girl for the part. The actress already chosen to play Emma was a pale blonde, and Rosie would contrast well. She'd had enough experience in the theatre, and her singing voice was good. Her accent was a little stronger than he would have liked and his astute ear picked up her origins.

'You're from Texas, aren't you?'

She blushed slightly, 'How did you know?'

'Your accent.'

'Oh gee and I thought my classes had cured that,' she said, with surprising candour.

'I don't know whether "cure" is the right word, but those classes weren't so bad – there's only a trace.' He paused reflectively for a moment. What the hell if her accent wasn't quite right. It was an American production after all. Did it matter if the English maid had a slight Texan drawl? They had plenty of time to work on her.

'Tell me what you had for breakfast, in your best English accent,' he said.

She obliged.

'Pancakes and maple syrup?' said Daniel, with a grin. 'Kippers and kedgeree would have been more appropriate.'

She smiled back, she had a nice smile. Hell, she'd do, and besides which, he was tired and hungry, and she *was* very, very pretty. He looked at his watch, it was ten to six. They could take in the cocktail hour at the Top of the Sixes, and then go on to dinner.

'Well Rosie, you've got yourself the job' – she flushed a delicate pink – 'so I reckon you and I ought to go out and celebrate, don't you?'

'I'd like that,' she agreed.

Daniel lifted the telephone. 'Mattie, could you book me a table for two at Charlie's around seven-thirty?'

'I already have,' Mattie said smoothly.

Daniel threw back his head and laughed out loud. The girl looked at him enquiringly, but he made no effort to explain.

They spent a pleasant enough evening. After a few drinks Rosie dropped her interview manner. She'd packed a lot into her eighteen years of life and she mildly amused Daniel with anecdotes from her already considerable past. It was after twelve by the time they were back in his apartment – a penthouse suite on Fifth Avenue overlooking Central Park. Like his office, it was decorated predominantly in one colour, but this time cream, rather than an austere white. Here and there were splashes of colour – apricot, brown, a little yellow. The effect was calm, uncluttered luxury.

Rosie let out a shriek of delight. 'Why Daniel, it's lovely,' she said. 'Wow, I do envy you.'

'I envy me too,' he said, gallantly, 'for being able to spend an evening with a gorgeous lady like you.' He kissed her neck, nibbling gently at her ear. 'A drink?' She nodded. 'Wander round, take a look,' he said, 'I'll just fix us some coffee and brandy.'

A few minutes later he returned, poured the coffee and put on some Mozart. For a little while they sat beside one another on the sofa, sipping their brandy. In the gentle lighting, Rosie seemed softer, younger – less of the hardened showgirl. The shadows emphasised the delicate shape of her face, her eyes were now a deep, deep blue.

Enough of the preliminaries, Daniel decided. Deliberately he set down his drink, taking hers too from her hand. Their eyes met and held, and slowly, carefully, Daniel began to undo the buttons of her blouse. He slipped his hands round the nape of her neck and slid them down her shoulders, marvelling at the smoothness of her skin. In a single movement, with an expertise born of considerable practice, he slid the blouse from her shoulders. Then, only then, did his eyes leave hers, as he gently traced the line of her breasts.

She uttered a single word of protest as he drew her to him,

but stayed unresisting in his arms as he kissed her, and gently removed the rest of her clothes. As she lay there naked beside him, so beautiful and so very young, for a moment he felt a stab of guilt. Then he dismissed it. She'd done this sort of thing before, he was sure of it. Rosie was a girl who knew the score. Absolved, at least in his own mind, he gave himself up to the pleasure of the moment.

Next morning Daniel headed his car out of town. He was to spend the weekend with his old college friend, Jim. Jim, his wife, Penny, and their young son, Chuck, had a house out at Scarsdale. Chuck was Daniel's godson, Jim and Penny his closest friends. He smiled to himself as he joined the freeway. He had a tough week ahead and this weekend was just what he needed to prepare himself.

By midday he was sitting in their kitchen, sipping a beer. He'd forgotten all about Rosie, and in a week's time, he wouldn't even remember her name.

Chapter Three

Oddly enough, Anna found the persistent rain rather cheering. She pulled the duvet cover higher, snuggled deeper into the bed, and gazed around the little room that was, at any rate for the time being, her home. It might seem drab on most days of the week, but compared with the grey dankness outside, it was almost cosy. She glanced at her alarm clock – it was eight o'clock. Monday morning meant understudy rehearsals at ten. She just had enough time to wash her hair, if she could only summon up the energy to get out of bed.

Sometime . . . Never was about to embark on its fourth triumphant week, and because of the play's success, Martin Peters was positively paranoid about the quality of the understudies' performances. His fear centred round Gerald's unpredictability of course. What if his drink problem returned – could Richard Manning, as understudy, keep the audience in their seats – could Anna cope with Gerald if Celia was taken ill? The success of the play depended on the absolute perfection of the players – there was no room for the mediocre, for the second rate. Thankfully, everyone understood this, and cooperated, as far as they could, with Martin's relentless pursuit of excellence. Indeed, the ecstatic reviews and the packed houses had affected the whole company. They were all pushing in the same direction, supremely grateful for the opportunity to be a part of theatrical history in the making.

Anna was slipping back into that glorious state of semi-consciousness when there was a thudding on her door.

'Anna!' came the shrill voice of Mrs Franks, her landlady. 'Anna! Are you in there?'

'Yes,' Anna croaked.

'Phone call for you, lovey.'

'Could you ask them to ring back, Mrs Franks? I'm still in bed.'

'I've tried that already, love. He says it's urgent and to get you to the phone double quick.'

Anna sat up in bed. 'Did he say who he was?' she called through the door.

'Didn't ask.'

Groaning, Anna staggered out of bed. She didn't possess a dressing gown and her slippers seemed to have completely disappeared. She pulled a big baggy sweater over her night-dress, and opening the door, started down the stairs. The patchy linoleum was cold and gritty under her feet. 'It had better be urgent,' she muttered.

Mrs Franks' telephone was strategically placed, mid-way down the passage, between the front and back doors of her old Victorian terraced house. On that particular morning, both doors were wide open. As a result there seemed to be a gale blowing down the passageway and the wind was bringing the rain in with it.

'This had better be important,' Anna grumbled into the mouthpiece, 'it feels like I'm rounding Cape Horn here.'

'It *is* important, darling,' replied Martin Peters. 'What do you mean, rounding Cape Horn?' Anna briefly described the scene. 'It sounds terrible, darling, but I may be just the man to take you away from all that.'

Anna giggled. 'Is this an improper suggestion, Martin?'

'Sadly no, darling, we haven't time. I want you dressed and in the theatre inside half an hour.'

'But you said rehearsals didn't start until ten this morning. I want to wash my hair.'

'You can wash your hair this afternoon. I want you here *now*, before anyone else arrives.'

'Why is it always me who's dogsbody?' Anna grumbled. 'Why can't Sophie come in early to help you sort out whatever it is?'

Sophie was the company's wardrobe mistress, an endearingly eccentric punk with nymphomaniac tendencies.

Between them, she and Anna coped with most of the mundane chores.

'Sophie is already here, although that's entirely beside the point,' Martin replied sharply. 'Actually, you can please yourself whether you come in or not because for the job I have in mind I don't think I'd have too much difficulty in finding a willing recruit. After all, who would turn down the opportunity of starring in the West End opposite Gerald Kingdom, in the smash hit of the decade?'

Anna suddenly felt faint. 'What did you say?' she said, in a small voice.

'What I'm saying, or rather trying to say despite the interruptions, is that Celia's throat infection has deteriorated over the weekend, to the point where she definitely can't appear tonight or tomorrow night – and possibly even Wednesday. I'm not saying *a star is born*, darling, but this is a chance for you to show us what you're worth.'

'You mean I'm actually going on for Celia *tonight*? I am really playing Sarah?' Anna could hardly hear his reply for the thudding in her ears.

'For an intelligent girl, darling, you can be terribly thick – how many more times do I have to tell you? Yes, you're playing Sarah to Gerald's Robert in tonight's performance of *Sometime . . . Never*, and right now, we're wasting valuable rehearsal time. You have twenty-five minutes to get here and don't you dare be late. I hope I've made myself clear . . . at last.'

The phone went dead. In a state of trance, Anna replaced the receiver, turned and mechanically began to climb the stairs. Suddenly, she was struck by the enormity of what had just happened. 'Yippee!' she yelled. 'Mrs Franks, where are you?' She began bounding up the stairs two at a time. 'Mrs Franks, Mrs Franks!'

'Whatever's the matter, lovey,' said Mrs Franks, coming out of one of the bedrooms. 'Do you have to make all that noise? You'll disturb my other guests.'

'Sorry,' said Anna, arriving on the landing breathless.

'Is something wrong, dear? Not bad news I hope?'

'No, no, quite the contrary. It's good news. Terrifying news, but definitely good.'

24

One of the reasons that Mrs Franks was such a successful landlady, despite the dilapidated state of her property, was because she had acquired the knack of being a good listener. It was an art she had developed over the years. She knew that people who lived alone liked to talk. Listening to what they had to say was quite as much a part of the service she offered as clean sheets once a week and a quick mop round on Thursdays. As a result of this strategy, her tenants were devoted to her and completely overlooked the irregular plumbing and peeling paintwork. Now, she leaned heavily on her brush, and waited for all to be revealed.

'You know I'm understudying the leading lady?' Anna said. Mrs Franks nodded. 'Well, she's off sick, just for a few days, so it means I'm going to be taking her place.'

'When?' asked Mrs Franks. She had been hoping for some juicy personal exposé, but she was far too professional to show her disappointment.

'Tonight, tomorrow and possibly even Wednesday. Celia has a bad throat. Just think, Mrs Franks – me, a leading lady in the West End!'

Mrs Franks looked Anna up and down, taking in the bizarre combination of the baggy sweater and lacy nightdress. Poor girl, she didn't look much like Mrs Franks' idea of a leading lady.

'That's very nice for you, lovey,' she said, kindly.

'Yes, it is, isn't it?' Must dash or I'll be late for rehearsals. Wish me luck, Mrs Franks.' Anna continued her noisy voyage up the stairs.

Mrs Franks looked after her and shook her head. Leading lady indeed . . . of course, some of her guests were a little odd. Living alone wasn't healthy really. Still, she couldn't complain, she made a good enough living out of those who did.

On the tube journey to Shaftesbury Avenue, Anna studied the script. She knew the part well, of course – Martin's persistence with understudy rehearsals had paid off, and Sarah's role was not an arduous one. *Sometime . . . Never* plotted the slow disintegration of a man named Robert who discovered his young wife, Sarah, was being unfaithful to him. The supporting roles of the butler, and even that of Sarah, were merely the props used to help illustrate what was going on in Robert's mind. The play belonged to Gerald and was mostly in monologue. Nonetheless the little vignettes created by his exchanges with the other two characters were vital, in their own way.

The Northern Line deposited Anna at Leicester Square and she began hurrying up Shaftesbury Avenue. Even during the day, without the lights, there was a glamour, a romance about the place. For an instant, she hesitated outside the theatre and stared at the posters. At that moment, it seemed impossible to believe that she would be on stage in the West End that very night – playing where so many famous names had played before her.

Martin was sitting alone in the stalls when Anna arrived. She walked to the front of the stage and peered at him through the half-darkness.

'You're late,' he said, accusingly.

She consulted her watch. 'Only three minutes. It's not bad, Martin, I was in bed when you rang and I've had to come all the way from Clapham.'

He stood up and walked to the front of the house, then paused and examined her in silence for a moment. 'Hmmm,' he said, 'good, you're looking quite bonny, except that your hair could do with a wash.'

'But you said . . .' Anna began.

'A joke,' said Martin, holding up his hands in mock protest. 'I'd like to run through your part before the others arrive, but first, let's have a talk in your dressing rooom.'

'My dressing room!' Anna's eyes grew wide at the mere thought.

'Stars do have them, you know,' said Martin, with a grin. Together, they walked backstage. 'We could do with some coffee,' Martin grinned, 'but I can't really ask you to make it bearing in mind your new status, can I? Sophie!' he roared. 'Coffee for two, in Celia's dressing room, and quick about it.'

'Yes, Master,' came a distant voice.

He grinned, almost sheepishly, Anna noted with surprise. 'That girl gets no better, but she's fun to have around,' he said indulgently.

'In an exhausting sort of way,' Anna agreed.

Anna had been in Celia's dressing room often enough in the last few weeks, but it took on an entirely new perspective when she realised, albeit briefly, that it was to be her own. It was large, by dressing room standards, and the inevitable drabness had all but been obscured by Celia's trappings. Flowers, cards, magazines, make-up, heated rollers and a selection of luxurious silk underwear which was carefully laid out. There were two comfortable chairs, and the room was blessed with surprising warmth.

'Cosy, isn't it?' said Martin, grinning at Anna. 'It helps, of course, being the producer's wife.'

They'd just settled into their chairs when Sophie arrived, and deposited, unceremoniously, two mugs of coffee on to the dressing table, spilling them as she did so. She eyed them both for a moment. 'Don't you go getting too cosy with 'er, Martin, just 'cos she's a star.' She winked at them, and disappeared out of the door with a commendable swagger.

'What a mess,' said Martin, looking at the spilt coffee with distaste.

'Never mind.' Anna gave him a quick smile, and began mopping up with some of Celia's tissues. Martin's passion for neatness was well documented by endless stories of his tantrums over back-stage disorder.

'Anna,' he said, 'I don't want you to become too excited about this opportunity. You have two days, possibly three, in the part, but no more. If you were getting a long run of several weeks it might be different.' He hesitated, 'Look, I'm going to talk off the record now, and what I'm going to say is strictly for your ears only – OK?' Anna nodded, wondering what on earth was coming. 'Celia Compton is a well-known name, because she's married to Alan Buckmaster. This production, in common with many others in the past, tolerates her because her husband is the producer. Luckily, her role in *Sometime . . . Never* is not too demanding. Everybody is so spellbound by Gerald, they hardly notice the rest of the cast.' He paused and sipped his coffee. 'Nonetheless, she's wrong for the part, Anna. I'm sure you must have realised that yourself.'

'Certainly, she's too old,' Anna agreed.

'She's too old, yes, but there's more to it than that. Because Gerald is an absolute wizard, he makes the audience believe that Sarah is the kind of woman who could cause a man to blow out his brains. But, looking at her performance in isolation, one wonders why Robert isn't actually celebrating the prospect of a divorce.'

Anna laughed. 'I think you're being a little hard on her, Martin.'

'Perhaps, but for a couple of nights, at least, I'd like to see the part played properly. I think it would be good for Gerald, too.'

'You mean, you think I can do better than Celia? I haven't had anything like her experience.'

'No,' said Martin, 'but I believe you're dead right for the part. We mustn't throw Gerald with too many variations, but I'd like to show Sarah as the author intended her to be shown. I want to change the emphasis, create just the right balance in the relationship and I honestly believe you're the right person who can do it, Anna.' He smiled, 'You never know, there might be someone out there on the other side of the footlights who notices you in the next couple of nights.' Anna nodded, feeling a sudden knot of excitement in her stomach. 'One of the things I'd like to do,' Martin continued, 'is to reintroduce the kiss.'

'The *kiss*?' said Anna, 'I didn't know there was one.'

'Yes,' said Martin, with a grin, 'just before the final scene. In fact we had a great deal of trouble with the author over it. You see, I believe it's a fairly vital part of the story really – a part which, without the kiss, even Gerald can't convey. In one last desperate attempt to win Sarah back, Robert kisses her so passionately he almost loses control – in fact, it's quite obvious he desperately wants to make love to her. Sarah doesn't reject him, indeed quite the contrary. One is supposed to form the impression that she is shocked by her own ardent reaction to her husband. It is *Robert* who withdraws, terrified at the humiliation of forcing his attentions on her, when she no longer loves him. Subtly, you see, it changes the ending, makes it more poignant. They can no longer communicate, but Sarah's spontaneous rection to that kiss does suggest there are grounds for saying Robert kills himself unnecessarily.'

'I see,' said Anna, 'that's very good. So why isn't it in?'

Martin grinned. 'Gerald refused to kiss Celia with the necessary passion.'

Anna grimaced, blushing a little. 'Do you think he's going to feel any differently about me?'

'I don't think, I *know*. I've already spoken to him this morning, and he says he'd be delighted to kiss you, with as much passion as I consider necessary.'

'And I thought today was going to be another wet Monday,' said Anna ruefully.

Martin hesitated. 'There's just one other thing . . .'

'Go on,' said Anna, 'spit it out, you might as well tell me the worst.'

'By reputation, Gerald is awful with understudies. He adores teasing them and making their life hell. Certainly he was absolutely thrilled when he heard this morning that you would be on stage with him tonight. So . . . well, don't expect him to make things easy for you.'

'You're not exactly filling me with confidence,' Anna said.

'Sorry, but forearmed . . .' Martin stood up. 'I'll leave you in peace now for a few moments, and I'll ask Sophie to pop in to check out your wardrobe. We'll have a run through,' he glanced at his watch, 'in, say, ten minutes.'

By the time Gerald arrived on stage, Anna had been through her part twice with Martin, and was feeling relatively confident. 'Ah, the intrepid Miss Wetherby,' Gerald said, giving her a mock bow. 'May I say what a pleasure it will be to play opposite you tonight.'

'Thank you,' Anna stammered.

Slowly, Gerald looked her up and down. 'Is she word-perfect then, Martin?' he asked, without taking his eyes from her.

'Absolutely,' Martin replied.

Gerald smiled. 'Good. Well, let's put it to the test, shall we? As they say, let's take it from the top.' Anna nodded and scurried off stage, relieved to be escaping from Gerald's presence. On stage, even in casual conversation, his magnetism was overpowering. The words, *born to act*, came into her mind, as she stood in the wings watching him prepare for the

29

first scene. The problems of the whisky bottle seemed far away now – indeed nothing to do with the man standing on stage. Gerald Kingdom was where he belonged and the thought of joining him in his world was intimidating to say the least.

In years to come, Anna was always to remember that rehearsal. For the first time in her life she felt she was really acting. Undoubtedly, some of Gerald's greatness did wear off. 'Acting is very like playing a game of tennis,' she was to become fond of saying. 'If your opponent is a good player, your own performance benefits from the reflected glory.'

Even the kiss went well. Gerald's ardent embrace, the passion of his kiss, took Anna completely by surprise, knocking the breath from her body, leaving her trembling and bewildered – it was just what Martin wanted.

At the end of the rehearsal, everyone crowded on stage. The reactions to Anna's performance were interestingly varied. 'Not bad,' said Martin. 'You need to work on that second scene a little more, but with luck, we should have it right by lunchtime.'

'You were spaced out,' said Sophie. 'Man, that kiss! It was really something – I wish I'd got a load of that.' She openly ogled Gerald, making them all laugh.

'Very nice, dear,' said Richard. 'You made me feel quite misty-eyed.'

Everyone looked expectantly at Gerald. He studied Anna in silence for a moment. 'You're better than the Old Boot,' he conceded, 'but I don't want you getting ideas above your station. Now . . .' He glanced at his watch. '. . . where's my bloody whisky,' the whole company chorused, laughing with relief.

'Sophie is in charge of your refreshments for the next couple of days,' Martin said firmly.

'No,' thundered Gerald, heading towards his dressing room. 'No, I'm not prepared to put up with that. I'm used to having Anna around, and that's the way I want things to stay.'

'Fuckin' charming,' said Sophie, under her breath.

Gerald whirled round. 'See what I mean? I'm not having that foul-mouthed brat in my dressing room. Anna, fix my drink . . . *now*.' No one dared argue.

It was nearly two o'clock by the time Martin finally released Anna. 'Now,' he said, 'go home, have a bath, wash your hair, and for goodness' sake, eat something. That last run through was just right, so all you have to do now is to relax. I'd like you back here at six. We don't want any last-minute panics, do we darling?'

'Six! I need to be in earlier than that – what about the props?'

'Darling, sod the props – someone else is handling those. You're a star – remember.'

Anna nodded. 'OK,' she said, with a grin. 'Six it is, then. I just have a couple of phone calls to make before I leave.'

'Mummy, it's Anna.' There was a pause at the other end of the telephone. Anna was used to this. May Wetherby did not find emotional relationships easy – she always needed plenty of time to formulate a reply.

'Anna, my dear,' she said, at last, 'how are you?'

'I'm fine, Mummy, and you?'

'Yes, yes – busy, of course.'

Anna knew at that moment her mother would be pushing her glasses further up her nose, frowning a little in concentration. The telephone always made her nervous. 'Why are you ringing, dear,' she said, a little peevishly, 'nothing wrong, I hope?'

'No,' said Anna, 'everything's fine . . . in fact, you know I'm understudying the leading lady in this play with Gerald Kingdom . . . well, Celia Compton, who I'm understudying, is sick and I'll be playing the role anyway for a couple of nights.' She paused, but her mother said nothing. 'I was wondering whether, well . . . you and Daddy could come down to London and see the play. You know, give me some moral support.'

'Which days are we talking about, dear?' her mother asked, vaguely.

'Tonight and tomorrow night.'

'Oh, I'm afraid we can't, dear, you should have given us more notice. Your father is lecturing tonight, and tomorrow we're going to dinner with the Dean.'

'Couldn't you cancel the dinner?' Anna asked impatiently. 'I'm sure he'd understand, in the circumstances.'

31

'I don't think your father would approve of doing that. Won't you be playing the part again sometime?'

'Possibly on Wednesday,' Anna said. 'It just depends how Celia's throat progresses.'

'Wednesday, Wednesday . . . yes, we could make it then, I suppose.'

'All right,' said Anna, slightly mollified, 'I'll give you a ring on Wednesday morning and let you know whether I'll still be in the play or not. If so, I'll organise you some tickets.'

'Fine, dear.'

'You won't forget, will you, Mummy?'

'Forget? No, of course not.'

Anna's second telephone call was more satisfactory.

'You mean you're actually acting with Gerald Kingdom!' Sally shrieked down the phone.

'Yes, and I even get kissed by him – very soundly indeed,' Anna said, laughing.

'You don't! Heavens, some people have all the luck.'

'Sally, I was wondering . . . you wouldn't come down and see the show tonight, would you? I'd just like to feel there's one friendly face out there.'

'Of course I will, Anna. Let me see, where are we . . . Monday. Yes, I can even get away from the office early. What time does it start?'

'Seven-thirty.'

'No problem,' said Sally. 'Wild horses wouldn't keep me away.'

'Bless you,' said Anna. 'I'll leave a ticket for you at the box office. We're playing to absolutely packed houses, so I'll organise you a house seat.'

'A house seat – that sounds very grand,' said Sally. 'Oh Anna, I *am* excited for you. Are you nervous?'

'No, terrified.'

'You'll be great, you see. The loudest clapping will be coming from me – OK?'

'OK. You'll come backstage afterwards, won't you Sally?'

'How do I do that?'

'Out of the foyer, turn left and left again. The stage door is clearly marked, and I'll tell Freddy to expect you.'

'Can't wait. Must fly, the old man's on the warpath. 'Bye.'

'Goodbye,' said Anna. She replaced the receiver with a smile, basking a little in Sally's evident enthusiasm.

By half past three the same afternoon, while Anna was lying in a steaming bath in Clapham, in Fulham Sophie and Martin had just made love for the second time.

'For an old buffer, you're not half bad,' said Sophie, stretching her magnificent body lazily, like a cat.

Martin lit a cigarette and squinted at her through the smoke. Everything about Sophie was over the top. Her hair, *this week*, was green one side and purple the other, with a single white line dividing the two colours, starting at her forehead and running over the top of her head down into the nape of her neck. She adored food, drank like a fish and smoked like a chimney – yet her skin had a healthy, rosy glow to it and her eyes were crystal clear, the whites standing out startlingly in contrast to the deep green of her irises. Martin placed the cigarette between her lips, and ran a hand down the voluptuous curves of her body. 'How old are you, Sophie?' he asked, suddenly.

'Nineteen, lover. Why?'

'Nineteen,' he mused. 'As if I haven't enough problems, I plunge myself into an affair with a nineteen-year-old, sex-mad punk.' He collapsed back on the pillows. 'I must be out of my mind.'

'Hey, what's all this talk about *having an affair*?' Sophie asked, leaning over him menacingly. 'Why make it sound so heavy?'

'Well, what would you call it?' Martin asked. 'I'm married, I'm old enough to be your father, and yet we end up spending every afternoon like this.'

'We're spending the afternoon making out because it's a wet Monday.'

'It was Sunday and dry, yesterday,' Martin reminded her.

'Everyone makes love on a Sunday afternoon,' Sophie replied, confidently.

'I didn't, until I met you.' Martin reached for the bottle of wine beside the bed, and topped up the glass. 'Mind you, there's a lot of things I didn't use to do before I met you.'

'Marty, what's with you this afternoon – you're one hell of an old grouse.'

He took a sip of wine thoughtfully, and passed it to Sophie. He sighed. 'Nervous, I suppose.'

'What about?'

'The play, you dope – Anna's first night.'

'She's OK – in fact she's great!'

'Yes, that's just it,' said Martin, thoughtfully. 'Potentially she *is* very good. She could have quite a future that girl. It's a damn shame someone like her doesn't have the part permanently. With Gerald heading the cast, we don't need any other celebrities.' He shrugged his shoulders. 'I don't know what's eating me. I think it's just that I like the kid, and I want her to do well for her own sake as well as mine.'

'Don't you start screwing around with her,' Sophie said. 'What you've got, you save for me – right?'

'She's hardly my type,' said Martin. Suddenly he was struck by the comedy of the situation, and started to laugh. 'Though goodness knows, I could hardly describe *you* as my type, now could I?'

'Thanks a bundle.'

He gently removed the glass from her fingers and kissed her. He cupped her great breasts in his hands, burying his face in them, savouring the sweatiness of her flesh. Making love to Sophie was like drowning in her big beautiful body, yet it gave him a release he'd never before experienced.

The girl was a godsend. *Sometime . . . Never* was the most demanding play he'd ever directed. He walked a tight-rope in his relationship with Gerald. One false move and the production could fall about his ears. His position wasn't helped by the fact that he knew few other directors could manage Gerald as he needed to be managed. Martin's tension came, not from doubts as to his own ability – it was his very ability that made him so aware of the potential hazards.

He smiled to himself, his lips exploring the soft plains of her breasts – Sophie was more responsible for the success of *Sometime . . . Never* than she, or anyone else, would ever know.

'Mind you, Marty, while you were making it with Anna, I could suss out Gerald.'

Her voice interrupted his thoughts. He looked up, startled. 'Don't tell me you have designs on Gerald. I may be old enough to be your father – he's old enough to be your grand-father.'

Sophie winked, gathering Martin closer to her. 'There's very few men I don't fancy, lover boy, and Gerald really is something else. You must admit, it would be very interesting to see whether he can live up to his reputation.'

'A reputation, he certainly does have,' Martin agreed. 'He surprised me today, actually. I expected him to give Anna a hard time, but he was surprisingly, well – kind.'

'Perhaps he fancies her too.'

'Oh for heaven's sake, Sophie, can't you ever get your mind above your waist?'

'Not right now, darling.' He felt her hand on his thigh.

'Oh no, not again,' he groaned.

'Haven't you the strength, lover?'

He raised himself on one elbow and stubbed out his ciga-rette. Then he turned to her, smiling slightly. 'I rather think I might. Let's see, shall we?'

Two hours later, a tall, slim figure, in jeans and an anorak, slipped through the stage door. Her face was scrubbed clean of make-up and with her hair scraped back in a pony tail, she looked about sixteen.

'Good evening, Miss Wetherby,' said Freddy.

'Hello,' said Anna. 'It's a beastly evening, isn't it, Freddy. Do you think it'll keep the audience away?'

'Certainly not when there's a new star to come and see.'

Anna laughed. 'That was kind of you, even if we both know it's not true. Freddy, a friend of mine, Sally Braham, will be coming backstage after the show. Could you point her in the general direction of my dressing room?' The words sounded unreal – *my dressing room*, could this really be happening?

'Of course I will, Miss, and Miss, if I don't see you again, best of luck. They tell me you're very good.'

'Let's hope *they* are right. Thanks Freddy.'

The sight that greeted Anna when she opened the dressing-room door stopped her in her tracks. Someone had tidied away Celia's trappings, but far from looking bare, the room was a mass of flowers.

'Not bad is it, being a star?' said Sophie, following her into the room.

'But who did all these come from?'

'Take a look,' said Sophie.

There was a bunch of pale pink roses from Richard. 'Bless you, my dear,' the message read – 'all the luck in the world.' There was an enormous bouquet from Alan Buckmaster – it was a kind thought, but the message was irritating. 'I know my wife's part couldn't be in better hands. Good luck, Anna. A.B.'

'Bloody sauce!' said Sophie.

There was a bouquet from Martin. 'Sock it to 'em, darling,' it read.

'Typical,' said Sophie, with the trace of a smile.

From Sophie herself there was a pot of blackberry jam. 'Sorry,' she said, 'not really appropriate, is it, but I picked the blackberries myself back in September. I made the jam too – it's quite good, really it is.'

'Bless you, Sophie,' said Anna, giving her a kiss. 'I think it's a lovely present.'

'And look what Gerald's given you.' A bottle of vintage champagne stood on Anna's dressing table. A note with it read – 'I'm only making this offering on condition you split the bottle with me after the show. I think you know where to find the ice. Gerald.'

'A real charmer, ain't he?'

Anna grimaced. 'Whatever you do, Sophie, don't let me forget to fix his drink for him at six-thirty.'

'Let him fix his own drink. Fucking hell, you've got enough to think about tonight – the miserable old bugger.'

'Look, Sophie, I'm not just doing it for him, I'm doing it for me as well. If I'm not there to give him the right dose, he might overdo it. As you rightly point out I've got enough to cope with . . . I need Gerald being drunk tonight like a hole in the head.'

'Point taken, love. Come on then, let's have a crack at turning you into a star.'

Anna viewed her shabby appearance in the mirror. 'You're going to have a job.'

'It'll be a bloody sight easier than with some I've known,' said Sophie, firmly.

Promptly at six-thirty, with hair and make-up done, Anna was ready to give Gerald his drink. What to wear – was the problem.

'Haven't you got a robe?' Sophie asked.

Anna shook her head. 'I didn't think of bringing one.'

'All stars have robes,' Sophie said reprovingly. Suddenly she noticed Celia's hanging on the back of the door. It was pink satin with a hideous feathered collar.

'Hey, wear Celia's – go on. I dare you.'

The two girls eyed the robe with mutual distaste.

Anna shook her head. 'I'll just have to wear my shirt. I wouldn't be seen dead in that thing.'

Sophie pouted. 'Spoilsport – still you'll give the old bugger a thrill in that shirt – it barely covers yer bum.'

'Come,' said the voice from within, responding to Anna's knock. Gerald's dresser was fussing round him when she entered. 'Leave us for a few minutes, would you, Ben?' Gerald said. Left alone, they stared at one another in silence. Gerald studied Anna's shirt and raised an eyebrow. 'Very fetching, Miss Wetherby.' As always in his presence, Anna felt uncomfortable and somehow out of control. She could think of nothing to say. 'Funny,' said Gerald, at last, 'I didn't think you'd remember to come tonight.'

'Of course, I remembered,' said Anna, walking over to the tray of drinks, grateful for something familiar to do. She mixed the drink in silence and handed it to him.

He took a sip and grimaced. 'They don't make them like they used to.'

'No, thank goodness,' said Anna firmly.

'Anna . . .' Gerald hesitated; he'd never directly addressed her by her Christian name before, and Anna was aware that a subtle change was taking place between them. At this moment he was treating her like an equal. 'Anna, you did remarkably well this morning,' he said, shortly. 'Repeat the dose and you've got nothing to worry about. I, er . . . I know it can be

37

nerveracking, having to take over, especially your first time in the West End, but I'll be there – remember that.'

And that's the most terrifying part, Anna thought privately. Aloud she said, 'Thank you, and thank you, too, for the champagne.'

'A pleasure,' said Gerald, bowing his head slightly.

'I'd better go,' said Anna, 'I still have a lot to do.'

She started to open the door. 'You will do splendidly, I don't doubt it,' said Gerald gently.

Anna turned and smiled. 'Thank you for . . . everything.'

The last hour seemed to fly by, and as it did so, Anna's tension mounted. Everybody kept dropping in to see her, to wish her luck, to offer advice, when all she really wanted to do was to be left alone. Martin was the last to pop his head round the door. 'I'm going front of the house now, all the best, darling.' After he'd gone, she felt deserted – almost betrayed. At the five minute call, she sat alone at her dressing table and studied her face in the make-up mirror. She'd forgotten all her lines, every single one – she couldn't even remember how the play began. Terror gripped her in a vice and she stared back with enormous eyes, at her own horrified reflection.

'Beginners please, Miss Wetherby, Mr Kingdom, this is your call.' Hearing her own name being called alongside Gerald's terrified Anna still further. She heard Gerald's footsteps go past her door. She stood up, trembling, smoothed her dress and checked her hair. Taking a deep breath, she walked out of the dressing room.

She stood in the wings waiting for her cue while Gerald made his opening speech. She didn't know whether she was going to faint or be sick, but one of them seemed inevitable. Her cue came. She flashed a brief look at Richard, who was standing by her side. He smiled reassuringly.

She moved forward, and as she did so, it was as though she stepped out of the cloak of her own insecurities. She walked to the centre of the stage. The spotlights blinded her and even through the darkness, she was aware that the auditorium was crammed to bursting. She opened her mouth to speak. The words that came out were steady, assured . . . it felt like coming home.

Chapter Four

'Anna, you were wonderful, brilliant – gosh, I'm so proud of you. Give us a kiss.'

'Sally, I can't, I'm covered in cleansing cream.'

'A hug then, give me a hug.' The two girls embraced. 'I couldn't believe it. My old chum up there on the stage. I cried and cried – look at my make-up, has it run?'

Anna studied her friend. The two girls could not have been more different. Sally was short and plump, with a pink and white complexion and blonde curls. She beamed with good nature. 'No,' said Anna, 'you look great, positively blooming.'

'I'm not at all happy about being *blooming*,' said Sally, 'blooming suggests expanding and I know I am – I just can't lose weight whatever I do. How I wish I was thin like you – and tall, I would *love* to be tall.'

'You're just right as you are,' Anna insisted.

'You must be so thrilled.' Sally was beside herself with excitement. 'How do you feel? You were so good – you *were* good, weren't you? I mean, you must know it yourself.'

'Martin seemed pleased,' Anna said, vaguely. turning back to her make-up mirror to start removing the cleansing cream.

'Don't come that *couldn't care less* attitude with me,' said Sally. 'You're thrilled to bits, go on, admit it.'

Anna stopped removing her make-up and turned to face her friend. For all her outward calm, she had never felt more exhilarated in her life. 'You know me too well,' she admitted. 'I *am* excited, of course I am, but a little shell-shocked too.'

'But everyone thought you were marvellous, didn't they?' Sally insisted.

Anna grimaced. 'I've had everybody's verdict except Gerald's.'

'Hasn't he said anything?' Sally's eyes widened at the mention of his name.

Anna shook her head. 'He had plenty of opportunity to do so when we were taking the curtain calls, but he didn't say a word. He was too busy turning his devastating smile on the audience, I suppose,' she added, with a touch of irony.

'I'm sure he must have been pleased,' Sally said, loyally.

Anna sighed. 'I hope you're right.'

Gerald's view really did matter, Anna reflected, as she began brushing her hair. And strangely enough, it wasn't purely because he was a great actor whose opinion was professionably valuable. That was part of it, of course, but the main reason centred on the growing relationship between them. Anna knew instinctively that over the last few hours, she had gained his respect, and respect was something, she judged, Gerald Kingdom didn't hand out too often. Once gained, it seemed vitally important to her not to lose it.

'That kiss!' said Sally, breaking into her thoughts. 'Gosh, what I would give to be kissed like that by Gerald Kingdom. You do realise, don't you, that you've been kissed by one of the greatest screen lovers of our time?'

'Our mothers' time,' Anna corrected.

Sally frowned. 'It's not like you to be bitchy, Anna.'

'I'm not being bitchy, just factual.'

'You looked fairly shattered by it, if I may say so.'

'I was supposed to,' said Anna, shortly. 'It's part of the script. I don't know why everybody makes such a fuss about the kiss. Sophie goes on and on about it, too.'

'Who's Sophie?' Sally asked.

'Our wardrobe mistress. You'll meet her shortly I expect. She's fun in a rather bizarre sort of way.'

As if on cue, there was a knock on the door – it was Martin and Sophie. 'We wondered if you'd like to come out for a drink,' said Martin. 'I do think a celebration is in order – you were really sensational, darling.'

Anna shook her head. 'Thanks awfully Martin, but to be honest I'm absolutely knackered. Would you mind if I said no. Perhaps tomorrow night . . .'

'Oh, do go,' said Sally. 'Don't mind me.'

'I don't know who you are, love, but you come too,' said Martin, smiling at Sally.

'Sorry,' said Anna. 'This is Sally – Sally, this is Martin and Sophie. Look, you're all going to think I'm a dead bore, but it's been quite a day, one way and another, and the answer's still no. Bless you for the thought, though.'

'That's OK.' Martin turned to Sophie. 'It looks like I'm going to be stuck with just you then.'

The doorway was suddenly crowded by a third figure. 'My dear Martin,' said Gerald, 'I can hardly imagine a worse fate.'

'The last of the great romantics strikes again,' Sophie said, glowering at Gerald.

He ignored her. 'I can see grounds for getting rid of you two, but who's this third person, threatening to spoil my intimate little drink with our new leading lady?'

'We can take a hint,' said Martin cheerfully. 'See you in the morning.'

Anna had completely forgotten about the bottle of champagne. 'This is my best chum, Sally. She came down from Oxford especially to see the play – you wouldn't mind her joining us, would you?' Anna knew how much Sally wanted to meet Gerald, and glancing at her friend, she saw that Sally was staring at him, absolutely transfixed.

'A best friend, how perfectly ghastly,' Gerald murmured. 'From school days, I assume?'

'That's right,' said Anna, firmly.

Gerald glanced briefly at Sally and obviously dismissed her. 'Well, I suppose I'll have to put up with both of you, if I must,' he said ungraciously.

Sally looked crestfallen and Anna could have cheerfully killed him. 'Sally is a fan,' she said. 'You should be nice to your fans.'

'I'm always nice to my fans,' Gerald said, wearily.

He had brought with him two exquisite Waterford glass champagne goblets. A cracked mug was found as a substitute for a third glass, which with ill grace Gerald insisted on using himself. The champagne cork came out with a satisfactorily emotive thud, but there was no accompanying sense of occasion. The three of them sat uneasily in the small dressing room. The champagne was warm, Anna had forgotten the ice, and when Gerald pointed it out she was instantly irritated.

'It was *your* gift,' she said. 'Shouldn't you have arranged for it to be chilled.'

'You know where the ice is kept – I don't.'

'You could have asked,' Anna said. 'I had a lot to think about this evening.'

Gerald ignored her, took a sip of champagne, and grimaced. 'At this temperature, I might just as well have brought you some ghastly gassed sparkling wine. You probably wouldn't have noticed the difference anyway.' His voice was heavy with contempt.

'Certainly good company means more to me than good wine,' Anna replied.

Sally looked from one to the other, clearly horrified by their bickering. 'What did you think of Anna's performance tonight, Mr Kingdom?' she said in a desperate attempt to steer the conversation on to safer ground.

The question dropped like a single stone into a silent pond. Anna and Gerald forgot their argument and both turned their attention to Sally. 'It's a subject I would prefer to discuss with Anna, without the benefit of an audience.' Gerald's voice was icy.

Anna was instantly on her feet, her eyes blazing with rage. 'How dare you speak to my friend like that. How *dare* you! Have you so lost touch with reality that you think you can treat people anyway you like?' She picked up the half empty bottle of champagne together with the two glasses and thrust them into his lap, spilling them as she did so. 'Here, take these, I don't want them, and please leave my dressing room. As an actor I admire your talent enormously, as a man I – I utterly despise your appalling bad manners.'

Gerald stood up with commendable dignity. 'I imagine someone must have told you that a display of temperament is tantamount to proficiency in acting. I fear you have been sadly misinformed.' He left the room without another word.

When he'd gone, Anna collapsed in a chair, feeling weak and shaken.

'Anna, I'm so sorry,' said Sally, clearly very distressed. 'It's all my fault. I should have gone as soon as he arrived.'

'*No, you should not!*' Anna thundered. 'You're the dearest friend I have in the world. How dare Gerald walk in here and assume he has some sort of monopoly over me just because he's the big star. I'm very sorry you had to be witness to this scene, Sally, very sorry.'

'Would you like to go out for a drink after all?' Sally asked tentatively. 'I'm sure there'll be somewhere still open.'

Anna shook her head. 'No thanks, really, and *you* ought to be going – you have a long drive back to Oxford.'

Anna dressed, and ten minutes later the girls parted. There was a constraint between them but Anna felt incapable of dealing with it. She was too tired.

On the spur of the moment she decided to take a taxi home. She sat hunched in one corner of the cab, trying to take stock of what had happened to her during the day. The elation she had felt immediately after the performance had been dimmed by her altercation with Gerald – dimmed, but not destroyed. She'd been good tonight, she knew it, and tomorrow she would be better . . .

'All right, break for ten minutes,' said Martin, wearily. 'Anna, could you come and see me in your dressing room.' Anna followed him backstage. 'OK,' said Martin, as soon as they were alone, 'what's with you and Gerald this morning?'

'Does it show?' Anna asked, surprised.

'Of course it shows,' said Martin. 'Tonight's performance is going to be an absolute disaster unless you two can pull yourselves together.'

Anna averted her eyes. 'I'm afraid we had rather a set-to last night.'

'Again . . .?' Martin sighed. 'Was it about drink?'

Anna made a face. 'Ironically, in a way, yes. He left a bottle of champagne in my dressing room last night, and suggested we should share it after the show. When he found my friend Sally was backstage, he took exception to the fact that we were a threesome and started being extremely rude to Sally . . . so, well, I'm afraid I chucked him out.'

'You what?' said Martin.

Anna had the grace to blush. 'I, sort of, threw him out of my dressing room.'

'Anna, you can't do things like that to Gerald Kingdom.'

'It is evident from his behaviour that it's something that doesn't happen to him too often, or at any rate, often enough,' Anna said angrily. 'It's because no one will stand up to him that he's so insufferable.'

'So what are you trying to do?' Martin asked. 'Set yourself up as a one-woman campaign to save Gerald Kingdom from his own personality? Because, if you are, you're choosing one hell of a time to do it.'

'I'm not the least bit interested in saving Gerald. He can behave as he likes so far as I am concerned. All I ask is that he should not inflict his more obnoxious characteristics on to me.' Even to herself, Anna realised the words sounded pompous and ill advised.

Martin stood up, his normally pale face flushed with anger. There was a tic in his left eye. He was exhausted from another hectic night with Sophie, and he was not feeling at his most tactful. 'So far as I'm concerned, Anna, Gerald can behave how he likes. *He's* the star, *he's* the man with the talent, *he's* the person round whom this show hangs. Without him, you, I and everyone else in this company could be out of work. If you upset that man once more, you're out. Do I make myself quite clear?'

'Perfectly,' said Anna, sullenly.

Rehearsals were abandoned for the day in an atmosphere of building crisis. Anna was just leaving to go home when Richard caught her in the passageway. 'How about a quick drink on the way home, dear – just to drown our sorrows?' Angry and humiliated by Martin's words, it sounded like a very good idea. He took her to a wine bar just round the corner from the theatre, and soon they were sitting cosily in a corner, sharing the contents of a small carafe.

For a while they didn't speak, as if Richard sensed Anna needed a little time to settle the turbulence of her feelings. At

44

last he broke the silence. 'Prepare his whisky sharp at six-thirty, just as usual. You'll find that will solve the problem.'

Anna was startled from her thoughts. 'Are you talking about Gerald?'

'Of course I'm talking about Gerald,' said Richard, uncharacteristically impatient.

'He can pour his own whisky tonight,' Anna replied.

'Anna dear, you are two stubborn people, and I realise that neither of you will ever be prepared to say sorry. If you take him his whisky, honour will be satisfied without either of you losing face.'

'Did Martin put you up to this?'

'No, he didn't. I'm suggesting it purely for selfish reasons. It would be a tragedy if you two ruined tonight's perform-ance because of some tiresome quarrel. I couldn't stand the strain.' He smiled slightly. 'You must remember, I'm an old man . . .'

'I don't think I can pander to him to that extent, Richard, even for you.'

'Then you're a fool, my dear,' said Richard gently.

Anna mixed Gerald's whisky precisely at half-past six, and handed it to him.

'Judging by the colour, it's a little stronger than normal. Is this to ensure I'm good-humoured?'

'No,' said Anna, 'my hand must have slipped.'

'Would you care to join me? I have some wine if you would prefer it.'

It was a peace offering and Anna recognised it as such. 'No, thank you very much, I still have a lot to do. I'll see you on stage.' She met his eyes and found them surprisingly compassionate.

'Do as well as you did last night and between us, we'll have them on their knees,' he said softly. Then his sudden kindness seemed to trouble him for he glanced at his watch, feigning panic. 'Is that really the time? Out of my sight, girl, you're not the only one with a lot to do.'

Despite the abrupt dismissal, it was obvious things were back to normal. Richard had been right.

Anna was better, they were both better that second night – more sure of each other, and yet still wary. The volatile nature of their relationship spilled over into their performance. The poignancy of their loving and hating brought the audience out of their seats when the final curtain fell.

Anna was exhausted. She removed her make-up quickly, and slipping on her jeans and an old sweater, started for the door.

Sophie met her in the doorway. 'There's a guy to see you. He's a fan, how about that?'

'Oh Sophie, get rid of him. I don't want to see anyone tonight, I just want to go home to bed.'

'Do you mean it?' Anna nodded. 'Only he is dreamy . . . I mean gorgeous.'

Anna grinned. 'Well, he's all yours.'

'Right on,' said Sophie, enthusiastically.

Anna found her anorak, zipped it up against the cold and started walking along the passageway.

Sophie was back. 'He says I'm wonderful, but it's you he wants to see. He says he has a proposition for you.'

'Is he a nutter?' Anna asked.

'He must be to turn *me* down.' Sophie grimaced, and then relented. 'No, I reckon he looks a regular guy.'

'Where is he?'

'With Freddy.'

'Well, I have to walk that way.'

Anna, used to Sophie's extravagant descriptions of men, was totally unprepared for the man who greeted her at the stage door. Even in the dim light, his good looks were startling – a tall, powerfully built man, not someone who could be brushed off in an instant.

'Good evening,' she said. 'I gather you wanted to see me?'

He hesitated. 'I'd like to talk to you, Miss Wetherby – in fact I was hoping you would join me for dinner.'

'I'm awfully tired . . .' Anna began.

'I realise that. Let's go somewhere quiet and quick.' He smiled. 'It's not purely pleasure, there is a business angle as well.'

'Who are you exactly?' Anna asked.

'I'm a theatre producer – on Broadway.' Anna threw back her head and laughed. 'Why are you laughing?' the man asked, amused at her reaction.

'Some years ago,' said Anna, 'when I very first joined the theatre, a well-known actress, who I think should probably remain nameless, took me under her wing. She gave me a lot of fantastic advice, and one of her great sayings was – "never trust a man who wears gloves or who claims to be a Broadway producer." '

The man grinned and held up his hands. 'No gloves, I'm half-way there.'

Anna looked at him doubtfully for a moment. 'You evidently know who I am. Am I being stupid – *should* I know who you are?'

He shook his head. 'No, Ma'am. Let me introduce myself. My name is Daniel Chase of Chase Productions, New York City.'

Chapter Five

Standing in the shadows was not a natural role for Gerald Kingdom – but he did so now. He watched intently as the two tall figures walked down the street together. Even in the dark, their bright hair – one fair, one rust – shone like twin beacons. The steps they took were youthful, full of vigour, and he heard the girl's laughter ring out as they rounded the corner.

Once they were out of sight, Gerald turned up the collar of his overcoat against the persistent drizzle, and started walking in the opposite direction, towards his car. Who was the man with her – some tiresome boyfriend, he supposed. A callow youth no doubt, certainly not serious competition. The thought halted him in mid step for a moment. What was he thinking of – Anna was not his type. He liked his women glamorous, submissive, hanging on his every word, and yet there was a quality in Anna Wetherby which attracted him, but which he couldn't quite define. He found it disturbing.

A feeling of depression stole over him, as he climbed into the seat of his big Mercedes. His performance that night had been the best yet. He was comfortable in the role now, of course, but the catalyst had been Anna. It was her presence as his wife, which had inspired his performance to still greater heights – and she was damn good too, there was no denying it. He started the engine, but made no attempt to drive away. He was reluctant to go home. Home had every possible material comfort – a luxurious flat in Princes Gate overlooking Hyde Park – but it was a lonely place.

There were at least half a dozen women he could ring at this moment, who in response to his call would come round to his flat – who would flatter him, pamper him, and would gladly join him in his bed. But it was not what he wanted, not tonight. He wanted a *real relationship*. He said the words out loud, as if speaking them would help him understand what he meant by them. He shook his head, bewildered, and with a sigh, swung the car out of its parking place. He would ring no one tonight. He would have a few whiskies and then a bloody good sleep – that should put him right.

The restaurant in Greek Street was perfect – small, cosy and informal. They were given a table in the window, with a good view of the street. Anna smiled at Daniel. 'Do you know, I think I could stay up all night watching the world walk by – particularly here in Soho, there are the most wonderful collections of people.'

'I hope that means you like it here,' said Daniel.

'Yes, I do,' said Anna. 'It's a terrible trait of mine, but I do adore watching people. I was on holiday in Paris last year, and I spent nearly the whole time sitting in cafés, just studying the passing traffic. I'd like to pretend it was useful for my work, but really, I think I'm just inquisitive.'

'Would you believe, I did exactly the same thing?' Daniel said, unaccountably excited by the discovery. 'I was over in Paris in the Fall. The weather was beautiful, golden, and *I* just sat in cafés, watching the world go by, I loved it.'

'I've never thought of Americans as being observers,' Anna said, genuinely surprised. 'I've always thought of them as people who dash around *doing* things, far too high-powered to just sit and watch.' She grinned at him, 'Especially Broadway producers.'

'Ah,' said Daniel, 'but I'm only half American, the other half's English.'

'Which half?'

'My mother . . . my mother was English.'

'Was? Has she died?' Anna asked gently.

Daniel nodded. 'I never knew her. She died in childbirth – mine.'

'Oh, I'm so sorry,' said Anna. 'I probably shouldn't have asked you – it's my inquisitive nature again, you see.'

49

'It's OK,' said Daniel, but Anna could tell it wasn't. Despite their brief acquaintance, she had caught a glimpse of a deep hurt in some dark corner of his mind.

He was talking again. 'Yes, I suppose because the country is in my blood, I've always loved England, and Europe too. It'd odd really – I had an all-American upbringing. You know – I chewed gum, ate hamburgers, played baseball, went to college – yet I feel, in a crazy kind of way, there's an Englishman trying to get out.'

The waiter arrived. 'Are you ready to order?'

They both looked at him in surprise, they hadn't even begun to study the menu. 'I guess not,' said Daniel, 'we've been too busy talking.'

'I tell you what I'd love,' said Anna, 'just a simple steak and a salad.'

'Make that twice,' said Daniel. 'Rare?' She nodded. 'And a carafe of your house wine – red, I guess.'

The waiter disappeared and Daniel turned to Anna once more. She was struck by his good looks and somehow, his strength – not only physical, a mental resilience was evident too. Indeed, she formed an immediate impression that here was a man who got what he wanted. There was a toughness about him, and yet strangely at odds with this apparent characteristic, she felt there was a vulnerability too. Perhaps her view was coloured by the reference to his dead mother. It was odd that, the way they had immediately started talking so intimately.

'It's strange,' said Daniel, putting a voice to her thoughts, 'but already it feels as though I've known you a long time. Oh hell, that didn't come out right – it was a real schmaltzy line.' He frowned in concentration. 'How do I explain – it's just that somehow you have extracted more information from me in the first five minutes of our conversation, than I normally disclose in a couple of dozen dates.' He smiled. 'In the circumstances I think it's only fair to tell me something about yourself.'

'No,' said Anna, firmly, 'not until you tell me why you've invited me out tonight.'

For the first time, in as long as he could remember, Daniel

felt an over-riding desire to tell the exact truth. He looked down at his hands for a moment, trying to collect his thoughts. Absolute candour with women didn't come easily. He looked up at her and met her eyes. 'You were partly right about not trusting my motives. I am genuinely a Broadway producer. I work for my father,' his voice sounded hard, a little bitter, even to himself. 'I'm over here because I'm interested in taking *Sometime . . . Never* to Broadway. I realise, of course, that you were only understudying the part of Sarah tonight for Celia Compton, so I guess my plans don't really affect you.' He paused, speculatively, for a moment, and then smiled. 'Hey, but I thought you were great, by the way.' Anna started to protest. 'No, genuinely. You are an extremely accomplished actress, but I have to admit, I don't have any parts to offer an English girl right now.' He sighed, all this honesty was a strain. 'I asked you out to dinner for two reasons – the main one being I thought you looked the kind of person I'd like to spend an evening with, and secondly, I thought you might be able to give me little background information on the various personnel involved in *Sometime . . . Never.*'

'Do you know something, Mr Chase,' Anna said, 'you've just gone up in my estimation enormously.'

'I have! Great, that's very generous of you. May I ask why?'

'Because I think you've just told me the truth.'

'Ma'am, I have that,' said Daniel, laughing.

'And you know what else?' Daniel shook his head. 'Although it was quite clearly an effort, I don't think it was as painful as you had anticipated.'

Daniel stared at her in amazement. 'It's kind of spooky having one's mind read, but I guess I might get to like that too.'

While they ate, Anna talked Daniel through the details of the company. 'What about Martin Peters, the director?' she asked. 'Presumably you'll want to take him too?'

'Do you think I should?'

'Most definitely. It takes a very special man to handle Gerald Kingdom. Gerald is wonderful, brilliant, with enough talent in his little finger to rate him as a first-class actor, but

51

he's a very difficult man to understand.' She took a sip of wine. 'It's a question of handling him right. Up to a point he needs to be pandered to, in order to protect his ego, and yet with too much rope, he'll hang himself. Martin plays him like a fish.'

'You sound as though you know Gerald Kingdom pretty well.'

'I'm starting to,' Anna admitted, 'though I think you could say our relationship has not been without incident.'

'Oh really!' said Daniel, raising his eyebrows.

'No, not that kind of incident,' said Anna, grinning. 'Seriously Daniel, I think you'd be making a big mistake to separate Gerald from Martin. He needs very careful direction, particularly in a play as sensitive as *Sometime . . . Never*.'

'I guess you're right,' said Daniel slowly. 'Certainly Gerald's legendary problem with booze is going to cause a lot of hassle, when I approach the Angels. If I present them with a successful actor/director partnership, they may feel more confident.'

'Angels,' said Anna thoughtfully. 'I know they're the people who put up the money for theatre productions, but who *are* they exactly – I've always wondered?'

'That's the fascinating part. They can be almost anyone – business men of course, but also doctors, lawyers, farmers, little old ladies – in other words, a complete cross-section of society. Some of them form themselves into syndicates so they can command a big stake in the production – others invest just a few dollars. Obviously every producer has his tame Angels – people who respect his judgement.'

'It *is* fascinating,' Anna agreed, 'and we humble players think we have all the headaches!'

The steak finished, they ordered coffee and brandy. 'Now, I've fulfilled my part of the deal,' said Daniel, 'it's time *you* came across with the goods. I want to hear all about Anna Wetherby, starting with the day you were born.' He noted with surprise the sudden change in Anna's expression.

'I don't know anything about the day I was born,' she said quietly.

He smiled. 'Well, I guess you wouldn't remember too much about it.'

'No, I don't mean that . . .' she hesitated.

Daniel sensed immediately that there was some sort of problem ahead. 'Go on,' he said encouragingly.

'Well, you see, I'm adopted. Like you, I have never known my mother . . . my real mother.'

Daniel's expression was serious too now. 'So, what happened to you?'

'I was very lucky,' Anna said, quietly. 'I was adopted when I was just over three weeks old. My parents, my adoptive parents that is, live in Oxford. My father is a university don.' She smiled indulgently. 'His subject is ancient history. He's awfully sweet, but one feels he would be far more at home among the ancient Greeks than he is in the twentieth century.'

'And your mother?'

'Same as Daddy, only slightly less exalted. She's a university lecturer.'

Daniel was acutely aware that he was treading on dangerous ground, but for some reason he had to know more. 'It must have been great, growing up in Oxford. It's a wonderful city.'

'Yes, it is,' Anna agreed.

Daniel tried again. 'Do you mind being adopted?'

'It came as an awful shock,' Anna admitted.

'You mean, your parents didn't tell you from the beginning?'

She shook her head. 'I don't think they were trying to be deceitful or unkind. I think it just never occurred to them that it was important.'

'Tell me about it,' Daniel asked.

'I was eleven,' said Anna, after a moment's pause. 'The date was December 10th and it was the day of our Christmas school play.' She smiled shyly at Daniel, a smile he found quite delightful. 'I've always had this long, rather unruly hair, and my mother was brushing it for me. It needed to look especially good since it had to be put up for the play.' Her eyes were suddenly full of pain. 'We were standing in front of a full-length mirror in my mother's bedroom. She has this habit of looking over the top of her glasses. Anyway, she squinted at my reflection in the mirror, and said – "You'll be too tall, of course, but I think you're going to be quite a good looking girl Anna, when you grow up." '

'She was right,' said Daniel, softly.

Anna ignored him, too caught up in the drama of the past. 'And I replied – "I can never make up my mind whether it's you or Daddy I look most like." Then, then, my mother simply stopped brushing my hair and said, almost crossly – "Don't be silly, dear, you obviously can't expect to look like either of us, bearing in mind you're adopted." '

'Jesus, did she really say that?' Anna nodded. 'That is incredible! How did you react?'

'I was stunned,' Anna admitted, 'shocked, horrified, frightened.' She smiled at him sadly, 'And I forgot all my words in the school play that afternoon. I kept going over and over it in my mind – it seemed such a terrible thing. You see, at the time, I thought it meant they couldn't love me, like proper parents do.'

'Poor little girl,' said Daniel, softly. 'Did you ever want to find your natural parents?'

'Not for years,' Anna said, 'but then when I started going through the usual teenage traumas, I suppose it was inevitable I should do so. Of course, I decided my natural parents would understand me far better than my adoptive ones, and in fairness there are some grounds for taking that view. As parents go, mine are awfully sweet, but they live in a different world from the rest of us. It's always been a source of astonishment to me that they actually wanted to adopt a child when they discovered they couldn't have any of their own. They are far happier in some stuffy old library, with their noses in a book, than they are building sand-castles, or playing Monopoly.'

'Finish the story,' Daniel demanded. 'Did you try to locate your natural parents?'

Anna nodded. 'I ended up talking to a social worker in Torquay. I found out I'd been born there, and the social worker was able to tell me that my mother had been twenty at the time of my birth, was unmarried, and . . .' she paused.

'And . . .?' said Daniel.

'An actress.'

'I see,' said Daniel, slowly, 'and did you find her?'

Anna shook her head. 'I got no further than the social worker. Although it was quite possible I might have been able to trace my mother, the social worker talked me out of it. We spent hours going through the whole saga but her advice was not to pursue my search. She considered my motives to be somewhat suspect, and in the end I had to admit she was right. You see, I was simply reacting against my adoptive parents—punishing them for not telling me sooner about the circumstances of my birth. I was, I suppose, in a crude way trying to pay them back for the hurt I'd felt. She also asked me to consider things from my mother's angle. Since my mother was only twenty when I was born, almost inevitably she must have married at a later date, and probably now has a new family. Apparently in these cases, it is highly probable that her husband and other children know nothing about me. The arrival on the scene of an illegitimate daughter could ruin her life.'

'Yes, I can see that,' said Daniel, gently.

Anna smiled at him. 'So I abandoned the search, but I'm afraid I hurt my parents dreadfully by pursuing it in the first place. I think they felt they'd failed and somehow we've never really been close since.'

'That's sad,' said Daniel. There were so many other questions he had wanted to ask her – whether she had become an actress because it was what her mother had been, whether she still felt insecure, whether there was a special man in her life. He sensed, however, he'd asked enough – for the time being at any rate.

Anna, too, had apparently decided it was time to end the conversation. 'Heavens, I talk too much. I hope I haven't bored you.' She glanced at her watch. 'You know, I really think I ought to go home now. I may be required on stage tomorrow night again. Celia is going to give us a verdict on her throat tomorrow morning, but just in case I am needed, I ought to get some sleep.'

'No, you didn't bore me, and yes, I do understand your

needing to get home – I'll ask for the check . . .' he paused, '. . .and Anna, I am really grateful to you for joining me – I've had a great evening.'

Anna smiled back at him warmly. 'So have I,' she said.

'I'll order a cab,' said Daniel, as he paid the bill, 'then I'll ride with you to your apartment, and then take the cab back to my hotel.'

'You can't do that,' said Anna, genuinely appalled. 'I live in Clapham.'

'So?' said Daniel.

'It's south of the river. Where are you staying?'

'The Ritz,' Daniel replied.

Anna was amused. 'I might have guessed,' she said. 'Broadway producers can't really stay anywhere else, can they?'

They talked little on their journey out to Clapham. Both were shocked by the suddenness of their intimacy for neither of them were used to talking about themselves.

'I must see you again, before I go back to the States,' Daniel said, at last. 'I'll be tied up tomorrow morning in negotiations, but what about tomorrow evening? Can I take you out again?'

Anna shook her head. 'I'm hoping my parents are coming up to see the performance, in which case we'll have dinner together afterwards.'

'Well, the following day for lunch then – how about the following day?'

'I don't know what rehearsals there'll be yet, but can I say yes, tentatively? When are you going back to the States?'

'Friday, I guess,' said Daniel.

That silenced them. Without being able to put a name to it, they both felt something momentous had happened to them. Yet, it was obvious that fate had decreed they would never find out what – it hardly seemed practical to even consider conducting any sort of relationship three thousand miles apart.

When they arrived at Mrs Franks' house, Daniel jumped out of the cab and held the door open for Anna. She stepped down beside him and for a long moment they simply stared at one another. At last Daniel held out his hand. 'Goodnight

Anna, and thank you for a very special evening.' Formally, they shook hands, yet both seeming reluctant to let go. It was Anna who finally tore her hand away and began climbing the steps to the front door.

'Goodnight,' she called, 'thanks again.'

'I'll pop in to the theatre tomorrow so we can fix up Thursday.'

'OK,' Anna called.

Daniel smiled to himself in the darkness, as the taxi wound its way through the dreary south London streets. He couldn't remember ever having shaken hands with a girl in order to wish her goodnight. Come to that, he couldn't remember the last time he'd taken a girl to dinner but not to bed. Perhaps he was losing his touch. Whatever the cause, he didn't care. He was feeling good – good about being in England, good about the play but most of all, at that moment, good about Anna.

The room was icy. Anna couldn't afford to leave the electric fire on while she was at the theatre. She threw off her clothes and dived into bed, which was cold too. She pulled her knees up to her chest to try and keep warm, and waited for sleep.

It wouldn't come. It had been a long, difficult day, but she felt strangely alert. The evening with Daniel had disturbed her. The theatre was a place of short-term, shallow relationships. There had been a steady stream of friends, both male and female, in Anna's adult life, but no relationship had ever touched her. Probably her most intimate friendship, in terms of discussing her true feelings, was with Sally. And even with Sally, it was a question more of habit than choice – that, and loyalty. Sally after all had been the confidante to that bewildered eleven-year-old, who had just discovered the truth about her parentage. Sally had been a tower of strength then and Anna would never forget it. Sadly though, they had little in common now – the other night had proved that.

Yet here was this strange American who had walked into her life just a few hours before, and with whom she'd started to share the most intimate details of her life. It was unnerving, yet exhilarating. They were worlds apart – she thought of him now, in the extravagant comfort of the Ritz, while she

57

fought a losing battle to keep warm. Yet something special *had* happened between them, hadn't it . . .?

Five miles away, at Princes Gate, the empty whisky bottle crashed into the grate, sending splinters of glass in all directions. Gerald watched it fascinated, but detached. He glanced up at the photograph on the mantelpiece, showing a young boy in cricket pads. 'Chris,' Gerald addressed the photograph, his voice thick with drink. 'Your father is nothing but a drunken old sod and there's only one thing that will sort him out. You know what it is, don't you, old boy? The love of a good woman, that's what I need. The trouble is, I don't know any good women.' He paused, and took a sip of his whisky. 'There's the delectable Miss Wetherby, of course. Have I told you about her, Chris? Not my type really, but she needs someone like me, someone to soften her sharp edges. I wonder what she actually thinks of me – she probably throws all those tantrums in the hope of making an impression. Women are odd creatures, Chris, bloody odd. Still it's not something you'll ever have to worry about now, is it?' He stood up, swaying dangerously, and raised his glass towards his son's photograph. 'To Miss Anna Wetherby,' he said, 'the only good woman I know.'

Tears began to course down his handsome face, but he was too drunk to brush them away.

Chapter Six

'So far as I'm concerned, the sooner the better,' Gerald announced.

His two companions reacted in totally different ways.

'That's great,' said Daniel Chase.

'It's ridiculous,' Alan Buckmaster countered. 'There's no need to transfer for at least a year – this play will run and run.'

Gerald ignored him and addressed himself to Daniel. 'When would you like to make the transfer?'

'In three months' time,' Daniel replied. 'I'd like to open on Broadway at the beginning of March so that the play is well established in time for the Easter break.'

'That would suit me very well,' said Gerald, shooting a challenging look at Alan.

'But why, Gerald?' The veteran producer stood up and started restlessly pacing the floor. 'It doesn't make any sense. When we orginally discussed the concept of *Sometime . . . Never*, your one idea was to re-establish yourself on the British stage. Now, at the first possible opportunity, you're hot-footing it back to the States.'

'My dear Alan,' said Gerald, 'I really can't see why you have any objection. After all, we've proved the point. *Sometime . . . Never* is a howling success, which is why our young friend here wants to be part of it. The deal he's offering us all is generous to a fault – surely, it's a natural progression?'

'Ultimately, yes.' Alan paused in his pacing and ran a hand through his thick, white hair. 'But why so soon? This play is doing us all a lot of good. Being associated with a smash hit lends enormous credibility in the eyes of the British public.

It's good for your reputation, for mine, for Celia's . . .'

'Celia!' Gerald spat out. 'What in God's name has Celia got to do with anything? The only reputation she has, is as . . .'

'Stop!' Alan roared, his face suddenly suffused with anger. 'I'll put up with just about anything from you Gerald, but you are not to insult my wife.'

'If you don't want her insulted, you shouldn't bring her into the conversation. She can't act, she's too bloody old and quite frankly, she hasn't any sort of reputation to maintain.'

'Celia has a considerable following.'

'I suppose you could describe it as that,' said Gerald, nastily. 'Certainly, her audiences are frequently heard to say – ' "oh no, not that silly old bitch again".'

Daniel saw it was time to intervene. 'Look, you guys, this is getting us nowhere. You can exchange insults any time, but right now, let's get back to business.' The two older men turned and glowered at him, and Daniel had to struggle to stop himself smiling. Quite clearly, the scene he'd just witnessed was a ritual affair, which they both hugely enjoyed . . . and he'd had the audacity to interrupt it.

He began to talk quickly to stem any further interruptions. 'It's really as simple as this. We have a theatre available at the beginning of March and that's when we'd like to transfer the play. So far as future commitments are concerned, I can't make any guarantees. We might be interested in the play in a year's time, we might not. You could run for another twelve months here and then find *Sometime . . . Never* has no place to go. The opportunity on Broadway is *here, now*.'

'Precisely,' said Gerald, triumphantly, 'and it's an opportunity we can't afford to ignore.'

'If *Sometime . . . Never* continues to play to full houses during the next twelve months, we'll have no trouble in transferring to Broadway,' Alan insisted. 'Even if Chase Productions don't want us, someone will. We'll have a proven product to sell. I just don't understand this unholy rush, Gerald.'

'Money,' Gerald replied.

'What?' Alan stared at Gerald, his brow wrinkled.

'Money, dear boy. You know, the stuff that rules your life . . . and mine. Young Mr Chase will be paying me precisely 'four times what I'm currently receiving from you.'

'But you can't be short of a bob or two,' Alan protested.

'I have plenty of everything, including creditors,' Gerald replied drily.

Alan walked over to the window and stared down into the street below. Gerald's exposé had surprised him. All those films should have amassed him a fortune, yet quite clearly he must have squandered the lot. What a waste – Alan despised the misuse of money. What had Gerald spent it on, he wondered – three divorces, women, booze – they must all have taken their toll. He sighed. He knew he'd lost the battle and it was a shame because he'd looked forward to the relative peace of a long run in the West End. The role was perfect for Celia. She could enjoy all the glamour and notoriety of being a smash hit, without having to play a part which was beyond her. Whatever he told the world, Alan Buckmaster was under no illusion as to the true extent of his wife's talent.

He turned round to face the room. 'I'm not sure how Celia is going to react, she was looking forward to spending the coming year in London.' He grimaced. 'She's never really taken to Broadway.'

You mean, Broadway has never taken to her, Daniel thought privately.

'I suppose this is something I should have mentioned before,' Gerald said suddenly, 'but there is a condition to my accepting your offer, Mr Chase.'

'A condition?' Daniel was suddenly apprehensive.

'I will make the transfer if, and only if, Anna Wetherby comes with me. I'm not prepared to play on Broadway with Celia, or anyone else, come to that. I want Anna in the role of Sarah. No one else will do.'

Anna managed to reach the telephone without really opening her eyes. 'I hope you're not going to make a habit of this,' she grumbled.

'Darling, don't be grumpy, I am the bearer of good news. Incidentally, how's Cape Horn this morning?'

Anna forced her eyes open and stared down the passageway to the front door. It was a brilliant sunny morning. It was also perishing. 'There's no wind or rain,' she conceded, 'but the temperature is sub zero. Tell me, Martin, do you get some sort of sadistic pleasure from hearing how the other half lives?'

'We've all been through it, darling. Now listen, there's good news, and good news. You're playing Sarah for one more night. Celia will be back tomorrow, but for tonight the part is yours. Secondly, there'll be no rehearsals this morning. Gerald is having some sort of set-to with Alan Buckmaster, and besides which, what is there to rehearse? After last night's performance, I feel anything I said would be entirely super-fluous.'

His words slowly filtered through. 'Does that mean I can go back to bed?'

'It means you can go back to bed.'

Daniel paid off the taxi. Dodging the traffic, he crossed Park Lane and started striding across Hyde Park towards the Serpentine. It was a beautiful morning, the air was crisp and clean and the frost crackled under his feet as he walked. It was hard to imagine that he was in the middle of a city.

He was hardly interested in the beauty around him though. He walked briskly, with his hands thrust deep into the pockets of his trousers, his head bent, his shoulders hunched against the cold.

So she was just like all the rest. Why was it that women thought the only way to stardom was on their backs? He was angry with her – he was angrier still with himself for being so gullible. After all this time, he should have known better. What he'd taken for innocence, was just play-acting – her apparent honesty was simple cunning. He'd allowed himself to be completely taken in with all that stuff about being adopted. It was probably a pack of lies – just another way of ensnaring his interest. Well, she'd clearly got her man in Gerald Kingdom. Quite a scoop for a young actress, Daniel thought bitterly.

He reached the Serpentine, and paused, caught up momentarily, in the beauty of the scene before him. Then he hurried on. Damn and blast all women – still he knew what to do. Anna Wetherby would be put firmly in his file marked 'disappointments'. There had been plenty of those in Daniel Chase's life.

He glanced at his watch. It was just after eleven. He'd better hurry. He had an appointment to see Martin Peters in his Fulham flat, at eleven-thirty.

Sophie answered the door. 'Oh, it's you,' she said, 'I thought you'd got away.'

Daniel struggled to remember where he'd seen her before, and the bewilderment showed on his face.

'You've forgotten me!' said Sophie, accusingly. 'I'm the one you turned down last night, in favour of our new star, Anna. Remember?'

Daniel smiled. 'Yes, I remember. I guess I screwed it up. I clearly made the wrong choice. Do you think another time I could take you up on your very kind offer?'

Sophie smiled, delighted. 'I'm dead sure you could – anytime you like,' she said, her voice husky with suggestion.

'Sophie, what are you doing?' Martin called from somewhere in the flat.

'Seducing your visitor!' she shouted back cheerfully.

'Oh, that's all right then.' Martin appeared in the little hallway and the two men shook hands, both immediately liking what they saw. Martin could understand Sophie's interest in Daniel – the man had film star looks, but also a strength of character showed in his face. Here was a man, Martin felt, in whose life there was little room for compromise.

Daniel watched fascinated, as Martin dashed around his sitting room, patting cushions, tidying away newspapers, and grumbling at Sophie for her untidiness. His quick, deft movements spoke of a restless energy, his passion for neatness suggested perfection in all he did. At last Martin was satisfied with the room. He straightened up and grinned at Sophie. 'To make amends for being such a slut, go and make us some coffee, darling.'

'Try "please",' Sophie suggested.

'Bugger off,' said Martin, good naturedly and Sophie went,

without apparent resentment. 'Now,' he said, turning to Daniel, 'sit down and tell me what this is all about?'

Daniel didn't waste time with preliminaries. 'I'm taking *Sometime . . . Never* to Broadway in March, and I'd like you to come too and direct the play. I could employ a director from my own stable, of course, but I have a feeling your handling of Gerald is kind of crucial to the play's success. Do you read me?'

'Yes . . .' said Martin, slowly, 'and I think you're probably right. When did you say, though – March?'

'Yes, it's imperative we open before Easter. I'd like to get the play settled in by the holiday period, which means opening around the 3rd or 4th. In other words, we'll close the play here towards the end of February, and move to New York right at the end of the month.'

'Sod it,' said Martin, clearly agitated. 'I can't do it, I'm sorry.'

This was something Daniel hadn't bargained for. 'Can't – why on earth not?'

'I'm committed to a television project over here during February and early March.'

'How long does it last?' Daniel asked.

'Six, maybe eight weeks.' Martin sighed. 'I'd assumed *Sometime . . . Never* was set for a long run in the West End. Had I known what was in store I wouldn't have committed myself so soon, but as it is, I confirmed the timing with the television company only last week. There's no way it can be altered now.'

'Surely you can do *something*,' said Daniel. 'Can't you skip it? Bearing in mind your importance to *Sometime . . . Never*, I think we would be susceptible to helping you break contract. Hell, Chase Productions can afford to pay a few damages.'

'I can't do that,' said Martin. He was clearly not trying to negotiate – there was no room for compromise in his reply.

Daniel was curious. 'It must be a big deal to have you turn down the opportunity to direct on Broadway. What is it exactly?'

Martin smiled slightly. 'It's a documentary I do every year about a group of mentally handicapped children in a specia

64

school. We've traced their progress since babyhood, and seen how they've developed. They're eight years old now – this year should be particularly interesting.'

Daniel shook his head in disbelief. 'Hey, Martin, I really admire you for your commitment, but this has to be crazy. There must be any number of directors who could handle the project – at any rate, just for this year.'

'No, that's quite impossible,' said Martin. 'I have to do it myself.'

'You *don't* have to do it,' Daniel said impatiently.

'Look,' said Martin, standing up, 'would it help to explain the situation if I told you that one of those kids is my son, Robin.'

It was something that hadn't occurred to Daniel. 'Oh shit, I'm sorry,' he said, 'I guess I put my foot in it. Your kid's mentally handicapped, right?'

Martin nodded. 'Robin has Down's Syndrome – you know, that means he's a Mongol.' He shrugged his shoulders. 'Obviously I became involved in doing this programme because of Robin, but now it's not simply about him any more. You see, I think the programme has a real contribution to make. Year by year, it shows people, ordinary people, the kind of anguish parents have to go through when they have a severely mentally handicapped child. It's a very sensitive subject and it's not one I can simply hand over to anyone else. There's no script, no real pre-planning – I simply move into the home with a camera crew for a few weeks, and see what happens. The story emerges as we go along. I'm sorry, Daniel, but that's the way it is.'

'I understand,' said Daniel, 'and I'm sorry – it must have been very rough on you and your wife.' This was obviously where Sophie fitted in, Daniel thought. It rather looked as though she provided Martin with much needed light relief.

They sat in silence for a few moments, both lost in thought.

'Couldn't you hold back the transfer until April?' Martin suggested, suddenly.

'No,' said Daniel, 'it's out of the question, I'm afraid. It's too late in the season to open on Broadway and in any event the theatre is available from end February. My father would never agree to keeping it dark for two months. A couple of weeks is too long by his standards. As it is, he'll be looking for any excuse he can find to avoid running *Sometime . . . Never*.'

It was Martin's turn to be curious. 'So, why are you persisting with the play in the teeth of such opposition?'

'I'm beginning to wonder,' Daniel admitted. 'First I'm going to have to fight my father tooth and nail, now it looks as though I can't have you, and if that wasn't enough, Gerald is insisting on bringing along his floozie.'

'His floozie?' Martin frowned. 'Who's that?'

'Oh, the young understudy, Anna Wetherby.'

'Gerald's floozie? You've got to be joking!'

'Who's Gerald's floozie?' said Sophie, arriving with a jug of coffee.

Martin smiled. 'Trust you to come in at this moment. I think Daniel is about to tell us all about it.'

'There's nothing to tell really,' Daniel replied shortly, 'it's just that Gerald is insisting on Anna playing Sarah on Broadway. If he can't have Anna he says he won't transfer.'

'Oh, I *see*,' said Martin. 'Well, that's not entirely surprising. Anna's performance is much better than Celia's, and Gerald positively loathes Celia anyway.'

'No, there's more to it than that,' Daniel insisted. 'Gerald made it quite clear that he had plenty of plans for Anna, on and off stage. These girls make me sick. They think they an screw their way to the top, and they don't seem to care what they do to themselves in the process.' His voice sounded so bitter that Sophie and Martin both looked at him in surprise.

'I'm sure you're not right about Anna,' said Martin. 'What do you think, babe?'

Sophie shrugged. 'Still waters and all that – it wouldn't surprise me.'

Martin took the coffee pot from Sophie's hands. 'I'll pour,' he said, with a smile. 'I know I'm an old-fashioned type, but I rather like drinking my coffee out of mugs, rather than lapping it off the floor.'

Sophie walked over to Daniel and draped an arm round his shoulders. 'You wouldn't treat me like this, would you?'

'No,' Daniel agreed, 'if there was any chance of your spilling

66

coffee on my floor, I'd have chucked you out long ago.'

'Fuckin' men,' said Sophie, morosely.

'So what are you going to do?' Martin asked.

'I guess I'm going to press ahead without you – in fact, I've already started drawing up the contracts.' Daniel sighed. 'It's a risk, but I know March is the right time for this play to hit Broadway. There's such a lot of crap on at the moment – *Sometime . . . Never* will make a refreshing change.'

Martin studied him in silence for a moment. 'I'd like to think you are going to succeed. Certainly I admire your spunk, but I honestly believe you're making the wrong decision. You're stacking the odds against success too high. Frankly, with all due modesty, I think you need me to make it work – Gerald is a sod of a man to handle.'

Daniel nodded his head, but quite clearly his decision was made. 'I guess we'll just have to hope he remembers some of the lessons you've taught him.'

'Amen to that,' said Martin, sagely.

'What!' said Anna.

'Don't be tiresome, Anna darling, you heard me the first time.'

'To Broadway – with you?'

'Yes, to Broadway, with me.' Gerald smiled. 'You see, in the end, your patience and persistence have been rewarded. After all these years of toil, thanks to a little help from this particular friend, at last you are going to receive the recognition that should be yours by right.' He bowed gallantly.

'I don't know what to say . . .' Anna stammered. 'I really am incredibly grateful.'

'How interesting it will be,' said Gerald, 'to find oneself the recipient of your gratitude, rather than your wrath.'

Anna blushed. 'Yes,' she said, with a smile, 'in the circumstances, you really have been most forgiving.'

'I shan't continue to be unless you pour my whisky. It is now three minutes overdue.'

Anna mixed his drink in silence. A million questions were coursing through her mind. How long would the run last, how much money would she earn; would Richard, and indeed Martin, be coming too?

Gerald correctly interpreted her silence. 'The official announcement will be made tomorrow morning,' he said, 'but I expect you'd like to know some of the details in advance. I was wondering whether you would join me for dinner after the performance tonight.'

Anna looked crestfallen. 'I'm awfully sorry, I'd love to have done, but my parents are coming down to see the play tonight. I don't really think I can abandon them when they've travelled all the way from Oxford.'

'Most certainly you can't,' said Gerald, clearly at his most expansive. 'I'd be delighted to take all three of you out to dinner.'

'Oh no, really, you mustn't.'

'I must, I insist,' said Gerald.

'But they're not your type, honestly, it will be a disaster.'

'When I entertain people to dinner, it is never a disaster,' he said, confidently, 'and besides which, your parents ought to meet me in order to see what sort of man their daughter will be mixing with in the months to come.' Clearly, he was not going to be dissuaded.

'Thank you then,' said Anna, 'it's very kind of you. I'd better be going, I'll see you later.'

'Most certainly you will,' said Gerald, giving her the benefit of his brilliant smile.

As Anna walked back to her dressing room, she tried to imagine Gerald Kingdom and her parents at the same dinner table. It was an impossible picture. She sat down thoughtfully at her dressing table and began applying her make-up. Strangely enough, as she worked, she did not think about Gerald nor indeed about the possible career opportunities this marvellous new development might offer. Her thoughts instead returned again and again to Daniel Chase. What seemed to be important to her was the fact that for some months to come she and Daniel would be working together . . . and living in the same city.

Chapter Seven

Anna felt extraordinarily comfortable on stage the third night. The knowledge that the role of Sarah was to be hers on Broadway gave her a proprietorial feeling towards the part. She wore it like an old friend, blossoming with new-found confidence. The fact that her parents were in the audience added a further fillip. She wanted to prove herself – to show them that her decision to become an actress had not been the emotional reaction of a teenage girl, but the mature decision of someone who'd known what she was doing and where she was going.

'We're going to miss you,' Richard whispered in her ear, as they took the final curtain call.

Anna grimaced at him. 'Yes, it's back to making the tea tomorrow.'

'You do that very nicely too, dear,' said Richard, grinning wickedly.

Gerald caught her arm as they were leaving the stage. 'I've arranged a little surprise for you, Anna,' he said. 'Champagne on stage in five minutes.'

He put his finger to his lips. 'It's not to celebrate the transfer,' he said, 'it's your farewell party – remember, the Old Boot's back tomorrow. Now go and change and bring your parents with you, of course.'

Thank heavens I've got something decent to wear, Anna thought, as she began to change. She'd been shopping that afternoon in anticipation of having dinner with her parents. The dress she'd bought was wildly extravagant. Made in pure cashmere, the colour of clotted cream, it was a perfect foil for her chestnut hair. She slipped the dress over her head and

69

stared critically at her reflection. The effect was just right – it had been money well spent. For once, she felt a genuine surge of confidence. 'You're on your way, Anna,' she whispered into the mirror.

There was a knock on the door. Sophie was standing outside with Anna's mother and father in tow. 'I've just told them that it's tuppence to speak to you these days,' said Sophie. 'Still, I expect since they are your parents, you'll let them in for half price.'

'Get lost, Sophie. Hello Mummy . . . Daddy.'

Sophie was not to be deterred. 'I gather there's a piss-up on stage,' she continued conversationally. 'Take a nice long time saying hello to yer Mum and Dad, and then, with a bit of luck, I'll get your share – of the champagne, I mean,' she said, giggling.

May Wetherby's astounded gaze followed Sophie out of view. 'What an extraordinary girl! Is she half-way through dying her hair or is it always like that?'

Anna laughed. 'I think it's supposed to be like that, Mummy. How are you?'

'We're fine,' said May, 'aren't we, Stephen?'

Anna's father nodded, absentmindedly. He, too, was clearly still attempting to recover from the effects of Sophie.

'Come in a moment,' said Anna. 'I'll just put on some war paint and then, as you probably gathered, we've been invited to a party on stage. After that, Gerald Kingdom is going to take us out to dinner. I hope that's all right, but I couldn't really refuse.'

'Well, I suppose so,' said May, doubtfully, 'but I had rather hoped we'd have a quiet family supper. I shan't know what to say to the man.'

'It'll be fine, Mummy, there's a lot to talk about. You see we have something to celebrate. You mustn't tell anyone yet, because it hasn't been announced, but I'm going to be offered the opportunity of playing Sarah on Broadway.'

May looked blank. 'Broadway?'

'New York, dear,' said Stephen, helpfully.

'Good heavens,' said May. 'When are you going? How long will you be away?'

'I don't know any more than you at present,' said Anna, 'but I'll be told all the details tomorrow. Mummy . . .?' She paused midway through applying her lipstick. 'Did you . . . did you like the play?' Her confidence suddenly seemed to have deserted her as she waited for her mother's reply.

There was a long pause. 'It was rather a gloomy subject,' May suggested.

'*I* was very proud of you,' Stephen said suddenly. 'I had no idea you were so good, Anna. I think you played your part magnificently.'

Anna smiled at her father. 'Thanks Daddy,' she said with relief.

Everyone was already on stage by the time they arrived. Gerald saw them enter and began to clap, and soon everyone joined in. Gerald drew Anna to his side. He silenced the company and then began to speak – his beautiful voice holding everyone spellbound. 'The reason I've invited you all here tonight is to remind you of something that we, veterans of stage and screen, all too easily forget. Talent in the performing arts is not the exclusive property of the experienced, of the well tried and tested. There should be room *always* for fresh, new, exciting talent, and it is our job, not only to recognise it when we see it, but actively to seek it out. Anna has brought a new dimension to *Sometime . . . Never* during the last three nights. She has demonstrated that you can have star quality without being a star. As of tonight, very few people have ever heard of the name "Anna Wetherby", but in five years' time, I am confident that she will be enjoying her rightful place as one of the most celebrated young acting talents of this generation.'

Everyone clapped. Someone handed Anna a glass of champagne. She felt her cheeks burning with excitement. So this was what it felt like to be a success – the feeling was heady, intoxicating.

Richard drew her on one side. 'Congratulations again, my dear. Do you know, I think you've just scored a first.'

'What do you mean?' said Anna.

'In all the years I've been associated with Gerald, I've never heard him make a speech about anyone but himself.'

Anna laughed. 'Oh, Richard, that's rather cruel.'

'Cruel it may be, my dear, but true nonetheless. You've been good for him. It's a very healthy sign that he's showing an unselfish interest in someone else for a change.' Richard frowned, suddenly. 'At least, I assume it's unselfish.'

'What do you mean, Richard?' Anna asked.

Richard shrugged his shoulders, casually. 'You know me, dear, I ramble on . . .'

Anna gazed around the room. Gerald had whisked her parents away. Her father was now in conversation with Martin and seemed quite happy. Her mother was being subjected to a heavy dose of Gerald's charm and though flustered, was clearly loving it. Suddenly, in the far corner of the stage she saw a familiar fair head, taller than the rest. It was Daniel. He was standing as she was, watching the proceedings. Their eyes met and held. Anna smiled but there was no answering warmth in Daniel's eyes – indeed, there was barely even recognition. Troubled by his lack of response, Anna hurriedly excused herself from Richard and walked over to him. 'Hello, Daniel.' He stared at her coldly, making her feel unaccountably nervous and unsure 'I – I just came over to say thank you again for such a lovely time last night. I don't know when I've enjoyed myself so much.'

'Oh, I'm sure there are plenty of great evenings ahead of you now, evenings which you will find far more enjoyable than last night.' His tone was sarcastic and there was an unmistakable bitterness in his voice. Anna recoiled from him, shocked by his hostility. 'What is it, what's wrong?' she asked, shakily.

'Oh, nothing's wrong,' Daniel replied, 'in fact everything's just wonderful, isn't it? You've charmed the Great Man into taking you to Broadway and in the process you've bought yourself instant stardom.' He looked her up and down. 'I suppose he bought you that dress too. Certainly, there's been a dramatic change in you in the last twenty-four hours. Me, I prefer the street look – Anna Wetherby in jeans and anorak.'

Anna stared at him. 'Daniel, I don't know what you're talking about. Could you please explain why you're so angry.'

'Oh, don't play the innocent, I really can't take that. At

least have the integrity to admit what you are. Christ, if you start deluding yourself, you really are finished.'

He was starting to make her angry. 'What exactly am I supposed to admit?' she asked.

'Look, honey, when a man like Gerald Kingdom makes it a condition of a big dollar contract that some unknown actress should play an insignificant part in his play, one doesn't have to be Einstein to work out what's going on.'

'You mean . . . Gerald made *me* a condition of the contract?' Anna said, slowly.

Daniel let out a great sigh, and ran a hand through his hair. 'Jesus, Anna, are you really expecting me to believe you didn't know?'

'Yes I am. Of course I didn't know, though I'm certainly going to find out why he did it.'

'You know why he did it, *I* know why he did it. He enjoys screwing you and you've convinced him there's plenty more to come once you're installed in some cosy little pad in New York.'

Anna stared at him in disbelief. 'You mean, you think I'm having an affair with Gerald, in order to further my career?'

Daniel sneered at her. 'Perhaps I've been underrating your acting abilities – this is certainly some performance.'

'How dare you!' Anna said. She couldn't believe this was the same man who'd made her feel so good only the previous evening.

'Oh I dare,' said Daniel. 'How you choose to run your life is up to you. In ordinary circumstances, I wouldn't give a damn if you slept with every jock backstage, but for some reason, last night, you made me think you were different. Oh, you were good. You had me daydreaming, would you believe? I actually thought that you and I might be going to have something special. I just don't know how I could have been so dumb.'

'Daniel . . .' Anna began.

'Shut up,' he said, roughly. 'What I hate most about this whole mess is your dishonesty. Take . . . what's the broad's name . . . Sophie, over there. She's nothing but an unpaid hooker, but she has the honesty to admit it. You – you make

73

me sick to my stomach.' He turned on his heel and left her, slamming down his empty champagne glass on the tray Sophie was holding. Anna watched his retreating figure, her heart hammering in her chest.

'Hey, what's with glamour boy?'

'How do you mean?' Anna tried to focus her attention on Sophie.

'Why did he leave in such a hurry? What on earth did you say to him?'

Anna ignored her question. 'Sophie, you don't think I'm sleeping with Gerald, do you?'

Sophie avoided her eye. 'It's none of my business whether you are or not, love.'

'That wasn't the question,' Anna insisted.

Sophie shrugged her shoulders. 'Can't say I've really thought about it much. It seems logical though,' she conceded. 'Most of us have heard about the transfer and it seems the old bugger made quite a song and dance about you going too.'

'I'm *not* involved with him,' Anna said, vehemently. 'I don't know why he was so adamant that I should go with him, but it's not because there's anything between us.'

Sophie shrugged her shoulders again. 'If you say so. I'd better go and collect some glasses, or this lot will be here all night.'

She doesn't believe me either, Anna thought. Suddenly, all the excitement of the evening seemed to have drained away. The truth was almost irrelevant – if everyone *believed* she had been given the part because she was having an affair with Gerald, her triumph was a hollow one.

Anna found dinner that evening a terrible strain. Gerald took them to Langan's Brasserie. The food was wonderful and the atmosphere dazzling – the place was full of celebrities of one sort or another.

'I thought I'd bring your daughter here to improve her education,' Gerald said to May. 'She has to start thinking now like a star rather than a tea girl, so she needs to become used to rubbing shoulders with the rich and famous.'

Anna managed a smile, and that was about all she did

manage to do that evening – smile. Luckily, her mother was unusually animated, and even her father became fairly chatty. Gerald's charm was irresistible.

At last it was time to go. As they were standing up, May said, 'Gerald, we've had a wonderful evening and really would like to repay your hospitality.'

Gerald smiled, 'There's no need really, I've enjoyed the evening too.'

May hesitated, obviously embarrassed. 'We're having a party to celebrate our twenty-fifth wedding anniversary on the last Sunday in January. Why don't you come up to Oxford and join us. We're holding the party in one of the colleges and we have plenty of room if you'd like to stay the night.'

Anna was horrified. 'Oh, Mummy, it's hardly Gerald's sort of thing,' she burst out.

'On the contrary, I should love to come,' Gerald said firmly. 'Thank you, May, for asking me, I'd be delighted to accept.'

May Wetherby blushed to the roots of her hair.

At last, Anna's parents were reunited with their car and Anna and Gerald were left alone. 'Where to now?' Gerald asked. 'Do you want to go straight home to bed, or would you like a nightcap?'

'I'd certainly like to talk to you,' Anna replied.

'Then a nightcap at my flat it shall be.' Anna hesitated and Gerald could not resist a smile. 'My dear girl, after the day we've had, I'm sure neither of us are up to any heavy seductions tonight.'

Gerald's flat came as no surprise to Anna. It was stylish and elegant, like its occupant. There was a quiet air of laid-back luxury. Everything was in good taste, and thanks to the ministrations of a faithful housekeeper, in excellent order, too. Only the library surprised Anna. It was a comfortable room, cosy even, with books and papers spilling out of shelves onto the floor. Even the armchairs had that well lived-in look of slightly collapsing springs.

'I hope you don't mind my bringing you in here,' said Gerald, 'but we can light a fire, and anyway, it's a very relaxing room.' He poured them both a brandy, put a match to the gas fire and they sat for a while either side of the fireplace, in a companionable silence.

'Well,' said Gerald at last, 'you've been extraordinarily quiet all evening. What's going on underneath all those chestnut curls?'

Anna looked up and met his eyes. 'It is being said that the reason I've been given the chance to go to Broadway is because you and I are having an affair.'

'Is it now?' said Gerald, clearly delighted.

'You may find it funny, but I don't. Apart from the fact that we both know it's not true, it also doesn't say much for my acting, does it? I'd like to think I was given the part on merit, and that being the case, I'd prefer the record to be put straight.'

'I can see your feathers are well and truly ruffled,' said Gerald. 'What a shame. We could have given the performance of our lives, gazing into each other's eyes, sending each other little notes . . .'

'Stop it,' said Anna, close to tears.

'Look, darling,' said Gerald, 'you really mustn't take life so seriously. Why does it matter a damn what people think – they're only jealous, anyway! This is a unique opportunity for you. Sit back and enjoy it, and to hell with everyone.'

'But why did you insist on my transferring with you?' Anna persisted.

'Let me make one thing clear straight away,' said Gerald. 'You could look like Helen of Troy, Marilyn Monroe, Juliet or Cleopatra, and you wouldn't have stood a chance of getting the part if you couldn't act.' He shrugged his shoulders. 'As for my more sinister motives, let us just say I like having you around. Broadway can be a fairly lonely place – yes, even for someone like me. You make me feel comfortable,' he looked about him, 'like this room.'

'I'm shabby and untidy, you mean?' Anna couldn't help smiling.

'Perhaps a little,' Gerald conceded, 'but warm and comforting, definitely comforting.'

It was an odd sort of compliment but Anna felt surprisingly reassured by it. She stood up and wandered over to the fire place. She sighed. 'I'll try and do as you suggest and ignore the gossip,' she said. 'I just don't find it very easy.'

'Life isn't,' said Gerald, sipping his brandy.

Suddenly Anna noticed the photograph on the mantelpiece. Before she could stop herself, she said, 'I-is that your son?'

'Yes,' said Gerald, shortly, clearly inviting no further comment.

She guessed she'd probably gone too far already, but something drove her on. 'Richard told me a little about him. He . . . died, didn't he?' Gerald nodded. 'What was he like?' she found herself saying.

Gerald stared into his brandy glass. 'He was bright, amusing, good looking, strong and healthy – until he was seventeen years old. A pusher introduced him to heroin at a party. It took two years to kill him. In the end, he didn't even want to live.'

'It must have been terrible for you,' Anna said, quietly.

'I read somewhere,' said Gerald, so quietly that Anna had to strain to catch what he was saying, 'that the human mind can fully recover from any tragedy, except for the death of a child. That's the one you never get over – it's the guilt, you see.'

'And you have a reputation for being a person who only thinks of himself,' she said incredulously.

Gerald looked up and smiled. 'Well, grief is only self-indulgence, isn't it?'

She left him then. He wanted to ring for a taxi, saying it was too late to be out alone, but she needed to walk, and think. The night was dry and crisp, a blessed relief after the weeks of rain. She walked for nearly fifteen minutes and finally picked up a cab in Knightsbridge. All the while, she turned over and over in her mind the events of the day. She had received notice of the first big break of her career; she was still reeling from Daniel's rejection; she'd been branded as Gerald's mistress . . . Gerald – she couldn't get out of her mind the expression on his face when he'd spoken of his dead son. Yes, it had been quite a day.

Chapter Eight

Daniel watched her as she slept. Even in sleep, her strong features had the unmistakable mark of the English aristocracy. Her hair was glossy, her skin flawless and healthy from country living. He guessed she must be nearer forty than thirty, but he suspected she'd changed very little in the last twenty years. If anything, she was probably better looking now than she had been as a young girl – the slightly aquiline nose and high cheek bones suited a mature face.

They'd met the previous evening in the bar of the Ritz. She was staying there too – up from the country to do some Christmas shopping. They'd had a few drinks together, and because they were both at a loose end, they'd talked late into the night. He'd discovered that her name was Fiona, that her husband's name was Rupert, that they had two teenage boys, both at Eton, six horses, a well-preserved Georgian mansion and fifteen hundred acres in Northamptonshire. Fresh from his contretemps with Anna, he welcomed the diversion, rather than risk being alone with his thoughts.

So absorbed had Fiona seemed with her family, it had never occurred to him that their evening would end with anything other than a hearty handshake. He was surprised, therefore, when she invited him to her room for a nightcap, and still more so, when she'd started, quite blatantly, to seduce him. Her vigorous, enthusiastic love-making seemed out of character with the cool, elegant woman he'd met earlier in the cocktail bar. It had been a busy night – he'd read somewhere that horsy women were particularly randy and certainly, there appeared to be some truth in the statement.

She stirred slightly in her sleep and reached out a hand to

him. 'Jamie,' she murmured, 'Jamie, is that you?'

'No, Ma'am,' he said, 'Daniel Chase, at your service, as indeed I've been on and off all night.'

Her eyes snapped open and she smiled lazily at him. 'So you have,' she said. Her voice was deep, her accent polished. He found it very attractive.

They kissed, and it was some minutes before Daniel remembered the reference to Jamie. 'Jamie?' he said suddenly, 'who's Jamie? I thought your husband was called Rupert.'

She was not even slightly ruffled. 'Jamie is a friend,' she said, 'a good friend – we've known one another for many years.'

Daniel frowned. 'You mean you're having an affair with him?'

'Daniel, dearest, you make it sound so suburban. Let's call him my lover – it sounds far more exotic.'

'How often do you meet?' Daniel asked, surprised to find himself shocked at her ready admission.

'I come down to London one or twice a month, and I stay overnight, of course.'

'Of course,' said Daniel, sarcastically. 'So what went wrong last night?' A hard note had come into his voice.

'There was some beastly dinner in the city which Jamie simply had to attend.'

'So you picked me up instead?'

'That's not very gallant,' Fiona said.

'No, it's not,' Daniel agreed, 'and it wasn't intended to be.' In one swift movement he was out of bed and began picking up the clothes he'd discarded in such haste the previous night.

Fiona propped herself up on one elbow and stared at him. 'Where are you going?' she demanded. 'It's early yet, I thought we might have breakfast in bed.'

'Well you thought wrong,' said Daniel. 'Perhaps if you ring for room service, you can persuade the waiter to dally a while when he brings your breakfast. After all, there's nothing like variety, is there?'

'Oh, so that's what's wrong with you,' she said, 'I'm rather afraid you're threatening to be stuffy. Men are such

79

conservative creatures really.' Daniel zipped up his trousers and began pulling on his shirt, completely ignoring her. 'Daniel, will you kindly speak to me. I know Americans have a tendency to be brash, but your behaviour is moving into the realms of discourtesy.'

'Good manners at all times – even in the bedroom, right?'

'Of course,' she replied.

'It doesn't matter what you do as long as you are polite about it. Not content with cheating on your husband, you're now cheating on your lover, or whatever you call him. I think your life stinks, Fiona. I'm sorry that, however briefly, I was a part of it. Let's hope the mud doesn't stick.'

'Get out!' she shouted. 'Get out of my room. How dare you speak to me like that.'

'Don't worry,' said Daniel, 'I'm going.'

Back in his own room, he showered and then lay down on his bed. He felt tired and depressed. Why had he reacted so violently? he wondered. He'd enjoyed their night together, he'd known from the beginning that Fiona was married – so why this morning's scene? He was nothing but a hypocrite. Of late, he seemed to be increasingly jaundiced where his relationships with women were concerned. It was as though he was searching for something he could never find, something which always eluded him – and probably always would, he thought miserably. Involuntarily the image of Anna Wetherby came back into his mind. Despite the emotion of the moment, he couldn't help but remember how stunning she'd looked the previous evening – that rich chestnut hair, those enormous eyes. Although she was tall, there was a fragile quality about her – even in jeans she looked very feminine.

He glanced at his watch. In two hours' time he and Alan Buckmaster were due to announce to the company the transfer of *Sometime . . . Never*. Whatever his personal disappointment so far as Anna was concerned, he would have to try and make amends today. He had let his personal feelings run away with him the previous night, which was both inappropriate and unprofessional. In a few months' time he would be working with the girl – they had to create some sort of armed truce. He picked up the telephone and asked reception to call him in an hour. Then he slid wearily between the sheets and fell into a troubled sleep.

The meeting was a subdued affair. Alan Buckmaster spelt out the reasons for the transfer, confirmed the date the play would be closing in the West End, and Daniel gave Gerald and Anna a letter spelling out the terms and conditions of their employment with Chase Productions.

The money seemed fabulous to Anna. After years of struggling on an assistant stage manager's pay, this newfound wealth seemed almost unreal. She knew she should feel excited, but somehow she couldn't. There were too many clouds hanging over the whole affair. Alan's speech had come as a profound shock since she'd hoped that the whole company would be transferring to Broadway – the only change being herself replacing Celia. Instead she found that she and Gerald alone were involved. The thought of being without, not only Richard's company but, even more important, Martin's direction, made her feel understandably apprehensive. Coping with Gerald alone seemed a monumental responsibility. You're being stupid, Anna told herself. Gerald is Chase Productions' problem, not yours, but somehow she couldn't see it like that.

And then, of course, there was Daniel. His cool, polite manner of this morning was almost worse than his accusations of the evening before. He'd shaken her formally by the hand when presenting the letter. 'I hope you'll be very happy working for Chase Productions, Anna,' he'd said. The eyes that met hers were cold and impersonal.

When the meeting broke up, Anna followed Richard Manning into his dressing room. 'If I make the coffee,' she said, 'can we talk?'

'Of course, dear. You know I have a well-trained avuncular ear. What's your problem?'

'I thought you'd be transferring too.'

Richard shook his head. 'No, small parts like mine practically never cross the Atlantic, one way or the other – Union rules, you see. Chase Productions have to put up a fairly strong case for employing a British citizen rather than an American one.'

'But butlers are always English, Richard.'

He grinned. 'There are enough English butlers in the USA to sink a battleship,' he said. 'Besides which, I wouldn't have wanted to go – Alan knows that. Margaret, my wife, hates America, and I certainly wouldn't leave her behind.'

Anna handed him his coffee. 'You are a nice man,' she said. 'I wish there were a few more like you around.'

Richard smiled his sweet smile. 'After a sentiment like that, I'd better offer you a chair, hadn't I?'

They sipped their coffee in silence for a few moments.

'But if the small parts don't normally transfer, why am I being allowed to go?' Anna asked.

'Well, rules are there to be broken, aren't they?' said Richard. 'Gerald, I understand, made your transfer a condition of his accepting the role. There's bound to be a Mr Fix-it in Chase Productions who can square things with the Union.'

'People think I'm having an affair with Gerald,' Anna said, in a small voice, 'but I'm not, Richard.'

'No, I know you're not, my dear, but you do need to be careful.'

'Why?' Anna asked.

'Gerald is a great deal older than you but he is still a very attractive man, and above all, he's an accomplished seducer. You'll find it lonely in the States, particularly at the beginning. This play and Gerald will be the only familiar things around. Take my advice, my dear, and don't get involved with him. *He's* a born survivor, but he has destroyed a lot of lives during the course of his chequered career.'

'Surely not . . .' Anna began.

'No, I don't mean he's committed any crimes,' Richard said, hurriedly. 'He doesn't even actively go out intending to hurt people. It's just that he's so wrapped up in himself, he habitually makes a mess of his personal relationships. You see the normal rules appertaining to loyalty and integrity don't seem to apply to Gerald. People get hurt.'

'He seems to have cared a great deal about his son,' Anna said. 'We spoke about him last night.'

Richard shrugged his shoulders. 'I don't know much about it. The boy could have been the one person who got through to Gerald, but even then, one is forced to ask the question, why did Christopher take to heroin?'

'You surely can't blame Gerald for that?' Anna said.

'I'm not really blaming Gerald for anything, my dear. I'm just saying that people who care about him seem to wind up in trouble.'

Anna finished her coffee and stood up. 'I'm going to miss you,' she said.

Richard smiled. 'I'm going to miss you too. Come here and give an old man a kiss.' She bent and kissed his dry cheek – it smelt of reassuring things, like tobacco and Pears soap. She drew away, smiling. 'Promise me . . .' Richard began, then he hesitated, staring at her, a frown suddenly forming a deep furrow between his eyebrows.

Anna quickly sensed his change of mood. 'What is it, Richard?' she asked. 'What's wrong?'

He pulled himself together with obvious effort. 'Nothing, nothing, my dear, it's just that . . . well, just for a moment, you reminded me of someone. All I was going to say was – be careful. Promise me.'

'I will, Richard, I can look after myself, you know.' She winked at him and then slipped out of the door.

Richard sat on alone, staring at the spot where she'd been, listening to the sound of her footsteps dying away.

'I hope you're right, my dear,' he said quietly.

'Anna!'

Anna whirled round. Daniel was standing on the edge of the stage. His face was in shadow so she couldn't see his expression, but she thought she could sense tension.

'What are you doing here?' she asked, alarmed. 'I thought everyone had gone.'

'I could ask the same of you,' said Daniel.

'I'm just going to set up the props for tonight,' Anna replied. 'It'll save doing it later on.'

'And I've been waiting for you,' said Daniel. 'I thought perhaps we might grab an early lunch together.'

'I wouldn't have thought you'd want to be seen having

lunch with a fallen woman,' Anna said, sarcastically. 'Thanks for the offer, but no thanks.'

'Look,' said Daniel, 'I'm here to apologise – I guess I was rude last night. Your private life is your own affair and I have no right to criticise.' He ran a hand through his hair. 'I'm not exactly a saint myself, heaven knows.'

'Perhaps that's the trouble,' Anna said, coldly, 'perhaps you judge everyone else by your own standards. Has that occurred to you?'

'Look, Anna, don't let's fight again,' said Daniel. 'It's been quite a week for us both. I'm tired, I expect you are too. All I really wanted to say was, I'm sorry and I hope what I said won't make it too difficult for us to work together.'

'Oh, so that's it,' said Anna. 'You thought you'd soften me up with a lunch, just to make sure there would be no problems with the production once we transferred. I may not be very old, Daniel, and I may not be very experienced, but I am a professional actress. Subject to my agent checking the details, I'll sign your contract. Once signed, so far as I am concerned I am committed to giving you my best, and that's exactly what you'll get, regardless of my feelings for you.'

Her eyes were bright with anger, her colour high. She looked magnificent when she was angry, Daniel realised. He shook his head. 'Oh God, I'm getting myself even deeper in the shit. Look, Anna, I'm sorry – I'm sorry for everything. I just don't like the idea of you throwing yourself away on that old guy.'

'I'm going to say this once more and then so far as I am concerned, the subject is closed for ever. I am not having an affair with Gerald Kingdom and I have no intention of ever doing so. You and everyone else can think what you like. I can't tell you why he insisted on my going with him to Broadway. I tried to find out last night, but he couldn't really explain himself. However, regardless of his motives, I am not prepared to go on and on justifying myself when there's nothing to justify.'

'I want to believe you,' Daniel said, quietly. He sounded sincere, even to Anna's somewhat jaundiced ear.

'Then perhaps you should try,' she said. 'Haven't you ever heard of trust?'

'Oh, I've *heard* of it,' said Daniel, bitterly. 'But I also know it's something a guy can't afford to have too much of in this life. In my view, trust merely represents taking an unnecessary risk with one's peace of mind.'

'Perhaps you should try taking that risk,' said Anna. 'You might find trusting someone quite a revelation.'

'Someone like you?' Daniel asked.

'Why not like me? To you, I'm just another unknown actress, using any way she knows how in order to further her career . . . but I'm not like that, I'm *not*.' There was a catch in her voice.

Daniel moved out of the shadows and, taking Anna by her shoulders, turned her to face the light. 'You're crying,' he said, bewildered.

'What if I am?' said Anna angrily, trying to wipe away her tears.

'Why are you crying?'

There seemed little point in not telling him the truth, since quite clearly there could be nothing between them now. 'Because, like you, the other evening meant something special to me. For some reason I seemed to be able to talk to you and . . . and I don't think I've ever met anyone, man or woman, who I've liked as much as I liked you that night. I know it sounds ridiculous, but it felt straightaway as though you were my friend.'

'I felt the same,' Daniel said, softly, 'and that's why it hurt so much when I found out about you and Gerald. I felt . . . well, betrayed.'

'I haven't betrayed you,' Anna whispered, her voice a little steadier.

'I'd like to believe that.'

They stared at one another in silence. Daniel still held Anna by the shoulders. Carefully, gently, he pulled her to him until her head rested on his shoulder, and her arms slid round his waist. In an instant, the raw emotions of the moment before were replaced by a feeling of warm comfort. They relaxed against each other. Anna's body felt soft and inviting against his own and Daniel longed to kiss her, but he knew the moment was wrong. The thread that bound them was too fragile, too easily damaged beyond repair.

'When you come out to the States,' he whispered against her hair, 'do you think we could try again – try to be friends? Strange as it may seem, I need a friend.'

'So do I,' Anna replied.

They drew apart, awkwardly, both aware of the strong undercurrents between them, both terrified of making a wrong move.

'Do you write letters?' Anna asked, suddenly.

'Only business letters. I just call friends when I've got something to say.'

'Why don't we write to each other?' Anna suggested. 'That way, we could keep in touch over the next couple of months. I'd feel awkward if you rang me, I wouldn't know what to say – I'd get flustered.'

'I think that's a fine idea,' said Daniel. 'I probably won't be very good at it, though. I don't think I've written a proper letter since high school.'

'Nor me,' Anna admitted.

They sat down on the edge of the stage and exchanged addresses.

'When are you leaving?' Anna asked.

'I'm catching a flight out at three o'clock this afternoon.'

'Oh!'

Their eyes met and held. 'I guess I'd better go,' Daniel said. 'We don't feel like lunch, do we?' Anna shook her head, and he stood up.

'Will you take care?' she said, in sudden panic.

He held out his hand, she took it. 'So long as you make sure you do too. I'll write you a letter on the plane.'

'Will you?' she said. 'Will you really?'

'I promise.' He bent forward and, fleetingly, his lips brushed hers in the smallest of kisses.

'Goodbye,' Anna whispered.

'Goodbye, little one. See you in two months.' He turned and walked away from her, down the corridor towards the stage door. It took all her strength not to call out to him, not to say – don't go, hold me again.

When he was out of sight, Anna sat down on the stage once more. She glanced at her watch. It was barely ten minutes since she'd left Richard's dressing room. Ten minutes which had changed her life – for she knew, without a shadow of doubt, that nothing would ever be the same again, now Daniel Chase was her friend.

Chapter Nine

'Jesus, Dan, you've done what?' Matilda Jackson was appalled.

'Oh, come on Mattie, you heard me the first time, it's in the bag – *Sometime . . . Never* is ours.'

'You . . . you mean, you've actually issued the contracts?'

Daniel grinned rakishly. 'Yep, and the copies are here in my briefcase. I've got a good deal too. Alan Buckmaster, the English producer, is a fair man – I didn't have any trouble.'

'But Walter will go bananas, I mean . . . spaced out.'

'Well, he's just going to have to learn to live with it, because this deal is going through.' Daniel's face was grim – then suddenly he smiled, looking around his office with obvious pleasure. 'It's nice to be back, Mattie, and good to see you too.' He gave her a quick hug but she was not to be mollified.

'But why didn't you just agree terms, as your father instructed? Why did you have to sign them up?'

'Mattie, don't tell me you've gone over to the enemy while I've been away.'

'No, of course I haven't. I just don't understand why you've rushed into this.'

Daniel sighed, and slumped down into his chair. 'It's a complicated situation – the most complicated part about it being, of course, Gerald Kingdom. Not only is he the star, and a volatile one at that, but he owns thirty per cent of the play as well. The rest of the ingredients are kind of crazy too – the producer's wife is currently Gerald's co-star, but Gerald has refused to bring her to the States. The British director can't transfer with the play, and at the last moment,

Gerald made it a condition of his contract that he brought over a relatively unknown British actress to play opposite him.'

'Let me get this straight,' said Mattie. 'We have Gerald Kingdom, but he's sacked his co-star. We have no director and we're stuck with some kid in the supporting role who Gerald enjoys screwing – but that's probably all she's good at. Christ Almighty, Dan, you must be out of your mind.'

'Actually, she's very talented, and she's not sleeping with Gerald,' Daniel replied, tersely.

Mattie studied him for a long moment.

'Oh,' she said, 'so that's the score. You've fallen for the kid.'

'Anna is just a friend,' Daniel said, defensively. 'She's nice, you'll like her, Mattie, but there's nothing between us.'

'Since when was there ever *nothing* between you and a female of the species – it's not your style.'

'Well, perhaps that's where I've been going wrong,' said Daniel. 'Now, for heaven's sake, quit grousing and get the hell out of my office. I've got a lot of work to do before I see the old man.'

Daniel and Matilda rarely quarrelled and when they did it never lasted long. Having furiously paced her office for five minutes, Mattie made some coffee and took the pot and two cups in to Daniel. 'Hey look, I'm sorry,' she said. 'That was one hell of a homecoming. I really want you to succeed with this play, I know how much it means to you . . . only I get worried.'

'It'll be OK, Mattie,' Daniel said, reassuringly.

'But the old man can be such a bastard and I hate seeing you get trampled underfoot.'

Daniel grinned up at her, 'I'm not a kid any more, Miss Jackson. Now, pour that coffee, and if you really want to help, let's try and get some sort of report down on paper. I'm due to see my father tomorrow morning.'

'OK,' she said, uncertainly.

'Oh, and Mattie . . . for Christ's sake, smile.'

The following morning was bitterly cold. Flurries of snow the previous night had frozen into treacherous icy patches. The traffic was slow moving; there were endless accidents and Daniel arrived at the office over half an hour late. It was not a good start.

'Go right on in,' said Freda, Walter's secretary. 'He's expecting you.'

'I'm sorry I'm late,' said Daniel. 'What sort of mood is he in?'

Freda grimaced, 'Interesting, I'd say.'

'Oh hell, that doesn't sound too good.'

Walter Chase was standing by the window, puffing his first cigar of the day. He turned as his son entered. 'Daniel,' he said, warmly, 'how was the trip?'

'Fine, thank you,' said Daniel. 'How are things here?'

'Great, never better.' It was an unusual response from Walter Chase who was not normally so jocular.

Daniel couldn't disguise his surprise. 'No kidding?'

'Yeh. I'll tell you all about it, but first, let's hear about your trip.'

Daniel launched straight into the presentation of his deal, bending the facts where appropriate. He told his father he had decided against employing the British director on the grounds that Chase Productions had access to more proficient talent. He knew it would be a popular argument, and it was well received. Walter liked to think Chase Productions did everything better than anyone else.

When Daniel had finished running through the details, he took a deep breath. 'So that's the deal,' he said, 'but there's something I haven't mentioned.'

'Oh?' He had his father's full attention now.

'I went ahead and issued the contracts while I was in London. There's nothing left to do except hand over the cash.'

'Oh, is that *all*?' Walter's tone was far from friendly. Daniel hurried on. He had one last card to play. Walter firmly believed that only Americans knew how to conduct a deal and he loved to knock the British for their lack of business sense. 'Well, you know the British,' said Daniel. 'I didn't dare leave town without tying them down to a contract. In America it's so easy. You just wave enough dollar bills and you have your deal. Negotiations in the UK are never that simple – there seem to be so many other influences besides making the odd buck.' Walter said nothing, and Daniel encouraged, pressed on. 'Look, I appreciate I shouldn't have gone ahead without your blessing, but I know I've done the right thing. This play will run and keep on running. Hell, we shouldn't have any trouble raising the money. With its track record in the West End, it should be a cinch. I'll handle the negotiations, you won't have to do a thing. I reckon this play could be one of the biggest things that's ever happened to Broadway. It's got quality, style and it's going to do one hell of a lot for the image of Chase Productions.'

'The only thing that's good for Chase Productions is profit,' Walter said sourly.

Daniel judged it was time to move on to the practicalities, to assume the decision to produce *Sometime . . . Never* had Walter's approval.

'Who do you recommend I go to first to raise the dough?'

'You're not going to any goddam Angels – I don't want my reputation shot,' Walter burst out.

'But we're committed.'

'*You're* committed. *You* issued the contracts, not me.'

'I issued them in the name of Chase Productions.'

'Do you remember Charlie Richards?' Walter said, suddenly.

'That sleazy childhood friend of yours – the porn artist? What the hell's he got to do with anything?' Daniel was getting rattled.

'Shut up a moment, will you,' said Walter. He strode over to his desk and viciously stabbed out his cigar in the ashtray. 'Sit down and listen,' he commanded. 'You never know, you might even learn something.' Daniel did as he was told – one false move now and he knew *Sometime . . . Never* would be down the pan. 'As you are aware,' Walter continued, 'my so-called sleazy friend and I have dabbled in the film business for some years.'

'Aren't I just,' Daniel said, sarcastically. 'Blue movies – it's one of your activities I prefer not to think about. What do you and Charlie call yourselves – "Fantasy Films"? It sounds like you're ripping off Walt Disney, but I guess you don't feature too many Snow Whites.'

Walter Chase leaned back on his chair and looked

speculatively at his son. 'They're very tastefully done,' he said, 'if you like that kind of thing.'

'Yeah, I'm sure – I just don't happen to.'

'How would you feel about the whole project if I told you that Charlie and I have just sold Fantasy Films for two million bucks.'

'What?'

Walter grinned. 'I thought that would shake you.'

'Two million dollars!' Daniel said, aghast, 'but the business must have grown hugely to fetch that kind of figure.'

'Yeah, it has. Some of us, sonny, don't let the grass grow under our feet. While you dream about putting on classy productions, I bring home the dough ... improving the image of Chase Productions – you make me sick. Chase Productions' image is just fine because the Corporation backs winners – at least it has up until now.'

It was the wrong moment to start a row. 'How does all this concern *Sometime . . . Never?* Daniel asked quietly.

'If you're going to make an idiot of yourself,' Walter said, 'I'd prefer you did it with my money, rather than someone else's. You think I'm a slob, you think I've got no taste, no class. You sneer because I prefer Mantovani to Beethoven, because I like my suits loud, because I prefer hamburgers and popcorn to fancy dinners. But I'll tell you this, Daniel, I can make money, and it's *my* money that's turned you into the flash guy you consider yourself to be. OK, so I don't fit into your world, so let's see how you fare in mine. I'll back this show, not just because I'm flush with cash, but because it's time you stopped standing on the sidelines giving me a lot of crap. It's time you did more than just put your goddam toe in the water.'

'That's not fair,' Daniel said, 'I've always wanted to take greater responsibility.'

'Not fair, not fair,' his father mimicked. 'You sound like some snivelling brat. Outside the nursery, kiddo, nothing's fair. Now this is the deal, and listen carefully. If the show flops you have to pay me back every dime I lose, plus interest. I'm not mug enough to be an Angel, and I am not prepared to take risks. I've worked too hard for my bread to have you lose it all for me. The money I'll be putting into this show of yours isn't Chase Productions' dough, it's mine and I want it back, all of it – is that clear?'

'OK,' said Daniel, 'that's fair enough but since I believe the play will make money, I'd like a piece of the action.'

'Well, you won't get it,' Walter replied.

'If I'm to make good the losses, surely it's only right I should have a share of the profits.'

'You'll get your share of the profits one day,' said Walter. 'When I'm dead, Chase Productions is yours. You'll collect then, but not before.'

'But . . .' Daniel began.

'Shut up. As far as I'm concerned, this conversation is over. You accept the deal as it stands, or I withdraw my offer.'

Daniel stood up, wearily. 'OK, we have a deal.'

After Daniel had left his office, Walter studied the paperwork his son had left behind. The boy had done well. He'd picked up the play for the right price. The contracts he'd issued were not text-book ones, they showed flair and initiative, and ensured Chase Productions a good deal. He must be a better negotiator than I thought, Walter mused, and yet it never came across in the meetings between father and son. Walter always managed to destroy Daniel's case, the boy always folded up under pressure, like he had just now.

It never occurred to Walter that he was a hard man to deal with at the best of times and that he was particularly tough with his son. No, Walter attributed Daniel's lack of negotiating skill to having had life too easy. He lit another cigar and thought back to his own first production. He'd borrowed money against security he didn't actually own and he'd worked night and day from one room in Harlem. If the production had failed, he'd have certainly gone bankrupt, he'd probably have gone to prison . . . so he'd made darn sure it didn't. Walter smiled to himself – it was all too easy for Daniel. He wouldn't be worrying about *Sometime . . . Never* tonight, Walter was sure of that. No doubt he'd be out with some broad, having a ball on Corporation expenses.

As it happened, Walter was wrong. Daniel spent that evening writing to Anna.

The next few weeks sped by for Daniel. He personally supervised all the preparations for *Sometime . . . Never* – particularly the pre-publicity. Chase Productions' Public Relations department was good, but it wasn't good enough for Daniel. He launched a massive attack on the media, and soon had Gerald's first week in New York heavily committed to publicity. There were television interviews, magazine profiles, chat shows – he lined them all up, checking the details thoroughly himself. Gerald was easy to promote but Daniel even managed to secure some good publicity for Anna. Several of the major women's magazines wanted to run an interview with her, and he fixed her a couple of television spots.

He spent Christmas with Jim and Penny in Scarsdale, in a blur of fatigue and alcohol, and by December 28th was back at his desk. New Year's Eve Daniel spent alone in his office. At the stroke of midnight, he opened a bottle of champagne and wrote a letter to Anna.

They had corresponded weekly, sometimes more, since Daniel had left London. The stack of letters he kept in the locked drawer of his desk was growing steadily, and with it so was his knowledge of Anna. The first letters had been stilted, difficult, but now, they told each other everything. For Daniel, it was a marvellous release to be able to express his true feelings without restraint. The bond was growing between them with each letter. In her last letter Anna had actually said she was longing to see him again. When he'd read the words, he'd wanted to ring her up there and then, but he knew it would spoil things. They were taking tiny tentative steps towards each other, but he had to be careful, very careful.

By January 15th, Daniel felt he had more than done justice to *Sometime . . . Never*. He felt better than he'd felt in a long time, if ever. The vibes were good for the play. The media was intrigued and willing to give Gerald a chance to prove himself . . . and in just five weeks, he would be seeing Anna again.

That particular morning it was snowing heavily. The sky had a yellow tinge to it, suggesting that there was plenty more to come. By the time Daniel arrived in the office, Matilda was already at her desk and there was a girl waiting with her.

Daniel called 'Good morning,' as he walked past them, but their response was oddly subdued. The girl was vaguely familiar, though he couldn't quite place her.

When Matilda joined him a few moments later, her face was serious. 'Daniel,' she said, 'can you spare Rosie Blake a few moments?'

Daniel stared at her blankly. 'Rosie Blake – who's she?'

'The kid in my office.'

'Do we know her?' Daniel asked.

'She's got a part in *Emma*. You auditioned her, just before you went to London.'

Daniel did remember – the girl from Texas. He looked uncomfortable. 'What does she want, Mattie?'

'I don't know. She's pretty upset though.' Mattie gave him a hard look. 'She seems a nice little thing, but then I expect you know that.'

'OK, I'll talk to her now, but could you try and make an appointment for me to see my father in, say, half an hour. I want to go through the advertising budgets with him.'

Something was wrong with Rosie Blake. Daniel could see that the moment she walked in.

Her face was unnaturally pale, there were great dark smudges under her eyes and she looked as though she hadn't been eating or sleeping properly. Daniel stood up. 'Hello Rosie, how nice to see you. Would you like a coffee?'

She shook her head. 'No, no thanks.'

'Sit down then. What can I do for you? No problems with the part I hope?' She shook her head dumbly. Daniel felt a strong sense of disquiet – the girl was just sitting there, her head hanging. 'Look, Rosie,' he said, impatiently, 'I don't want to seem unfriendly but I'm up to my eyes in work this morning. Is there something wrong?'

Rosie raised her head and met his eyes, hers were full of pain and unshed tears. 'I'm . . . I'm pregnant.' The tears began to spill out of her eyes.

Daniel left out a slow whistle and leaned back in his chair. He remembered the night now – she was young certainly, but surely to God she was experienced enough not to get herself in this mess. He stood up and began pacing the room.

Suddenly he turned on her. 'Let's get this straight – I assume you are saying that you're pregnant because of me, because of the night we spent together. How do you *know* it's me?'

She was crying hard now. 'Because I never . . . because I haven't . . . you were the first man, you see.' She didn't seem to be able to go on speaking, the tears were choking her.

Daniel stared at her. 'Are you trying to tell me you were a virgin that night?'

She nodded. 'That's right.'

'Jesus, Rosie, surely you're not going to try and swing a stunt like that. I may be a lot of things but I'm not a fool. You told me all about your life, remember? You can't start playing the innocent with me, not now.'

'I knew you wouldn't believe me,' Rosie wailed, 'I just knew it, but it's true, it's really true.'

Daniel slammed his fist down onto the desk. 'Well then tell me this, Rosie, if that night was your first time, why weren't you nervous or apprehensive? Shit, I'd have known, wouldn't I, and in any event, why didn't you tell me?'

'Because I wanted the part,' she said. 'I wanted the part so badly and I knew if I didn't play along with you, I'd probably lose it. I – I thought if you knew it was my first time you might just chuck me out and . . .'

'Jesus, Rosie, what sort of man do you think I am?'

'I don't know what sort of man you are,' she sobbed. 'All I know is that sleeping with you was obviously part of the deal. I had to have that part, I had no money, nowhere to live . . .'

'I'm sorry, Rosie,' Daniel interrupted, 'but I simply can't buy it. In this business eighteen-year-old girls who get themselves from Texas to Broadway in one easy leap, only manage it one way. I don't like the system any more than you probably do, but it's the way things are.'

'I'm not eighteen,' Rosie said, tears were still running down her face.

'Godammit, how old are you then?'

'Sixteen, just sixteen.'

Daniel let out a sigh, the fight had gone out of him. He studied the girl in silence for a moment. Her tears had washed her make-up away and without it she certainly looked no older than sixteen. He stood up and walked over to the drinks cabinet, took two glasses and poured them both a hefty brandy. 'Drink that,' he ordered, 'we've got some talking to do.'

Rosie obediently drank her brandy and a few minutes later was more or less composed. Daniel stood with his back to her, sipping his drink and gazing out of the window, staring with unseeing eyes at the snowflakes as they fell. 'Right,' he said, at last, 'first of all, you do want the baby?'

Rosie shook her head. 'I guess I'd like kids one day,' she said, 'but I can't cope now. I'm here because I need some money. My room-mate, well . . . she knows this woman – it costs about two hundred bucks.'

'No,' Daniel thundered. 'If it's an abortion you want, then we'll have it done right. We'll find a clinic who'll look after you properly, and then after the operation, somewhere you can stay for a few days while you recuperate.'

Rosie's tears had completely gone now. 'Thank you,' she said, humbly, avoiding his eyes. She hesitated, 'I don't want to lose my part.'

'You won't,' said Daniel. 'We're still six weeks away from opening *Emma*. I'll fix it so that you can take a week's paid holiday, and there'll still be plenty of time for you to rehearse when you get back.'

'Thank you,' Rosie said again, 'thank you very much.' For the first time she looked up and met his eyes. They stared at one another in silence for a moment.

'I don't believe your story about being a virgin, Rosie,' Daniel said, 'but I concede that the child you're carrying could be mine. Either way it's all fairly irrelevant. Abortions are no picnic, particularly at sixteen, but it's an experience you must put behind you. It's something you'll never forget, of course, but you're young and time will heal.'

The kindness of his words brought a smile to Rosie's face, she relaxed, looking suddenly almost cheerful.

'Now,' said Daniel, suddenly businesslike, 'you'd probably rather get it dealt with right away, wouldn't you?'

'Yes, please,' said Rosie.

'We'll see if we can get you into a clinic this afternoon.

That'll mean they'll probably perform the operation tomorrow. I'll also fix you a few days in a hotel, with room service, once it's over. By this time next week you'll be fighting fit.' He spoke the words mechanically, his voice sounded weary and resigned. 'My secretary, Matilda, will have your address. You haven't moved, I take it?' Rosie shook her head. 'OK – go home now and Mattie will get things organised for you and give you a call. I'll send her round in the car to pick you up and take you to the clinic, so you won't be alone.'

'Does she . . . does she have to know?'

'Yes,' said Daniel, 'it would be better if she made the arrangements rather than me.'

'I understand,' said Rosie. She stood up awkwardly. 'Well, goodbye, and thanks again.'

'Goodbye,' Daniel said, not trusting himself to say any more.

Matilda found him, a few moments later, staring out of the window. He didn't move, keeping his back to her as he spoke, so she couldn't see his expression. 'Mattie, I want you to find me a clinic that'll handle a pregnancy termination tomorrow, and I mean somewhere decent. Then I'd like you to arrange for Rosie Blake to be admitted. Once the operation is over, I'd like you to fix her up in a decent hotel, with good room service, for say, four days. Would you see to it that you arrange it all personally, and actually take her to the clinic yourself. Now will you just say yes and not ask me any questions?'

'I won't ask any questions,' said Mattie, quietly. 'I'll just say I'm glad you're doing the right thing by her.'

'The right thing by her?' Daniel exploded. He turned round to face Matilda, his eyes blazing, 'The right thing by her . . . do you know she tried to tell me she was a virgin until she met me. I'm darn sure that child isn't mine. I'm just the jerk who's paying the bills.'

'She's little more than a child herself,' Mattie said quietly.

'Oh, so you think I'm the shit who got her into this mess and that she's the poor little innocent.'

Mattie sighed. 'No, I don't necessarily think that, Dan. I just think you ought to take one hell of a hard look at your lifestyle. What, for Christ's sake, are you trying to prove – that you're the greatest stud in the history of the universe? Don't you think it's time you started looking for something more than an easy lay? You're not a college boy any more.'

'Oh great,' said Daniel, 'so now I'm getting a lecture.'

'Yes, you darn well are,' said Mattie. 'I take your point about this kid – if you hadn't knocked her up, someone else would. To be frank, it's not her I'm concerned about, it's *you* and what you're doing to yourself that scares the shit out of me. There's a lot of kindness in you, Dan – I see it, working with you every day – but so far as your relationships with all other women are concerned, it's just a quick fuck and away. You know, there's this thing called love – you ought to try it sometime.'

'What for?' Daniel said sullenly.

'Do you know,' said Mattie, 'that's about the saddest thing I've ever heard anyone say.'

It was still snowing the following morning as Daniel stood by his office window. He couldn't work, he couldn't concentrate on anything. This morning, possibly right at that very moment, a life was being destroyed, a life that could just possibly be that of his own child. He wondered suddenly whether it had been a boy or a girl. For a moment he considered which he would have preferred, and the thought brought a sudden flash of pain, so unexpected that he all but gasped.

He tried to change the direction of his thinking. It had been the obvious course to take. Rosie couldn't bring up a child, hadn't even wanted to. OK, so the baby could have been adopted, but that would have meant he'd have been forced to support Rosie for nine months. Inevitably the newspapers would have got hold of the story too, and his father would have given him hell . . . No, it had been the right thing to do. He glanced at his watch, it was only ten-thirty, but he walked over to the drinks cabinet and poured himself a large Scotch. He drank it in a single gulp, which momentarily took his breath away, then he poured himself a second and sipped it more slowly.

Daniel always thought of himself as having been alone all his life. His childhood had been watched over by a succession of nannies – all efficient in their way, but they had never really cared for him, or he for them. His father had been a remote figure, nearly always at the office. In charitable moments Daniel wondered whether Walter had stayed away from home because of the memories of his dead wife, which must have been there, and perhaps, were all too painful. At other times, it just seemed as though his father didn't care a damn about him. Whatever the reason, Daniel's childhood had been luxurious but lonely. There had been no home life, no sense of family. When he'd visited the houses of school and college friends, they had always stood out in stark contrast to his own sterile existence.

Mattie's words came back to him now. *Love* – she was right, there had been no room for love in his life. He was suspicious of it. When he thought of love he thought of pain in the same breath. Now, standing alone in his office, slightly drunk, he wondered if he could have loved this baby whose life he'd just destroyed. For the first time, he could have had someone to share things with, to come home to.

He shook his head, his mind confused. Mattie's words had upset him more than he was prepared to admit, especially to himself. He needed to talk but to whom? Suddenly, the answer seemed obvious – after all, what were friends for? He sat down heavily at his desk, drew out a sheet of paper and began to write. By the time he'd covered four pages, the pain in his heart had eased a little.

Chapter Ten

The café was small, dingy and far from clean. It was over-heated, but it needed to be, for every time anyone came or went, a blast of cold air ripped through the tiny room, making the customers hunch deeper into their overcoats. Steam from the coffee machine had collected as condensation on all visible surfaces, making everything unpleasantly damp.

Anna rubbed the window and peered out. It was almost dark, and certainly time to make tracks towards the theatre . . . but she couldn't face anyone yet. In front of her lay the discarded pages of Daniel's letter which had profoundly shocked her. Yet should it have done? The fact that he'd spent the night with a young actress was quite understandable. The fact that the girl had become pregnant, possibly by him, was very sad but not at all surprising. Even her extreme youth was excusable. No, it was the abortion which upset Anna, though she recognised her view might well be distorted. After all, she, herself, presumably had been an unwanted baby. Certainly, her research had indicated that her mother had been unmarried. What if *her* actress mother had made the same decision as Rosie Blake? She would have been denied a chance of life.

This aspect didn't seem to have occurred to Daniel. His letter was full of self-pity. Rosie had taken advantage of his position; Matilda, his secretary, had been unnecessarily harsh. He had, at least, looked after Rosie properly, but no mention had been made of the baby and its lost future. Anna could see that it was impractical for Rosie to keep the child, but it could have been adopted . . . not destroyed.

Anna sighed and took a sip of the beige liquid, which was laughingly described as coffee. She wrinkled up her nose in disgust.

'Awful, isn't it?' A middle-aged woman sat opposite her. A headscarf was knotted determinedly under her chin and she wore a sheepskin coat. Anna recognised her instantly as a devotee of the January sales.

She tried to force a smile. 'Yes, it is,' she agreed.

'You were looking terribly sad just now, dear, if you don't mind my saying so. Are you all right?'

'Oh yes,' said Anna, hurriedly. She began picking up the pages of Daniel's letter.

'Did your letter contain bad news?' the woman persisted.

'Not exactly,' Anna said. She could stand no more of this interrogation. She stood up, paid for her coffee and started to leave.

The woman was entirely unrepentant. 'Don't worry dear, every cloud has a silver lining,' she called, to Anna's departing back.

The cold air hit her as she stepped out of the café. With head down, shoulders hunched, she started towards the theatre. It wasn't *just* the abortion that had upset her, Anna decided. She minded that Daniel had been so recently involved with someone else. It was unreasonable of her, but she was jealous of Rosie, and the knowledge that he had been caught up in this mess somehow tainted her view of him.

During the last few weeks of their exchanged letters, their intimacy had grown considerably. Anna had told him things she'd never told anyone before, and she suspected that this was true for him too. Of course, he had been right to tell her about Rosie Blake, but somehow she felt the exposé threatened their own relationship. She wouldn't reply, she decided. Their correspondence had caused her to do a lot of day-dreaming about Daniel Chase and it was clearly foolish. His life was too complicated, too different from her own. 'Concentrate on your career and forget him,' Anna muttered under her breath, as she walked. But even as she spoke the words, she knew it was not going to be that easy.

'Oh Sally, it's entrancing!' May Wetherby gazed around the hall. It was a wood-panelled room, with four great chandeliers suspended from a high ceiling. The walls were covered with sombre oil paintings of former dons and famous graduates. It was an imposing room, but before Sally's transformation it had been dark and austere. Sally had simply filled the room with flowers. Great displays stood in every corner, ivy crept along the mantelpiece and round the pictures. Suddenly, the room looked festive.

'I'm glad you like it,' Sally said, warmly. 'You couldn't possibly have celebrated your twenty-fifth wedding anniversary in the room as it was – it was positively creepy. Now, what else is there to do?'

'Well, nothing much except for setting out the glasses,' said May. 'I think they could probably do with a polish at the same time.'

'Let's tackle that together then,' said Sally.

'Are you sure?'

'Yes, of course, I've got nothing better to do.'

'Thank heavens for outside caterers,' said May. 'I couldn't begin to cope myself. I'm absolutely hopeless domestically.'

'And by contrast, I love cooking,' said Sally, smiling. 'It's a good thing we're all different, isn't it?'

'I wish Anna was more like you.' May held up a polished glass to the light for inspection, before setting it down on the table which had been allocated for the bar.

'Certainly, Anna and I couldn't be more different,' Sally agreed. 'She's so ambitious about her career, and I'm sure she'll succeed. Whereas I . . . I can't wait to give up my job, get married and have babies.'

'It's Anna who should be here tonight, not you,' May complained.

'But Mrs Wetherby, that's not really fair. You know she has to work at the theatre tonight.' Sally would never hear a word against her friend.

'Yes, I suppose so, and I should be used to it by now. Her career has always come first.' There was a trace of bitterness in her voice.

'But isn't that the price one pays for being an actress?'

'Yes,' May conceded, 'but I'm not arguing about the way actresses have to live, I'm simply querying Anna's decision to become one.'

'But she's very good,' Sally protested. 'You must have seen that yourself, the other night.'

'She's good, but no better than thousands like her, and half the time, I wonder whether she's even happy. I just suspect her motives for going on the stage, that's all.'

They worked on in silence for a moment or two.

'You mean, you think she's only chosen to work in the theatre because her natural mother was an actress?' Sally chose her words carefully.

'Yes, something like that,' said May. There was pain in her eyes as she spoke. 'Do you know, Sally, it's a strange thing, but I can talk to you far more easily than I've ever been able to do with Anna. I wonder why that should be?'

'Anna cares about you and Dr Wetherby very much, I'm sure,' said Sally, 'but I think she's still hung up about being adopted.'

'Yes, we handled that all wrong,' May said, almost to herself. 'The trouble is Stephen and I aren't very competent where small children are concerned. Our work has always been so important to us, you see – that's the trouble. Looking back on it, I don't think I was a very good mother, not a very good mother at all.'

'I think you're worrying unnecessarily,' Sally said. 'Tomorrow you're going to have a party to celebrate being married happily for twenty-five years – that's no mean achievement in itself. You also have a talented daughter, who is about to take Broadway by storm, and . . . we've nearly finished these glasses.' They both laughed.

'Yes,' said May, 'you're quite right. We have a lot to be thankful for.'

'What time are Anna and Gerald coming down tomorrow?' Sally tried to sound casual, but wasn't too successful.

May gave her a sharp look. 'About tea-time,' she said. 'Why don't you come to tea too? In fact, why don't you bring your dress, change with us and stay the night afterwards. It certainly would be more sensible than trying to go home after the party.'

'Oh, I'd love that,' said Sally. 'I'm dying to see Gerald again. I don't know why really, because he was awfully rude last time I met him.'

'Was he?' said May, surprised. 'He was charm itself when Stephen and I had dinner with him.'

'I expect his moods vary a lot,' Sally said indulgently.

'Promise me one thing,' Gerald said, as he eased the car away from the kerb, to the ecstatic waving of Mrs Franks.

'Try me,' said Anna.

'When, and if, you ever take up residence in London again, could you make sure, *absolutely sure*, that you don't repeat the mistake of living in Clapham.'

'Clapham is very nice, in places,' Anna said defensively.

'Yes, but this isn't one of those places, is it, darling?'

'No, but you try living anywhere better on an ASM's pay.'

'All that is nearly behind you,' said Gerald, expansively. 'Soon, the entire world will be positively littered with your luxury apartments.'

Anna laughed delightedly. This is just what I need, she thought. A day out with Gerald *and* my parents' party. Anything to forget Daniel's letter. 'So what's the plot,' she asked. 'What are we going to do today?'

'We're going to drive to Woodstock,' Gerald said.

Anna groaned. 'Oh no, you're not going to make me go round Blenheim Palace, are you?'

'No, of course not. Why?'

'Remember, I was at school in Oxford for fourteen years. I've been round the Palace so often, it almost feels like home.'

'Fear not,' said Gerald, 'I had in mind lunch at The Bear. In fact, so confident was I that this would be acceptable to you, that I have actually booked a table for two, at one o'clock.'

'That sounds lovely,' said Anna, 'but won't you be mobbed by the adoring matrons of Oxfordshire?'

'Oh no,' said Gerald. 'The devotees of The Bear are far too respectable for that. They will simply stare and stare.'

He was right. Anna began by being embarrassed at everyone's concentrated gaze, but after the second champagne cocktail, she ceased to care.

'Did it take you a long time to get used to being recognised everywhere you go?' she asked.

'Not really. It's something that creeps up on you. I can

remember the first time it happened though.'

'Where was that?' Anna asked, intrigued.

'A bar in Los Angeles. This guy came up to me, shook my hand, told me I was great and asked me to sign his autograph book.'

'Gosh,' said Anna, impressed.

Gerald smiled. 'The trouble was, he thought I was Richard Burton, so he was somewhat disappointed with my signature.'

Anna laughed out loud. 'Oh no, did he really?'

Gerald nodded. 'I didn't mind though. He knew I was someone and that's what mattered.' He smiled at her. 'I hope I'm with you the first time it happens to you. It's quite a high.'

'Oh, I'll never be recognised when I'm with you. Just look at them all,' she whispered, 'they can't take their eyes off you. They don't even notice I exist.'

They went in to lunch – smoked salmon, followed by partridge. Gerald lifted his wine glass. 'Here's to May and Stephen Wetherby on their twin triumphs – their twenty-fifth wedding anniversary and their beautiful daughter.'

Anna sipped the wine – it was a very dark red and so smooth it slipped down her throat like milk. She turned the bottle towards her and looked at the label. 'Chateau Latour,' she said. 'My God, Gerald, that must have cost a fortune.'

'Nothing is too much trouble for my lady,' Gerald said, inclining his head in a small bow.

Anna looked at him sceptically. 'Gerald, you're being very kind to me. Do you have some ghastly ulterior motive?'

'What an awful child you are,' Gerald said. 'I'm just, how shall we say . . . encouraging our relationship, so that when we are thrown onto Broadway, like two orphans in a storm, we'll have something, or rather someone, to whom we can cling.'

The mention of Broadway reminded Anna of Daniel. Slightly drunk, she found herself suddenly saying, 'Gerald, what are your views on abortion.'

Gerald looked stunned. 'I don't know what prompted that question, Anna, but if you want my view, in most circumstances I'm dead against it.'

Anna blushed. '*I'm* not pregnant,' she said, hastily, 'I . . . I just know someone who has had an abortion recently, and the whole affair is rather playing on my mind.'

Gerald stared at her quizzically. 'You're a funny little thing, and if I may be permitted to say so, oddly naive. The pros and cons of abortion are something you should have sorted out at twelve. Certainly at your age, you should know your own mind on the subject.'

'It's different when it involves someone you know,' Anna said, defensively.

'I suppose so,' Gerald conceded. 'It's odd actually, I have been in all sorts of trouble during my life, but in that respect at least, the gods have smiled. So far as I am aware, I only have three children – had three children,' he corrected himself, 'and they were all born legitimate.'

'Do you see much of your other two children?' Anna asked.

'No.'

'Do you miss them?'

'Not in the least,' Gerald replied.

'Gerald, you are awful, that can't be true.'

'I'm afraid it is, darling. They're two girls, you know, and the problem is, they are the absolute spitting image of their mother. She's a ghastly woman, a first-rate bitch. I can't think what on earth possessed me to marry her.' He paused reflectively. 'In fact, now I come to think of it, she only has one redeeming feature.'

'What's that?'

'She's an Australian.'

'So?' said Anna, somewhat confused.

'Don't be thick, darling. When our differences became irreconcilable, as they say, she packed her bags and returned to her native land. Australia is such a gloriously long way away – I can't tell you the thrill it still gives me, even now, to think of the thousands of miles which separate us. Sheer bliss!'

'I expect she feels the same,' Anna said, a little tartly. 'Tell me, Gerald, when was the last time you actually saw your daughters?'

'About nine years ago.'

'But that's terrible! For all you know they may have turned into really nice people.'

'Not a hope under their mother's influence, I'm afraid.'

'Well, I think it's very sad,' said Anna.

'If you're right and it *is* very sad, we certainly shouldn't be talking about it. I don't know about you, but I've eaten myself to a standstill. What shall we do now?'

'A walk,' said Anna, 'in Oxford. I'll take you to the Parks. They're just down the road from my parents' house and it should be a lovely walk this afternoon.'

They drove to North Oxford and stopped in one of the quiet streets leading to the Parks. The sun was setting in a wintry sky and the air was cold. Anna shivered, 'We'll have to walk fast, or we'll freeze.'

Gerald slipped an arm round her shoulders. 'Keep close to me, my love, and I will shelter you from Winter's wrath.'

'That sounds like a quotation,' said Anna.

'Yes, it is,' said Gerald. 'I have acted in some truly bloody awful plays over the years.' He looked around him. 'This is wonderful, Anna, I'm glad you brought me here.'

They walked in silence for a while, as dusk began to settle. There were few other people around and no one disturbed them. The park was still and peaceful, their silence companionable. They were on their way back to the car, when Anna suddenly clutched Gerald's arm. 'Oh, look, Gerald, look at the swans.'

'But they're black!' said Gerald, astounded.

'Yes, they're the black swans of Blenheim. I knew they sometimes flew into Oxford, but I've never seen them before. Aren't they beautiful?' She turned to him. Her eyes were bright with excitement, her face flushed from the cold. The damp air from the river had caused little tendrils of hair to escape from the rest and curl to frame her face.

Gerald ran a finger gently down her cheek. 'Not as beautiful as you,' he whispered, 'not nearly as beautiful as you.'

Anna, of course, had some experience of Gerald's kisses, but this was different. This was not Robert kissing Sarah – that violent, desperate kiss, so full of despair. This was Gerald Kingdom kissing Anna Wetherby, on the banks of the River Cherwell . . . and it felt good. His lips were warm and firm on her own, his arms supported her – she felt comfortable, cared for, needed and not all all surprised at what was happening.

When at last they drew apart, Gerald's face was a mask. 'So, Miss Wetherby,' he said, with mock severity, 'you dragged me down to the Parks in order to seduce me – is that right?'

Anna blushed. 'No, of course I didn't, I most certainly wouldn't . . .'

Gerald laughed and stopped her mouth with the briefest of kisses. 'The lady doth protest too much. Come on, if we stay here any longer, we're going to be late for the party.'

They stood in silent homage for a moment, watching the swans as they glided under the bridge and out of sight. Then they linked arms and trudged back in high spirits. There was no constraint or awkwardness between them. What had taken place seemed, at the time, to be no more than a natural extension of their relationship.

The party was an enormous success, due, in no small measure, to Gerald. He charmed everyone, and drank in moderation, Anna noticed. He danced with May and Sally and did the rounds of the other female guests, from a dowager Duchess to the plain spinster daughter of the college chaplain.

It was well after three by the time Anna and her parents, Sally and Gerald, finally arrived back at the Wetherbys' rambling old house.

'May, Stephen, that party was an absolute triumph,' Gerald said.

'Largely thanks to you,' May said.

'Yes,' Sally gushed, 'you were wonderful, Gerald.'

Anna groaned inwardly at the hero-worship in Sally's eyes.

'Right,' said Stephen, taking charge. 'Bed for everyone, I think. I'll show you to your room, Gerald.'

With great ceremony, Gerald kissed the three women goodnight, and followed Stephen upstairs.

'Isn't he gorgeous,' said Sally, after Gerald had gone, 'and wasn't he terrific tonight? It was so kind of him to take such trouble to talk to everyone.'

'He wasn't being *kind*,' said Anna, 'he was having a wonderful time. Gerald positively basks in adoration, and the party tonight gave him a perfect captive audience. He was playing his favourite role – Gerald Kingdom, the star.'

'I think that's rather unkind, Anna,' said May.

'But factual,' Anna replied, shortly. 'I'm off to bed now. Thanks for a lovely party, Mummy. Goodnight.'

Despite the hour, Anna couldn't sleep. She lay in the little room that had been hers since babyhood, gazing round at the familiar objects that had always been a part of her life. The battered old rocking chair, the guitar, the complete set of Beatrix Potter – all very familiar, very dear, and yet, in a strange way, she felt detached from them now. She realised with a jolt that in all probability she would not be staying at home again before she left for the States, and once there, who knew what would happen? If work was available after *Sometime . . . Never*, it could be years before she returned. She felt excited, but apprehensive too. The road she travelled was of her own choosing, but it was a lonely one.

She was almost asleep when she heard the soft tapping on the door. At first she thought she might have imagined it, but then it came again, a little louder, more insistent. She jumped out of bed and opened the door cautiously. Gerald stood there, resplendent in a navy silk dressing gown. 'Thank God,' he said. 'It's taken me ages to work out which room you were in.' Before she could protest, he was inside her bedroom, closing the door quietly behind him.

'Gerald, what *are* you doing?' Anna said. 'Why on earth are you wandering about the house at this hour of the night?'

Gerald turned from the door to face her. His eyes, she noticed, were an even darker blue than normal. She stared into them, mesmerised by the intensity of his gaze.

As always, his timing was perfect. He paused just long enough before answering her question to give added depth and emphasis to his words. When he spoke it was in that deep, seductive voice which had wooed millions of women, across many continents, for over twenty years. 'Anna, my darling,' he said simply, 'you know perfectly well why I'm here.'

Chapter Eleven

'You've got to be joking!' Anna edged away from him, towards the far side of the room.

'I've never been more serious in my life.'

'Gerald, it would be madness. Casual affairs are not my sort of thing, and as for our getting seriously involved . . .' her voice trailed off.

'Anna, I love you.'

Anna looked up into his face – handsome, dangerous and immensely attractive. Whether the words he spoke were true or not, they could not fail to affect her.

'Gerald, you don't,' she said, softly. 'It's just that I'm here, now,' she tried a smile, 'and convenient.'

'No,' Gerald said, vehemently.

'Shhhh,' Anna said, 'you'll wake the whole household.'

'I'm sorry, but it's just not like that, darling Anna. You've made a wonderful difference to me in the last few months. You've . . .' he searched for the words, 'you've kept me off the booze, you've inspired me, you've shown me that my art is still intact and that I can still move people.'

'*I* haven't shown you any of those things,' Anna said, 'you've done that for yourself.' She shivered involuntarily.

'You're cold,' said Gerald. 'It's not surprising, this house is absolutely perishing.'

Anna smiled faintly. 'Yes, Mummy and Daddy aren't really into central heating. Actually, in fairness to them, it's probably just as well – they couldn't possibly afford to heat a house this size.'

'I refuse to stand in a bedroom with a beautiful girl at four o'clock in the morning, discussing central heating. Come to

111

bed, Anna. I won't, as they say, press my suit, I promise. Only let's at least talk somewhere warm.'

Anna came to him like a sleepwalker, and together fhey climbed into the narrow bed, Gerald pulling her to him so her head rested on his chest.

'That's better,' Gerald whispered softly, into her hair.

Their bodies warmed each other. Neither spoke, but as they lay there, Anna could not help but be aware of Gerald's astonishing magnetism. For a man who'd spent most of his life abusing his body with drink and high living, he was in remarkable shape. His shoulders were broad, his chest lean and tanned; the arms that held her, held her strongly with the sense of possession. She felt intoxicated by his closeness and was quite powerless to move away.

At last she felt him stir beside her. 'Anna,' he whispered, 'darling little Anna, I'm going to kiss you.' It didn't occur to her to protest, as his lips met hers – gently at first and then with mounting passion, that had her clinging to him like someone drowning in a dark, unknown sea. With consummate skill, he slid the nightdress from her shoulders. She knew she should stop him but she didn't know how to begin. He seemed to be everywhere, making her feel no longer a separate person, but more an actual extension of himself. She was naked in his arms and his kisses sweet, hot, demanding, were driving all conscious thought from her mind. He moved away a little, and with hurried fumbling fingers, struggled with the knot of his robe. It was in that one, fleeting moment, that sanity took possession over madness.

'No, Gerald, no.'

He froze. 'What do you mean, no?'

Anna took advantage of his surprise, and jumping out of bed, picked up the eiderdown that had fallen on the floor, and hurriedly wrapped it round her. 'Gerald, I'm sorry, but I can't . . . we mustn't.'

'Good God, girl.' He was struggling to compose himself. She could see that momentarily he felt at a disadvantage and it didn't suit him. He quickly recovered, pulled his dressing gown around him and ran a hand through his hair.

Then, sitting up, he leaned back against the bedhead in apparent casual indifference.

'I'm sorry, Gerald,' she said again, feeling awkward and stupid standing there, naked but for the eiderdown.

'*Sorry* is barely adequate,' Gerald said. 'You invite me into your bed, allow me to get all steamed up, and then turn off the tap. It's not really cricket, darling.'

'If you recall,' said Anna, 'you invited me into my bed.'

'But you came.'

She nodded miserably. Cautiously, she sat down on the edge of the bed, she felt too weak to stand. 'Gerald, I'm the last woman you should get involved with. I'm . . . well, I'm really rather a serious sort of person, I suppose. I don't want a relationship which represents nothing more than sex. I've tried that and it's not right for me . . . and to fall in love with you, Gerald – that would be a disaster.'

'No, Anna, you're wrong, it wouldn't. It's what I want – I've spent all my life looking for the right woman.'

'But I'm not the right woman,' Anna insisted. 'I'm not wise enough to cope with you, Gerald. Being . . . like that just now, felt good . . . lovely. If we made love tonight, we'd make love tomorrow, and the next day. By this time next week, I'd be totally committed to you, trapped and vulnerable.'

'Are you afraid of commitment?'

'Commitment to you, yes.' She searched her mind for the right way to express what she was feeling. 'Gerald, I could never trust you. I could never be sure of you. You would destroy my confidence, which in turn would destroy me and, ultimately, our relationship.'

'Has it occurred to you, Anna, that if I had you, I wouldn't need anyone else?'

'No, it hasn't,' Anna answered truthfully, 'and I think if you believe that to be true, you're deluding yourself.'

'And I think *you* are underestimating yourself. People change, you know, Anna.'

'No, they don't, not really,' Anna said. 'I can't risk it Gerald, I *daren't*.'

'Then I suppose there's nothing more to be said.' Gerald climbed off the bed. Even at that moment, he managed to look suave, elegant and totally in control. Yet his face was expressionless. Anna could read nothing there.

'I'll bid you goodnight,' he said, his hand on the door handle. He smiled faintly. 'It may be of some satisfaction for you to know that you are the first woman who has ever turned me away from her bed.'

Once the door was shut behind him, Anna picked up her discarded nightdress from the floor and put it on. She was trembling from head to foot but it was nothing to do with the cold. She climbed into the bed, still warm from where they had lain, and switched off the light. Why had she rejected him? she wondered. Was it for all the reasons she'd said, or was it the shadow of Daniel Chase which stood between them? Her tired mind refused to function, and at last sheer exhaustion brought blissful oblivion.

At ten-thirty the following morning, the Wetherbys sat over the remains of breakfast.

'I can understand Gerald sleeping late,' May said indulgently, 'theatre people always do, but I thought Sally would have been down by now. I don't know whether to leave the breakfast things, or clear them away.'

It was linking the two names in a single sentence that prompted the thought in Anna's mind. Once lodged there, it became an obsession in seconds – she had to reassure herself. Making her excuses, she ran quietly up the stairs and turned down the corridor towards Sally bedroom. She opened the door softly, her head pounding. They were asleep – two heads, one dark, one fair, close together on the pillow. Anna just managed to shut the door and reach the bathroom, before she was sick.

She waited until they had joined the motorway before speaking. 'So, this undying love you feel for me, did not prevent you from making love to Sally last night.'

Gerald appeared quite untroubled by her knowledge. 'Did you . . . did she tell you?' he asked, conversationally.

'No,' said Anna. 'Shall we just say I know.'

'Spying on us, very pretty.'

'Strangely enough,' said Anna, 'I don't mind for myself. You see, it only goes to confirm that I made the right decision last night. If you could go straight from my bed to Sally's, you simply can't have feelings like a normal person.' He said nothing, so she went on. 'It's Sally that breaks my heart. She worships the ground you walk on. She won't have a clue that last night was a one-off. She'll be day-dreaming right now about becoming Mrs Gerald Kingdom, about keeping you on the straight and narrow, about glamorous parties, and rubbing shoulders with the famous. I don't know how you could have done it to her, Gerald.'

'She's been asking for it ever since I met her. I made her very happy last night.'

'You've probably ruined her life,' Anna said, bitterly. 'She'll end up marrying some nice local lad who could have made her very happy, except that every time he takes her in his arms, she'll pretend it's you.'

'That's absolute rubbish,' said Gerald.

'Gerald, you just don't appreciate the havoc you cause.' Anna was close to tears, but she was determined not to give him the satisfaction of seeing how much he'd hurt her. 'You . . . you're an incredibly attractive man anyway, but the starmakers over the years have turned you into a sort of demi-god. Sally didn't make love to a flesh and blood man last night, she made love to an idol. Can't you appreciate the difference?'

'My amazing powers didn't seem to have too much effect on you,' Gerald said, coldly.

'Are you always going to be throwing that back in my face?' Anna asked.

'Very probably,' Gerald replied. 'Now, I'm rather tired . . . if you wouldn't mind, I would prefer we travelled in silence.'

On the outskirts of London, Anna said, 'Please drop me at a tube station. I couldn't bear the long-suffering expression on your face, if I forced you to witness the delights of Clapham again.'

'As you wish,' said Gerald shortly.

He dropped her at Marble Arch. 'Goodbye and thanks for

the lift,' said Anna, as she stepped out of the car.

'Goodbye,' Gerald replied, not even taking his eyes off the road ahead.

Gerald had been in his flat less than ten minutes when the telephone rang. It was Sally, enquiring as to whether he'd had a safe journey. Gerald gave a very creditable performance, of which even Richard Manning would have been proud. He explained he was Mr Kingdom's butler. No, he didn't know where Mr Kingdom was, but certainly he didn't expect him back that night.

Anna sat hunched over her little fire for a long time that night. She was both miserable and confused. The thought of what had nearly happened between herself and Gerald terrified her, and yet she suspected that in some dark secret corner of her mind, she actually regretted rejecting him, and envied Sally her lack of restraint.

Two things particularly haunted her. Gerald's arrival in her bedroom reintroduced her professional insecurity – what were his true motives for insisting she came to America with him? Perhaps it really was nothing to do with her acting ability after all.

The second concern was the transfer itself. The move to Broadway without Martin was worrying enough, even when her relationship with Gerald was good. Now it had all but broken down, the future seemed all the more formidable.

The longer Anna sat there, the more monstrous her problems seemed to become. Even her tears provided no relief. It was shortly before midnight when at last she took from her pocket Daniel's crumpled letter and read it again. Suddenly, behind his stilted words, she felt she recognised the mirror of her own feelings – isolation, unhappiness, confusion. Had she any right to sit in judgement on what he'd done? Had she behaved so much better? She thought not.

She climbed into bed, armed with pad and pen, and began to write, faithfully recording the events of the last two days, leaving nothing out. By the time she'd finished, the tears on her cheeks had dried, and the pain in her heart had eased a little.

Chapter Twelve

'Would you like a blanket?' The stewardess's voice cut through Anna's thoughts.

'Oh yes, thank you.' Anna pulled the blanket round her, adjusted her seat and lay back. She was tired, but right now sleep seemed out of the question. There was so much to think about – the drama of the past weeks, the uncertainty of the future. At this moment, suspended mid-way over the Atlantic, she was between two worlds. It was time for introspection rather than sleep.

Since the weekend in Oxford, the relationship between herself and Gerald had been strained. In theory, it had not greatly mattered. The play had only a fortnight to run, and with Celia back in the role of Sarah, Anna and Gerald had very little contact – except, of course, for his nightly whisky. Even then, there was no need for conversation – the ever-present Ben, Gerald's dresser, made it unnecessary.

There was a strange atmosphere amongst the company, almost a holiday mood. Undoubtedly *Sometime . . . Never* had been a triumph, but its run was nearly over. Everyone, except Anna and Gerald, was moving on – looking to new work, to a future unconnected with the play. Martin was now heavily involved in his TV documentary and had not been near the theatre for days. Richard was busy rehearsing a farce and was very preoccupied. It was a successful play that had been running for some months at the Garrick. Richard was taking over the main supporting role – it was a larger part than he'd played for sometime and he was very anxious about it.

'Am I too old to drop my trousers, dear?' he'd asked Anna, nervously. Anna hesitated.

'You're never too old for that, ducky,' Sophie assured him. 'Just don't do it anywhere near me. I might not be able to control myself.'

Sophie was as cheerful as ever, but even she was absorbed with other interests. She felt oddly bereft without Martin. Now he was once more heavily involved in his family's tragedy, it was quite impossible for them to meet. Instead, Sophie plunged herself into designing and making the costumes for a student production in Notting Hill. 'There's no money in it, but the director, Stephen, is really tasty – fuckin' hell, talk about bedroom eyes!' Sophie confided to Anna.

In normal circumstances, Anna assumed that she and Gerald would have discussed their mutual future on Broadway, but they maintained their aloof silence making joint plans quite unthinkable. This left Anna in a sort of vacuum – under-employed and restless.

Only on the last night did something of the old spirit return. Martin was there – taking a welcome break from the stark reality of the children's home – as was Alan Buckmaster and Richard's wife, Margaret. The atmosphere, before, during and after the performance, was highly charged with emotion. When Gerald pulled the trigger for the last time, the entire company was in tears, and there were precious few dry eyes front of house. The applause went on and on – the audience simply would not let him go. Again and again he answered the curtain call to cheers and shouts. Most of the audience were out of their seats and flowers were thrown onto the stage. The old theatre had seen some triumphs in its time, but it was questionable whether any had been more spectacular than Gerald Kingdom's closing night in *Sometime . . . Never*.

At last everyone was persuaded to go home. Gerald stumbled off the stage, weak with emotion and exhaustion, and burst into his dressing room to find Anna already preparing his whisky. Their animosity temporarily forgotten, Gerald put his hands on her shoulders and shook her gently. 'Anna, can we do that to them on Broadway – can we, can we?' He was sweating profusely, his face was tearstained, yet dishevelled as he was, he'd never looked more handsome.

118

A sudden warmth of feeling coursed through Anna, melting the coldness that had been between them. This was his moment of triumph, and whatever the rights or wrongs of Gerald Kingdom, she was privileged to be sharing it with him. 'Of course we can,' she said, smiling. She leaned forward and kissed his cheek. 'There's nothing you can't do with an audience, you know that, Gerald.'

He smiled back at her, noting the sudden friendship in her eyes. He gently pulled her to him, so her head rested on his shoulder. 'Dear little Anna,' he whispered into her hair. 'Does this mean you've forgiven me? I've hated the last weeks – all those cold looks and silences. Life's too short, darling.'

'You deserved every cold look you got,' Anna muttered into his shoulder.

'I know, I know, I'm a sod, an absolute swine, but you're not going to be tiresome and continue to sulk, are you?'

'I should.'

'Darling, look at me.' He pushed her gently away, though his hands still held hers. 'Tonight was all right, the play is good, I was good – no, I was brilliant,' he smiled slightly, raising one eyebrow. 'Try as I will, though, I can't get it together with that old bat. There's no magnetism between us, there can't be. With you . . .' he groped for words '. . . Anna, when you play Sarah, I do believe Robert would kill himself for you. The love-hate works between us.'

'You don't think you're perhaps exaggerating a little,' Anna suggested with a slight smile.

'Of course not, darling, you know what I'm saying is right – we're going to be wonderful, you and I.' He leaned forward and kissed her gently on the lips. It was not a passionate kiss, more conciliatory – a kiss of friendship. 'Now,' he said firmly, 'I must wash and change, and so must you. There could be some press at the party tonight and you and I need to appear in a blaze of glory.'

'That's going to put Celia's nose out of joint,' Anna said. 'It's you and she who should be in the blaze of glory tonight – not me.'

'Anna, darling, you're awfully sweet, but terribly naive.

Alan Buckmaster may appear to have a blind spot where his wife is concerned, but he's not going to do anything to jeopardise his future earnings. There's not a penny more to be made out of *Sometime . . . Never* in the West End, but there's a hell of a lot of money to be made out of the play on Broadway. You and I will be all over the British press tomorrow morning, and in twenty-four hours' time, New York will have picked up the story. Alan will find a way to pacify Celia, you'll see.'

He was right. The party was held at Joe Allen's in Covent Garden, and the size of the press attendance at the restaurant surprised everyone. After a few preliminary shots of Celia, the reporters turned their attention to Gerald and Anna . . . How did it feel to get her first break? Had she ever been to Broadway . . . to New York . . . to the States? Was she intimidated by acting opposite such a famous name, had she a regular boyfriend, what was her greatest ambition . . . The questions came thick and fast and as she stood, surrounded by photographers and reporters, Anna couldn't help remembering that other party, just five months before, on the opening night of *Sometime . . . Never*. Then she'd been a nothing, a nobody, watching from the sidelines. She glanced at Gerald, standing beside her. She owed him a lot, she owed him *everything*. It was something she must never lose sight of again.

By three o'clock, the party had been reduced to six. Martin and Sophie sat in a corner, entwined and giggling, drinking champagne out of a pint beer mug. Gerald, Anna, Richard and Margaret Manning were in a separate group. Gerald kept a proprietorial arm round Anna's shoulders – she leaned against him, slightly drunk, but pleasantly so.

'Well, you two,' said Richard, 'I think this is the moment when I should raise my glass in a personal toast – Gerald and Anna, all the very best of luck on Broadway.'

'Yes,' said Margaret, 'I'm sure you'll knock them for six, good luck, my dears.'

They sipped their champagne in silence for a moment and Anna looked at the Mannings with interest. Like many married couples who have been together for a long time, they looked oddly alike. They sat now, close together in a state of perfect contentment, holding hands.

'I'm very envious of you, Mrs Manning,' Anna said.

'Really?'

'Yes, I covet your husband. I think he's absolutely gorgeous. You're very lucky.'

Margaret gave Richard's hand a squeeze. 'Yes, I know.'

'Hey, come off it, darling,' said Gerald. 'What about me? I'm far better looking than he is, and younger.'

'All true,' Richard said, 'which brings me on to the next point I wanted to raise. You'll look after this child, won't you, Gerald? I mean *just* look after her, you know what I'm saying.' Richard, normally so affable and easy-going, had a hard note in his voice. The two men exchanged a look Anna couldn't quite identify.

Margaret came to the rescue, easing the tension. 'The trouble with Richard is that our sons are both so grown up and independent now. Neither of them are even twenty-one yet, but they're far more worldly-wise than he is. The result is that he has no one to fuss over any more, so it's a great treat for him really to be worrying about you, Anna.'

'It's true,' Richard agreed. 'Our sons do seem to know everything. To be frank, most young people terrify me these days, present company excepted, of course.'

'I can't agree with you there,' Gerald protested. 'My God, I've had more bollockings from Anna in the past few months than I've had in the rest of my life put together.'

'It's done you good,' Richard observed.

Margaret laughed. 'Yes, it has. You're far more mellow, Gerald. If Anna keeps up the good work, there's a serious danger that you might become a normal human being.'

'I've had enough of this,' said Gerald, with mock severity. 'In any case, I need to have a little talk with Anna. We'll see you two later. Come on, darling.' He stood up and held out a hand to Anna. Together they walked through to the bar area, missing completely the look of concern that passed between Margaret and Richard.

'You're very fond of that girl, aren't you, Richard?' It was clearly in no way intended to be an accusation.

'Yes . . . she reminds me a little of myself when I was young. She's something of an innocent and rather lonely too,

121

I think . . .' Richard's voice trailed off uncertainly.

'But she has a family, presumably,' Margaret said.

'Oh yes, but I get the impression she's not very close to her parents – perhaps I'm wrong.'

'You're clearly worried about her and Gerald and I can well understand why, but Anna's not a child, Richard. She'll cope.'

Richard turned and smiled absentmindedly at his wife. 'I'm sure you're right, dear,' he said, but his words carried no conviction and he seemed oddly preoccupied.

'You're tired, it's time we went home,' Margaret said. 'Shall we just go and say goodbye to them?'

'No,' said Richard. 'No, let's just leave quietly. I hate goodbyes.'

Gerald poured two fresh glasses of champagne. The restaurant had emptied long ago and the bar area too was completely deserted. 'Come and sit in this corner, there's something I want to ask you.' Gerald patted the seat beside him.

'That sounds very sinister,' Anna said, laughing. 'I think the answer is almost certainly going to be no.'

'It's not sinister, but it is serious.'

Anna caught Gerald's mood and stopped laughing. 'What is it?' she asked. 'Has something gone wrong with the transfer?'

'No, no darling, nothing like that. I was just wondering whether you were going up to Oxford again before we leave?'

'As a matter of fact I am,' Anna replied. 'I'm going up tomorrow. I've more or less packed up my room and Mrs Franks' son has lent me his car for the day. I'm going to take all my stuff home to my parents, stay for lunch and drive back.'

'I see,' said Gerald slowly. 'Are you . . . are you intending to see Sally?'

Anna was instantly alert. 'No, I'm not.'

'I wonder, perhaps, if you would . . . for me.'

'Why?' Anna asked sharply.

'Because she's been ringing me very persistently and she seems upset. I don't know what to make of the girl, Anna. She

122

worries me. I just want to make sure she's all right before I leave the country.'

It felt to Anna as though he'd just thrown a bucket of cold water in her face. So that was his motive for the kindness he'd displayed all evening. Quite clearly it was little more than an attempt to soften her up so that she would deal with Sally for him.

'If you think I'm going to help you sort out your smutty little affair, you've got another think coming,' Anna said vehemently. 'You got yourself into this, Gerald, you get yourself out. If she's breaking her heart over you, then it's up to *you* to put things right, up to *you* to explain.'

'I wasn't asking for myself,' Gerald said, his face taking on the familiar mask it always assumd when he was under attack. 'I was asking for Sally. After all, she is supposed to be your best friend.'

'*Was* my best friend,' Anna said heatedly. 'And that's another thing I can't forgive you for, Gerald. You've broken up a friendship that has lasted years. Neither of us have been in touch with each other since that disastrous weekend – we're both too embarrassed.'

Gerald ran a hand through his hair. 'Look, I don't seem to be getting through to you, Anna, darling. I can't help wondering if she's pregnant, she seems so upset.'

This was something Anna hadn't even considered. 'Oh, my God,' she said, 'you don't think she is, do you?'

Gerald shook his head. 'I simply don't know, but it's possible. Neither of us had exactly anticipated the outcome of that night.' He raised an eyebrow, smiling slightly, and Anna turned away, sickened. 'She rings up my flat, sometimes three or four times a week. To be frank, it's been absolute hell. She bursts into tears and says she can't live without me. I've tried to explain the position as best I can, but the girl's so hysterical I can hardly get a word in edgeways.'

'I'm sorry it's been so tiresome for you,' Anna said sarcastically.

Gerald ignored her. 'So will you help?'

Anna thought for a moment. Of course, she had no choice. Sally had given her years of loyal friendship. 'Yes, I'll help,' said Anna, 'but not for your sake, for Sally's.'

'I said I wasn't asking you to do it for me,' Gerald said. He too was clearly angry now.

'Just as well,' Anna bit back. 'You know, Richard warned me about you. He said you went around destroying people's lives. At the time I thought he was being rather harsh. Now I've been witness to it actually happening, I can see his point.'

'You're being a touch melodramatic, darling,' Gerald said, 'and Richard's an old hypocrite anyway. I could tell you a story or two about him. He may play the saint these days, sitting all coyly, hand in hand with his wife, but he hasn't always been like that, you know.'

'Don't make things any worse, Gerald,' Anna said. 'What you've done to Sally is bad enough, without trying to drag Richard down to your level. I can honestly say he's one of the nicest people I've ever met, and frankly, he's worth ten of you.'

Her face was flushed, her eyes bright and angry. Gerald found himself looking at her mouth and wanting terribly to kiss her. He forced himself to concentrate on the argument. 'There's no point in us bitching away like this, darling, it's getting us nowhere. If you'd see Sally tomorrow I'd be most grateful, and perhaps you could telephone me and let me know how you get on.'

'You mean, let you know whether she's pregnant or not,' Anna said, belligerently.

'That too,' Gerald agreed, mildly.

Anna stared at him for a moment, lost for words. Then she stood up. 'I'm going through to join the others,' she said, 'I've had enough of this conversation, more than enough.' She walked away from him between the pillars, and Gerald followed. The restaurant was now deserted.

'Oh no!' Anna said, 'look, everyone's gone – I've missed them. I haven't said goodbye to Martin and Sophie or Richard. I especially wanted to say goodbye to Richard.'

'You can telephone them all,' Gerald suggested.

'It's not the same.' Anna's voice was tired and dispirited. Gerald tried slipping an arm round her shoulders, but she moved away. 'It's your fault,' she said, tears springing into her eyes. 'You mess up everything. These people . . .' she gestured round the empty room – 'these people are the best friends I've had in a long time and, because of you, I haven't even had a chance to say goodbye to them.'

Gerald shrugged his shoulders. 'You've still got me, darling.'

She stared up at his impossibly handsome face, his amused, slightly indolent expression. 'But I don't want you,' she said angrily, and turning, she ran out of the room.

The door slammed and Gerald stood for a moment alone in the empty restaurant. 'But I want you,' he said softly, and his voice was low as he lingered over the words.

Reggie Franks' car had seen better days. In fact, Anna suspected, each individual part had seen better days, in a variety of different vehicles. It could be loosely described as a Ford Cortina, but the ill-fitting doors and odd coloured panels had a strangely disjointed look. The engine noise was reminiscent of her mother's old treadle sewing machine. Still, it was transport, and sitting firmly in the slow lane of the M40, at a top speed of forty miles an hour, seemed relatively safe.

Anna had woken to a hangover and a sense of foreboding. After a temporary remission, her relationship with Gerald was back to square one. The parting with her parents promised to be stilted and awkward, and as for the meeting with Sally . . . heaven knew what she would find.

Anna waited until they were drinking coffee in the drawing room after lunch before mentioning Sally to her parents. 'Have you seen Sally recently?' she asked her mother casually.

'It's funny you should mention it, Anna, but no, we haven't. Of course, being Sally, we had a charming thank-you letter after our party' – this Anna knew was a dig at her own general lack of communication – 'but we haven't heard a thing from her since, have we, Stephen?'

'If you say so,' Stephen replied, not raising his eyes from the *Observer Review*.

'Odd that.' May Wetherby knitted her brows, pushing her glasses up her nose.

'I . . . er, I thought I might pop round and see her this afternoon,' Anna said tentatively.

May Wetherby looked up sharply at her daughter. 'Do you have to? After all, we're not going to see you again for goodness knows how long.'

Anna shifted uneasily in the chair. 'Yes, I know, Mummy. I'm sorry, only I haven't heard from Sally either and I am slightly concerned. Besides which, I'd like to say goodbye. I won't be long, honestly.'

There was a rustle of newspapers and Stephen Wetherby emerged from behind them. 'I've been thinking, if this play of yours is a success, I believe your mother and I should fly out to see you, and it, of course.'

'To America!' May's voice was shrill.

Stephen shrugged his shoulders. 'Why not? We could do one of those package trips – a week in New York. Who knows, we might even be able to fly Concorde.' His expression was jaunty.

Impulsively, Anna jumped up and threw her arms round her father's neck. 'Would you, would you really do that?'

'Hey, stop it,' said Stephen, predictably embarrassed by Anna's demonstrative affection. 'I'm too old for this sort of thing, you know, but yes, I really think we should come out.'

'But the expense,' said May.

'To hell with the expense,' said Stephen, expansively, 'besides which, we can afford it. Anna is our only child, May, and I'm damned if I'm going to let her star on Broadway without my being a witness to it. Anyway, I have a feeling she might be a little lonely out there, and might appreciate a little moral support. Isn't that right, Anna?' he squeezed Anna's hand, as she knelt beside his chair.

May looked at them in surprise. '*Will* you be lonely, Anna?'

Anna smiled, a little sheepishly. 'I shouldn't be surprised. I don't know anyone at all in New York, except Gerald, of course, and he doesn't count.' Her voice sounded positively venomous, but luckily no one challenged the statement.

'Do you know,' said May, 'that's something which has never occurred to me. I'd assumed all you theatre people had friends everywhere.'

Anne shook her head. 'I suppose that does happen once you're a well-established actor, but most of my friends are in repertory companies like Leeds or Birmingham – in other words, a very, very long way from Broadway.'

'Well, that's nothing to moan about,' said May unexpectedly, 'that means you're one step ahead of them, one rung further up the ladder.'

'That's right,' Anna agreed, very conscious that this was the first time her mother had acknowledged her achievement in any way.

'I'm going to pour us all a brandy,' said Stephen. 'And I tell you this, my girl – even if your mother won't come, I'll be out to see you.' He winked at Anna as he stood up. 'Still, she will come, she wouldn't trust me with all those glamorous chorus girls.'

She trundled the car through the narrow streets of Jericho, the district of Oxford where most of the arts struggle, and occasionally flourish. Anna always fancifully assumed that behind every gaily painted front door, there lurked a budding artist, writer or musician. Certainly a myriad talent had come out of Jericho over the years.

Sally lived in the ground-floor flat of a little house close to the Oxford canal. Originally she had shared with several other girls, but now she lived alone, and took great pride in her home. Anna drew the car to a shuddering halt outside 9 Nelson Street. For a moment she sat still, trying to steel herself for whatever lay ahead. Then reluctantly, she climbed out of the car and walked up to the front door. Her hand had hardly touched the bell before the door opened.

'Oh, Anna, it's you.' The expectant light in Sally's eyes died away, her voice sounded listless and tired.

Anna stared at her friend. The change in her, in just a few weeks, was extraordinary. She'd lost all her excess weight. Her face had thinned down to expose a surprisingly delicate bone structure, even her eyes seemed larger, and the redness had left her cheeks. Suffering certainly suited Sally, Anna thought irreverently. 'Sally!' she said warmly, 'I'm here in Oxford to make my goodbyes, since I'm off to New York on Tuesday, so . . . well, here I am.'

'Great,' said Sally, wearily. 'Come in.'

The flat was a shambles. In the sitting room there were discarded coffee mugs everywhere, ashtrays were overflowing and odd pieces of clothing were strewn around.

'Good grief, Sally, what's going on?' Anna burst out. 'This isn't like you – my houseproud friend who always puts me to shame.' Sally smiled distantly, but said nothing. 'And what's with all these cigarettes, you never used to smoke?'

'It calms my nerves, it's that or booze.'

'Heavens,' said Anna, trying desperately to sound cheerful, 'you do sound in a bad way, you poor old thing. What's it all about?'

Sally sat down heavily in a chair. 'You know perfectly well what it's all about. I seem to be obsessed with him, Anna, it's as simple as that.'

Anna looked around her at the disarray and the small crumpled figure in the armchair. 'I'm going to get you drunk,' Anna said firmly, 'but first I'm going to clean up the flat and feed you. Have you anything to eat here?'

'I don't think so,' Sally said. 'I finished off all the food and booze last week. When it ran out, I simply stuck to coffee.'

'Is there a shop round here that's open on a Sunday?'

'Yes, in Walton Street.'

'OK,' said Anna, 'you sit there and leave everything to me.'

It took Anna less than an hour to shop, clean up and coax Sally into eating a plate of scrambled egg and drinking a cup of milky coffee. Then she placed a packet of cigarettes by Sally's elbow and pulled the cork on a bottle of wine.

Sally eyed the packet of cigarettes suspiciously. 'You don't approve of smoking?' she challenged.

'No, but judging by the state of your ashtrays, you ought to be weaned off them slowly. Besides which, we have a lot of talking to do and I need every prop I can lay my hands on in order to persuade you to relax.' She poured out two large tumblers of wine and handed one to Sally. 'Now drink that, smoke a cigarette and then I want to hear all about it.'

Sally did as she was told, and soon, without prompting, she began to speak. 'G-Gerald came to my room that night, after your parents' party.'

'I know,' said Anna, gently.

'You know, did he tell you?'

Anna thought quickly. 'Sort of,' she said. 'Anyway, I guessed.'

'Oh Anna, it was so wonderful. He told me he loved me – those eyes, that body, I couldn't believe it was happening to me, it was like a dream. And then . . .' Tears were slowly slipping down her cheeks, but she seemed unaware of them. '. . . and then, when I woke up in the morning, and there he was lying beside me, I knew it was true.' Her face clouded. 'He was odd, sort of distant when he first woke up, even while we were still in bed. Then you had to get back to town and we never really had a chance to talk again, and . . . and I haven't seen him since.'

'But he gave you his telephone number,' Anna said.

Sally shook her head. 'No.'

'So how did you get it? Gerald told me you've been ringing him.'

'I did a shameful thing, I'm afraid,' Sally said. 'I rang the theatre. I remembered the doorman's name was Freddy, you'd mentioned it. So . . . well, I'm afraid I impersonated you. Freddy was quite taken in and gave me Gerald's number immediately. I said I, or rather *you*, had to drop something in to him, you see.'

'Oh Sally. Here, have some more wine.' Sally offered her glass and Anna topped it up. 'What does he say when you ring him up?' Anna asked, genuinely curious.

Sally shook her head. 'Oh a lot of stuff about how wonderful I am and how sorry he is that he can't come up to Oxford to see me, and no, he's too busy for me to go down to London. I know it's all excuses, Anna – the sensible part of me knows that, but it's just that after having made love to him I feel . . . oh hell, it was like one of his old movies actually coming to life.'

'Precisely,' said Anna, triumphantly. 'Isn't that where you're going wrong, Sally? You're not in love with Gerald Kingdom, you're in love with the image of Gerald Kingdom – just like hundreds and thousands of women all over the world. The only difference is you've actually slept with him.'

'That's quite a big difference,' Sally said, smiling properly for the first time.

Anna grinned back. 'Yes, of course it is. Don't think I don't understand, Sal, but you simply can't be in love with the real man because you don't know him. He's not a bit like you imagine, you know.'

Sally's eyes grew wide. 'Do *you* know him, the real him?'

'I'm beginning to,' Anna said, 'and believe me, Sally, the real him isn't very nice.'

'I can't believe that. He can't be so uncaring or he wouldn't have sent you down to see how I was. I take it that's what he's done.'

'Oh yes, he sent me down all right,' said Anna. She paused for a moment, wondering whether Sally was ready for what she had to say. 'Sally, there's only one reason why he wanted me to come – he was worried you might be pregnant. You're not, are you?'

Sally shook her head, tears pouring from her eyes again. 'No,' she said, 'w-was that really the only reason?'

'The only reason, Sally – and what do you think he would have done if you had been – married you, loved and cherished you and the child? Not a bit of it. He would have sent you to an abortion clinic and paid a large sum of money to stop you talking to the press.'

There was a long, tense silence, during which Anna wondered whether she'd just lost her friend for all time. Suddenly Sally smiled. 'Men are sods, aren't they, Anna? Give me a top-up, there's a dear.'

Two hours and three bottles of wine later, Anna rang Gerald's flat. 'Gerald?'

'Speaking.'

'It's Anna.'

'Ah, Anna, the redeemer of my soul.'

'I'm ringing about Sally, Gerald,' Anna said. There was silence at the other end of the phone. 'Well,' said Anna, 'do you want to hear about her or not?'

'I would be grateful,' Gerald said, carefully.

'You'll be thrilled to hear she's not pregnant.'

'Thank God for that.' His relief was evident.

'And what's more, though I know you're not interested, she doesn't care a fig about you any more. Like me, she thinks all men are shits, and you in particular.'

'Anna, have you been drinking?' Gerald's voice sounded reproving, and the irony of his words didn't escape her.

'Yes,' she said, 'I have. I can't think where I picked up the habit, it must be the company I keep.'

'We're getting a little bitchy, darling, aren't we?' Gerald said. 'I'll see you in New York, unless I can think of a way of excluding you from the contract.' There was a click and the phone went dead.

Anna's next telephone call was to her parents. 'Daddy, it's Anna. I've had too much to drink and I'm round at Sally's. Do you think you could come and fetch me, and could I stay the night? I'm not fit to go anywhere at the moment.'

'I thought you'd be very disapproving,' said Anna. She was sitting with her parents at the kitchen table, drinking black coffee.

'It was nice that you actually needed us for something,' May said, 'even if it was only a lift because you'd drunk too much. Since you began acting, since you decided to follow your natural mother's footsteps . . .' she could not hide the bitterness in her voice, 'you've seemed to want to be entirely independent of us. It's gratifying that this once you didn't.'

'Come on, May, that's not being very fair,' Stephen said. 'Your search for your natural parents did hurt us, Anna, but we were wrong to be hurt.' Anna stared at him, he'd never spoken like this before. 'We've talked to a lot of people since and it's quite obvious that your reaction was a perfectly natural one, and we were at fault for not recognising it as such. It's proved a long haul getting back to any degree of understanding between us, but you're an adult now and I think the time has come when we should all make a fresh start, and bury past unhappiness for good.'

Anna turned to her mother. 'Is that what you feel too, Mummy?'

May pushed at her glasses, nervously. 'Your father is right,' she said, avoiding Anna's eye. 'Your career is blossoming, and, yes, let's look on this as a new beginning.'

* * *

Anna left Oxford feeling much happier than she'd expected to. Sally was going to get over Gerald, she'd shown far more sense than Anna had anticipated. Yes, Sally would survive. The parting with her parents had gone well too – their relationship was warmer, friendlier than it had been in years. Nonetheless, sitting in a taxi on the way to Heathrow Airport, on Tuesday morning, with no one to see her off, she'd felt very apprehensive. Gerald, she knew, had flown out the previous day to start the publicity campaign. He was staying in a different hotel from her own, so she wouldn't be seeing him until they met at the theatre. She felt very much alone.

'Ladies and gentlemen, we will be landing at Kennedy in eleven minutes.' The voice coming over the tannoy made Anna start back into the present. Just eleven minutes away from a whole new life. She opened her bag and began repairing her make-up. Everything would be all right if Daniel was there to meet her, she was certain of that. She knew Chase Productions had been advised of her time of arrival, and bearing in mind their frequent correspondence over the last months, it seemed logical to assume that Daniel would be there, in person. But Anna was nervous. Since her letter telling him about the night in Oxford with Gerald, she'd heard nothing from him at all. She'd tried to find excuses for him – pressure of work, poor post, the imminence of her arrival in New York, but somehow his silence felt wrong.

'Please, please let him be there,' Anna whispered to herself, as the plane dropped height and lazily circled over New York City.

Chapter Thirteen

Daniel was not there. While Anna was fastening her seat belt, twenty thousand feet above him, he was fixing a drink – for Rosie Blake. She sat on the sofa in his apartment – the sofa where they'd made love nearly five months before. She smiled up at him, prettily.

'So . . . *Emma* opens at the end of next week – how do you feel about it?' Daniel asked.

'OK, though I'm really looking forward to the opening. I've had enough of rehearsals.'

'That's a pretty standard reaction, isn't it?'

'Yeah, I guess. Daniel, I – I feel real guilty about this – this evening, I mean.'

'You shouldn't do.' He handed her a glass of wine.

'I should too. The whole idea was to take *you* out to dinner, to say thank you – you know, for arranging everything.'

'Jesus, Rosie, if that tale you told me was true – not that I'm prepared to admit it, mind – the last thing you should be doing is thanking me. Surely, kicking my ass would be more appropriate?'

'You were very kind,' Rosie said, simply. 'Even though you didn't believe me, you *were* kind, and you really made sure I had the best of everything. They were so good to me at that clinic, and the hotel afterwards . . . wow! You know, my bathroom was bigger than our whole apartment back home.' She smiled, displaying dimples on each cheek.

Dammit, thought Daniel, if only she wasn't sitting on that sofa – it's the lighting on her skin. The desire to touch her was tantalising, almost irresistible.

When Rosie had called him to ask him out to dinner he had

nearly refused. He was only too aware that Anna was due in New York the same evening. Still, what the hell. It was a month now since Anna had ended up in Gerald Kingdom's bed in Oxford and by now the old rogue would have made it with her, Daniel was sure. So, why the hell *should* he meet her at the airport? The less he had to do with Anna Wetherby the better. In just a few short months, she'd hurt him more than any woman he'd ever known . . . and he hadn't even kissed her. She was poison, and all he had to do was to remember he was well out of it.

So, Daniel had accepted Rosie's invitation, in as much that he'd agreed that they should spend the evening together. The kid earned a pittance so there was no way he was prepared to take a meal off her, and arguing about the check would have proved an embarrassment for them both. He'd suggested dinner at his flat, as a good compromise – he loved cooking, and, in any case, the only kind of restaurant Rosie would have been able to afford would have given him food poisoning, no doubt.

Daniel glanced involuntarily at his watch. Anna would be landing at Kennedy about now. He dragged his thoughts away from her, back to the conversation in hand.

'So, you're fully recovered now, Rosie, are you?'

'Yes, I am.' She hesitated. 'They say there's no permanent damage or anything, so I guess one day I can still have kids.' She looked vulnerable suddenly, and very young.

'That's good,' said Daniel, 'and you'll make sure it doesn't happen again, I guess.'

'Too true.' Her face was serious. 'I don't like thinking about it, you know, the idea of taking a life, because that's what it was, wasn't it?'

'I suppose so, technically.' Daniel searched his mind for words of comfort but there were none. She'd put a voice to his own thoughts. He tipped back his head, drained his glass and then reached for the wine bottle. 'Rosie Blake,' he said, 'you and I are in serious danger of becoming morbid. Come on now, let me give you a refill, and then come through to the kitchen and watch me cook. We're going to have one hell of a good evening, you and I.'

'I'll drink to that,' said Rosie, her eyes sparkling with mischief.

Anna stood, bewilderd, in the midst of the airport beside her luggage, and looked helplessly around her. A grumpy-looking man in faded denims stood with a placard in his hand. She strained her eyes – *Miss Anna Wetherby* – it read. With a sigh of relief she trundled her luggage over to him. 'I'm Anna Wetherby,' she said.

'For Chase Productions?' She nodded. 'This way then, Ma'am. I'm to take you to your hotel.'

The journey into New York made little impression on Anna. It was dark, drizzling and very cold – in fact the weather was perfectly compatible with her mood. She had surprised herself by the extent of her disappointment at not seeing Daniel. What was wrong? Why hadn't he met her, or was she, perhaps, expecting too much from their correspondence?

They were well into Manhattan before it occurred to Anna to wonder where they were going. 'Where are you taking me?' she said to the cab driver.

'Wentworth Hotel, it's on 46th and 6th.'

The address meant nothing to Anna. 'Is it near the Chase Theatre?' she asked.

'Yep, just a block away. Chase is on 45th, just the other side of Times Square.'

A thought suddenly struck Anna. 'Is the Wentworth Hotel near Central Park?' she asked.

'Central Park's a big place, lady. Whereabouts?'

'Central Park Westside,' she searched her memory for the address, 'on the corner of 67th Street, I think.'

The cabby shrugged, 'It's not so far, not this time of night, on a Sunday.'

Unwittingly, it was his choice of words which decided Anna. Of course, it was Sunday. Daniel wouldn't be working, would he? It was only just after ten, so surely he'd still be up. 'Would you take me there, please, instead of my hotel? I have a letter in my bag here somewhere which will give me the full address.'

'Just as you like, lady. You'll have to pay me though. Chase paid to go to Wentworth.'

'That's all right,' said Anna. 'How long will it take to get there?'

'Fifteen, twenty minutes perhaps.'

The decision made, Anna leant back in the seat of the cab, suddenly feeling very nervous and apprehensive. If Daniel had wanted to see her he'd have been at the airport to meet her, so why was she forcing the issue tonight? She was dead tired. The only sensible thing was to go straight to her hotel, and yet . . . It was the memory of his letters that spurred her on. Someone who'd written as he had would surely be pleased to see her.

Nothing could have prepared Anna for the luxury of Daniel's apartment block – she was amazed by its opulence. The entrance lobby was the size of a ballroom, all glass, chrome and acres of deep pile, maroon carpeting. The porter, in a neat suit one shade darker than the carpet, sat behind an official-looking desk. 'Good evening, Miss. Can I help you?'

'I hope so,' said Anna. 'I've come to see Daniel Chase. The thing is there's a cab waiting outside with all my luggage in it. I don't want to unload it unless I know he's here.'

'Yeah, I think he's in. Hold on a moment would you? Anna waited impatiently while the porter dialled Daniel's number. 'Who shall I say wants him?'

'Anna, Anna Wetherby,' she said, nervously.

There was a lengthy pause. 'Sorry, Miss, there seems to be no reply. Funny though, I could have sworn he was in.'

The need to see Daniel, having come this far, was suddenly overwhelming. 'Can't I just go up to his apartment and check if he's in?'

The porter looked at her doubtfully. 'You can't go up on your own. No one's allowed to do that, not without being announced, and I can't really leave my desk to take you.'

'Please . . .' said Anna. 'I've just flown in from London. I'm so tired, and the cab's costing me money out there.' The porter hesitated. 'I don't exactly look like someone who's going to cause any trouble, do I?'

'OK, but have Mr Chase call me, if he's in, to let me know

136

what you want done with this cab. Take the elevator to the fourteenth floor apartment 247.'

With breathtaking speed, Anna was deposited on the fourteenth floor. Daniel's apartment was straight ahead of her. She took hesitant steps to the door and pressed the bell.

Everything about him was more impressive than Anna had remembered. Standing there in the doorway, he seemed better looking, taller, fairer. Anna felt her heart begin to pound just at the sight of him.

For a moment they simply stared at one another. 'Anna, what a surprise,' Daniel said, at last. His voice was apprehensive rather than welcoming, and he glanced nervously over his shoulder.

'I'm sorry,' said Anna, 'I knew, really, I shouldn't have come. It's obviously an inconvenient moment.'

'No, no,' said Daniel hastily. 'Come on in.'

The scene that greeted Anna inside the apartment stopped her in her tracks. The cream room was subtly bathed in soft apricot lighting, making it appear warm and intimate. Leaning back on a pile of cushions in the middle of the floor sat a girl, exquisitely pretty. She held a glass of wine in her hand and at her feet were obviously the discarded remains of a meal. Another glass, clearly Daniel's, stood on the carpet close by her.

'Hi,' the girl said.

'Hello,' Anna managed.

Daniel stood awkwardly between them. 'Rosie, this is Anna Wetherby, the actress I was telling you about. Anna, this is Rosie . . . Rosie Blake.'

Rosie Blake . . . Anna turned the name over in her mind. Of course, the girl who'd had the abortion. Anna stared at her, curious, even in her bewildered state. Rosie was everything Anna was not – small and petite, with her short-cropped, black curls and big blue eyes. Now she was smiling cheerfully at Anna, showing perfect twin dimples on each cheek.

'Anna's just got in from London,' Daniel said. His voice sounded strained. 'I guess you must be really tired, Anna. Let me fix you a drink.'

Anna's mind was reeling. So he'd arranged the abortion

137

and now that it was over, they had simply taken up where they'd left off. There was no doubt in her mind that she had interrupted the beginnings of a very intimate evening.

Feelings of hurt, humiliation and rage seemed to be assailing her from all directions. She knew she had to get out before she made a fool of herself. 'No thanks,' she said, 'I won't stay.'

'But you must, you've only just got here,' said Daniel.

'Yes, but I didn't know you'd be busy.' Her voice was heavily laden with sarcasm.

'I'm not busy,' said Daniel. 'Rosie and I have finished eating. Hey, would *you* like something to eat?'

'No, I would not,' Anna said, in a strangled voice, moving away towards the door.

Rosie was suddenly galvanised into action. She jumped to her feet. 'Look, you guys, it seems like I'm the one in the way.' She glanced enquiringly at Daniel. 'Time I was going, right?'

'No, it's not,' said Daniel, clearly agitated. 'For heaven's sake, Anna, come and sit down, . . . and relax.'

'No, I can't, I won't stay.' She turned, almost running out of the apartment. She reached the lift and pressed the button, looking wildly round her for some other means of escape, but Daniel was right behind her. 'Anna, don't be silly.' He tried putting a hand on her arm, but she shrank from him. 'I'm sorry if you found it embarrassing, Rosie being here,' he whispered, 'but I wasn't expecting you.'

'That's blatantly obvious,' said Anna. 'Masterminding an abortion is bad enough, but once it's over, to carry on as though nothing had happened . . . it's – it's horrible. I thought I knew you, I thought those letters meant something.' The lift doors swished open behind her, and Anna stepped in. She turned to Daniel, her face haggard with the effort of controlling her emotion. 'But I don't know you at all, do I? *I don't know you at all*.' The lift doors shut and Daniel turned from them and walked slowly back into his apartment.

'Gee, I'm sorry,' said Rosie. 'Is she your heavy date?'

Daniel shook his head. 'No, no, nothing like that. I'm sorry, let's forget it. Come on, have some more wine and I'll find a soothing tape for us to listen to.'

138

'I don't think so,' said Rosie, gently.

'Why not?'

'Well, judging by the look on your face, I guess you'd rather be alone.'

'What look on my face?'

'Well, you look kind of crumpled. That Anna Wetherby obviously knows how to hit you where it hurts.' She came up to him, put her hands on his shoulders, and standing on tiptoe, kissed him on the lips. 'I had a great evening, thanks for inviting me, and thanks again, too, for the other thing.' Rosie hesitated. 'I don't know whether this makes it better or worse, but I didn't lie to you, you know. It was your baby, I know you don't believe me, but it was, truly.'

Daniel looked down at the little face turned anxiously up to his. 'I believe you, Rosie,' he said, huskily, 'and just for the record, it makes it worse.'

Anna was too tired and distraught to take in her surroundings when eventually the cab driver deposited her at the Wentworth Hotel. She was vaguely aware that her room was big, with two double beds, and its own bathroom. She dumped the cases, threw off her clothes and climbed wearily into bed. She was desperately tired, but sleep eluded her. What a fool she'd been. What on earth had possessed her to call on Daniel unannounced? She tossed and turned, trying to make some sort of sense of her feelings, and it was almost dawn by the time she fell into an uneasy sleep.

Grey light seeping through the curtains woke her a few hours later. For a moment she wondered where she was, then she remembered – New York. She tried saying the words out loud, but they sounded unreal. She got out of bed feeling tired and heavy-lidded, the memory of the previous evening still painfully fresh. She bathed and ordered breakfast in her room, but even after several cups of coffee, she felt no better. A message with her breakfast tray had told her to present herself at the Chase Theatre at eleven o'clock. At ten thirty, Anna took the elevator to the ground floor and asked the girl in reception to direct her to the theatre.

'Oh yeah,' she said, 'Chase – that's on 45th. It's easy. Out of here, turn right, across Times Square, and you'll see it come up on your left.'

'I'd imagined all the theatres were actually on Broadway,' Anna said.

'Hell, no,' the receptionist replied, 'practically none of them are on Broadway. The theatres are *either side* of Broadway, in the forties and fifties like 45th.' She spoke slowly and kindly as if to a child, and Anna stared at her in bewilderment. So Broadway wasn't really theatreland, the Great White Way, as she'd heard it described, nor was it the first time that day that Anna was going to be similarly disillusioned.

Anna was never to forget her first walk from her hotel to the theatre. The cold was intense and from manhole covers and even cracks in the road, steam escaped from the city's underground heating system, making everything seem somehow unreal. In London, although theatreland and Soho lay side by side, they never overlapped. If you wished to visit a West End theatre there was no need to run the gauntlet of strip joints and prostitutes. Not so in New York. In New York, Anna discovered, the two areas intermingled. Her first shock was how dirty and unkept the streets were, and how noisy. The noise was incredible. She wondered if she would ever become used to it. Then, she saw her first body – a vagrant, perhaps a junkie, lay stretched out on the sidewalk, and everyone was ignoring him, simply walking round him. A few yards further on there was another, and yet another – simply lying there in the dirt and cold. They could be dead for all anyone cared, thought Anna with horror. Every few yards there was a strip joint or a sex show, and even this early in the morning, the prostitutes were out on the streets, very obviously plying their trade. Anna's inexperienced eye didn't even notice the dope pushers and their like, who openly traded on human misery. The noise, the cold, the steam, the garbage – both human and otherwise – made Anna wonder whether she had inadvertently stumbled into hell.

When the Chase Theatre came into view, it was familiar in one thing at least. It was shabby – but not shabby like the London theatres, *shabby modern* Anna said to herself. She found the stage door and opened it gingerly.

'Yeah?' A small, unshaven face peered at her through a haze of smoke.

'I'm . . . Anna Wetherby. I'm due here at eleven o'clock.'

'Oh yeah.' The doorman's cubby-hole was at least familiar, even if the doorman himself was eyeing her with deep suspicion.

Anna had been taught, early in her career, that making friends with the doorman was essential. 'May I ask your name?' she said, smiling warmly.

'What's it to you, lady?' It was not an encouraging response.

'I'm going to be seeing you every day, I don't want to be saying *hello you* all the time, do I?'

'Charlie,' was the gruff reply.

'How do you do, Charlie.' Anna held out her hand. Charlie simply stared at it in disbelief and made no move to shake hands.

'Oh darling girl, don't waste your time trying to be friendly with Charlie, he hates everyone.' The voice behind Anna made her jump and turn round. A tall man was walking towards her. He had blue-grey hair and wore tight satin electric green trousers and a pink ruffled shirt, open almost to the navel. If that wasn't indication enough, his mincing walk made his sexual inclinations only too obvious. 'Hi there, sweetie pie,' he said, 'you have to be Anna.'

Anna smiled. 'Yes, I am. Who are you?'

'Ralph, sweet child, Ralph St John Brooks,' he replied, taking her hand in his and kissing it with great ceremony. .

'Hello Ralph,' Anna said, wondering who on earth this strange creature could be.

He sensed her confusion. 'Wondering who I am, right? I'm the butler, sugar pie, and I look just delicious in all that gear. You simply won't be able to resist me – no one can.'

The butler! Anna groaned inwardly – Ralph playing dear Richard's part – she could hardly bear it.

Some of the horror must have shown on her face for suddenly Ralph drew himself up to his full height. His soft feminine features rearranged themselves into the inscrutable mask of the professional servant and he held up an imaginary tray. 'Madam,' he said, 'tea is being served in the drawing room.'

Anna burst into laughter. 'You're really very good,' she said, amazed.

'I am, aren't I, darling. Come on, let me show you to your dressing room. It's right next to mine – isn't that cosy?'

Anna followed Ralph's swaying green hips down a long cheerless, concrete corridor. 'In here, sweetie pie,' he called cheerfully.

Anna's dressing room was small, stuffy and extremely shabby. It contained a dressing table with peeling paint, a stacking chair and a little lumpy bed. Ralph watched her expression as she gazed around.

'Darling heart, remember your nationality – all an Englishman is ever supposed to need is his castle, and all that crap.'

Anna nodded sagely. 'It's ever so 'umble, but at least it's all mine.'

'Right on,' Ralph agreed. 'Now I'm going to mix you a delicious Daiquiri to make you feel at home – strawberry flavoured, just like those beautiful rosy red lips of yours.'

Anna consulted her watch. 'Ralph, it's not even eleven o'clock!'

'Darling child, you're in New York, anything goes. Be back in a teeny weeny minute.'

Anna drank two of Ralph's excellent Daiquiris, arranged her dressing table, put a photograph of her parents and a few books on the one and only shelf, and hung a poster of *Sometime . . . Never* over the damp patch on the wall. She was just wondering what to do next when there was an impatient knocking on the door. Before she had a chance to call out, a burly figure filled the doorway. He was a caricature of the worst type of American – a big, brutish man, with a coarse face topped by a greying crewcut. He wore an overtight T-shirt which accentuated his paunch, baggy jeans and filthy tennis shoes. To cap it all, he was chewing gum in a noisy fashion. 'Hiya,' he said, 'you Anna?'

Anna nodded. 'Yes.'

'I'm Brad, Brad Hotchkiss, your director. How are you settling in?'

Anna's heart instantly did a flip, not for herself, but for Gerald. The thought of the two men having even the slightest thing in common seemed quite out of the question.

'I'm fine,' she said. 'As you see, I'm trying to make myself at home.'

Brad eyed the *Sometime . . . Never* poster. 'Yeah, I guess you two think you've got all the answers.' He nodded to the poster. 'It was quite a wow in London, yeah?'

Anna nodded, 'Yes, it was.'

'American audiences are different, you know. You can't play the same old tricks and expect them to work over here. The audiences are more critical, more sophisticated, less . . .' he chewed thoughtfully on his gum for a moment, 'less impressed by mystique . . . and old movie stars,' he added after a moment. 'Jesus, they're two a penny round here.'

Anna bridled at the implied criticism of Gerald. 'There are all sorts of old movie stars,' she said.

'Yeah, including the kind that turn up late. Is it a fetish I've got to get used to?'

'Are you talking about Gerald?'

'Yeah, of course I'm talking about Gerald. He was due here at eleven o'clock, like you.' Brad consulted his watch. 'It's now twenty-five after.'

'He's not so very late,' Anna suggested.

Brad stared at her in silence for a moment, which she found most unnerving. 'Tell me, Anna, have you ever been to New York before?' Anna shook her head. 'No, I thought not. In this town, you only survive if you're good – the best. OK, I guess you've noticed a lot of things different from London in the street – the hookers, the dope-pushers, the dirt. That means nothing, that's just scratching the surface. Getting under the skin of New York – now that's really different. It's everything people say it is – a tough city where only the strong survive. In New York you can rise to dizzy heights you've never even dreamed of. In New York, when you fall, you fall lower than you would have believed possible, and then you still have some falling to do. What am I saying? I'm saying this. Twenty-five minutes counts in New York City. Got it?'

Anna was determined not to be intimidated. 'It's very unlike Gerald to be late,' she persisted. 'I know he has a lot of promotional work to do this week. Could he be giving an interview somewhere?'

'He did a breakfast show this morning, if that's what you're getting at, but I guess it's past breakfast time now.' Brad's voice was heavy with sarcasm.

'I'm sure he won't be long,' Anna said, soothingly.

'Yeah, well, I hope you're right, because I sure as hell can't rehearse without him, and I have enough problems with this production as it is. We have gypsy runs scheduled for Thursday, Friday, and Saturday this week and the play opens officially next Monday. Right now, apart from the fact that I have no star, I also have no scenery.'

'Gypsy runs, what on earth are they?' Anna asked, bewildered.

'Jesus, where have you been, Anna? Gypsy runs are . . . what do you call them . . . previews.'

'Oh, I see,' said Anna. 'Why haven't we any scenery, Brad?'

'This theatre is bigger than the one you played in. The stage layouts had to be redesigned and someone's cocked up the measurements.'

'And what about costumes?' Anna asked. 'I gather we're having new ones.'

'Oh yeah, that's a point, I'll send Amy along to see you. In the meanwhile, let's hope we meet on stage later in the day – that is if our star bothers to show up.'

Anna hesitated. 'Is . . . is Daniel Chase coming in today?'

Brad stopped chewing and eyed her speculatively for a moment. So that was the score. He'd wondered why this unknown English bit had been cast – that fucker Dan Chase never let up. Well, she was a pretty little thing, one just had to hope she could act. 'Yeah, I guess he'll be along later,' he said, not unkindly.

After Brad had gone, Anna collapsed in front of her dressing table and stared moodily at her reflection. She looked how she felt – tired and dispirited, and she dreaded the thought of seeing Daniel again. She also had a strong sense of foreboding. It seemed to her tired, jet-lagged mind that *Sometime . . . Never* on Broadway was doomed – Gerald and Brad, it could never work.

There was a tap on Anna's door a few minutes later. 'Come in,' she called.

A strange figure waddled into the room, dressed in the most extraordinary shift, covered in enormous bright red roses. 'I'm Amy Jones,' a voice boomed out from above several chins, 'and I guess I'm your dresser.'

Anna rose to her feet, more out of alarm than good manners. The woman was a formidable sight – six foot tall if she was an inch, black, and enormously fat.

'Well, now, just look at you, child.' She took a step backwards and eyed Anna from head to toe. 'My, my, it's going to be a real pleasure dressing you. Give your old Amy a hug now.' Before Anna had a chance to protest, two coal-black arms grabbed her and she found herself pressed against Amy's ample bosom. Eventually Anna surfaced, hot and flustered. 'Oh Jesus,' said Amy, 'I forgot, you're British. You have to know someone ten, fifteen years maybe, before you hug them. Right?'

Anna laughed. 'Right.'

'No fuss, you're in New York now and you look like you needed a hug. You missing your Mummy and Daddy?'

'I'm twenty-two,' Anna protested.

'So? I miss my Mom and I'm forty-three. Now take your clothes off, child, and let's try on this dress.'

The clothes needed very little alteration. On the last garment, a simple shirtwaister dress, Amy sighed, her mouth full of pins.

'What's wrong?' said Anna. 'Doesn't it look right?'

'You don't represent no challenge to me, child. I could wrap you in a table-cloth and you'd look good. You don't need Amy's skills at all.' She looked really upset.

'I'm sorry,' said Anna.

'And as for that old queen next door, he's another one – hips like a boy. I didn't have to alter his suit at all. No one needs Amy.'

'There's Gerald,' Anna suggested, 'he's very particular about his wardrobe.'

'Gerald Kingdom. Yes.' Amy nodded, slowly, her expression brightening. 'He must be fifty-five at the lowest call. Now that's a guy who must have a tummy on him, and old Amy here will camouflage it good.'

'Oh, no, he hasn't,' Anna said.

Amy threw back her head and roared with laughter, the sound seeming to shake the very walls. 'And how would you know a thing like that, child?'

Anna had the grace to blush. 'Well, I – I just know he has a good figure,' she said, awkwardly.

'Yeah, I bet you do!' Amy gave her an enormous wink, then she sighed. 'Well, you'd better get that dress off, honey, and I'll put a few old stitches in it.' She shook her head, 'I guess this isn't going to be my kind of play.'

Or anyone else's come to that, Anna thought.

During the next couple of hours Anna discovered all the necessary facilities for making life as tolerable as possible in the Chase Theatre over the next few months. The toilets, she discovered, were adequate, though needless to say, a good ten-minute walk from the actors' dressing rooms. The Green Room, as it is known in the theatre – the actors' rest room – was an airless cubby hole, sufficiently close to the stage that one daren't talk, even during rehearsals. Nonetheless, it contained a coffee machine, a pile of reasonable-looking sand-wiches, and best of all, an ice-making machine. This reminded Anna of Gerald's whisky. When by two o'clock, he still hadn't arrived, with directions from Charlie she slipped out of the theatre to the local drug store, and bought a bottle. She had a feeling he was going to need it.

Gerald arrived at precisely twenty past two, and before he'd even reached his dressing room, he was in the midst of a major row with Brad Hotchkiss.

'What fucking hell time do you call this?' was Brad's opening comment.

'Firstly, I'd be grateful if in future you'd clean up your language before addressing me. Secondly, perhaps you would have the good manners to introduce yourself.'

Anna, sitting in her dressing room, couldn't help but smile, the comment was so typically Gerald.

'Don't you come the smart-arse with me. You've kept this company waiting for three and half hours. I don't wait that

146

long for anyone, *anyone*, do you hear?'

'Do I gather, extraordinary though it seems, that you are our revered director, one Brad Hotchkiss?' Gerald lingered over the words, as though he was saying something distasteful.

'Yeah, that's me.'

'Right, Mr Hotchkiss, I'm not sure you're entitled to an explanation as to what I've been doing during the last twenty-four hours, but here it is anyway. Today is Tuesday. On Sunday I flew out from Heathrow. I arrived in New York at 6.30 pm. By 8.30 I was in a television studio. I was finally released from the studio at half-past eleven. I then slept. I was woken at 5.30 yesterday morning and spent all of yesterday through until nine o'clock in the evening, going from one interview to the next. This morning, I had another five-thirty call, this time it was a breakfast show. By the time the show was finished, it was about ten o'clock and I was good for nothing. I went back to my hotel, had a shower, lay down on the bed and passed out. I imagine you would have done the same.'

Brad was unrepentant. 'But you weren't in your hotel. We called it, you hadn't checked in.'

'Chase Productions, in their ignorance, had booked me into the St Regis. When I'm in New York, I always stay at the Algonquin.'

'So you switched hotels, without telling anyone?'

'I haven't had *time* to tell anyone. Now, would you show me to my dressing room, and is Miss Wetherby here?'

'Yes,' said Brad, 'like everyone else she's been here all day, waiting for you.'

'I will be ready for you in twenty minutes,' said Gerald.

'Twenty minutes . . .' Brad exploded, 'you'll have to do one hell of a lot better than that.'

'Twenty minutes,' Gerald said. 'I need coffee, a sandwich and a large whisky.'

'Look, buddy, we're not running a restaurant here. You get your arse on stage right now.'

'You speak to me like that once more and I'm going straight back to the hotel.'

Gerald was losing his cool and Anna realised it was time to move very fast. Picking up the bottle of whisky, she slipped out of her dressing room and found the two angry men glowering at each other in the passage. 'It's OK, Brad,' she said, 'I've got some whisky, and I'll fetch him some coffee and sandwiches.'

Brad was defeated, but Anna was uncomfortably aware that she and Gerald had just made an enemy. 'Fine,' he said, 'absolutely fine. You all take as long as you like. I've got nothing better to do – obviously.' He stormed off down the passageway towards the stage.

'Anna darling,' Gerald held out his arms, 'my saviour, my salvation – come here.'

'I'm not really speaking to you, if you remember,' Anna said weakly, but the sight of his familiar face after all the strangeness of the last twenty-four hours was too much. She allowed herself to be hugged and soundly kissed.

'Here's your whisky,' she said, handing him the bottle.

'Oh darling Anna, this is Bourbon, it's filthy stuff.'

Anna flushed. 'It was supposed to be a present – a sort of welcome to Broadway. I have to admit it *was* the cheapest bottle in the store, but I didn't dare spend any more – I haven't quite got the hang of dollars yet.' She hung her head. 'Anyway, I'm sorry you don't like it.'

'What a pig I am darling, it was a sweet thought. I shall drink it with relish.'

'At least there is an ice-making machine in the Green Room.'

'Thank heavens for small mercies.' Gerald lowered his voice to a whisper. 'Where in God's name did Daniel Chase find that gum-chewing gorilla?' He smiled his beautiful smile. 'Still, I don't expect he'll be much of a problem – after all, he'll never understand the script. Most of the words have more than four letters.'

Well at least his sense of humour is still intact Anna thought, forgiving him, grudgingly, for his tactlessness.

They chatted amicably while Gerald devoured his sandwiches. 'So, what's the rest of the motley crew like?'

Anna gave him a catalogue of impressions. When she got to

Ralph St John Brooks, Gerald let out a hoot of laughter. 'That old reprobate. I didn't realise we were going to be stuck with him.'

'You know him?' said Anna.

'Yes, we were in a film together years ago. Queer as a coot, of course, and totally amoral. I wonder if he still drinks Daiquiris.'

'He does,' Anna said, 'I've had two already this morning.'

'Well, I never.' Gerald gave Anna a shrewd look. 'Ralph won't be the father confessor dear old Richard was to you, of course – in fact, quite the contrary. I have to say, Anna darling, that any advice Ralph gives you must listen to very carefully and then you must do exactly the opposite. It's the only way to ensure your virtue . . . Old Ralph!' Gerald laughed again. 'Well, that'll be someone to have a few jars with.'

Oh no, Anna thought, the final straw. There had to be one, of course – Gerald had found a serious drinking companion.

The rehearsal was a disaster. Brad insisted on starting with the last scene. 'I want to get a feel of what this play's all about. As I understand it, the theme revolves around this old guy killing himself, so I want to see him doing just that.'

Gerald stood tall and elegant beside Brad. 'My dear chap,' he said, 'the last scene needs to be worked into – I can't simply turn it on for you. The play is about Robert's slow disintegration – it's a step-by-step process.'

'Are you directing this fucking play, or am I?'

'I abhor the use of foul language at all times, particularly when it's directed at me, I thought I'd made that clear. As for who's directing the play – I have a tendency to believe I'd probably make a better job of it than you will.' Gerald's face was contorted with anger.

Brad won, and they started with the last scene, in which neither Anna nor Ralph appeared. Gerald sat on a stacking chair in the middle of the stage, with no desk. Anna stood in the wings, full of apprehension as he began the final speech that would lead ultimately to his death. It was awful.

Ralph, standing close behind her, whispered in her ear. 'Sweet child, tell me if I'm terribly wrong, but isn't the Great Man hamming it a little?'

149

Anna nodded. 'He's just doing it to aggravate Brad,' she whispered.

'There'll be tears before bedtime,' Ralph replied sagely.

Gerald had been speaking for less than two minutes when Brad interrupted. 'Is this supposed to be theatre? If you've travelled three thousand miles to give us this . . . Man, I have to say you've been wasting your time.'

Gerald rose from the chair, his face flushed. He walked to the footlights and glared into the darkness of the auditorium. 'On the last night of *Sometime . . . Never* in London, the audience applauded for a full quarter of an hour. In the end, the company manager had to go front of house and beg them to go home. I ask you this, Mr Hotchkiss, has that ever happened in the Chase Theatre, has it ever happened to you – I very much doubt it.' He rolled the words out.

'It sounds more like *Hamlet* than a row,' Ralph whispered.

'We'll repeat the play's success on Broadway,' Gerald continued, 'but I must rehearse it my way. I need a warm-up. Either we start with Act One, Scene One or we don't start at all.'

'Look, buddy, it's time you cut out the primadonna stuff and started doing some work around here. I don't care a shit about your finer feelings. All that concerns me is that we're doing it for real on Thursday night and you're going to have to be ready for it . . . and ready for it on *my* terms.'

'I'm ready for it now,' Gerald replied. 'We have the play, we have the cast, we have the theatre and, without doubt, we'll have the audience. What we can do without . . . if I may quote from your charming vernacular . . . is a little shit like you.'

'Don't you start that, buddy, if you want to swap insults, I can . . .'

Suddenly a voice, louder even than the other two, came from the back of the auditorium. 'What, for Christ's sake, is going on?'

In the darkness his fair hair stood out like a beacon. Anna felt her heart give a flip.

Gerald peered. 'That, I take it, is young Mr Chase.'

'It is indeed,' came the voice. 'What do we have here, civil war?'

'We certainly do,' Gerald replied, 'and I tell you this, you

150

change your director, or you change your actor, you can take your pick.' He turned and walked off the stage, brushing past Anna in his haste. His face was like thunder and Anna knew exactly where he was heading. The only relationship Gerald would be having for the rest of the day was with a bottle of whisky.

Daniel had reached the front of the auditorium. 'What the hell's going on, Brad?' he asked.

Brad shrugged his shoulders. 'It had to happen sometime,' he replied. 'One of these days Chase Productions had to back a no-no and this, by Christ, is it. Dan, that guy has had it. He was three hours late, he drinks and he won't take any form of direction. He was a star when I was in nappies and you weren't even a twinkle in your Pop's eye. Now, he's all washed up. I can't direct this play, I *don't want* to direct this play. Hell, I've got my reputation to consider. I'm going to Charlie's to get drunk. You'll find me there if you want me.'

'Dear, dear,' said Ralph to Anna, 'things are getting very exciting, aren't they, sweetie?'

Anna didn't reply. She was watching the dark figure of Daniel as he left the auditorium, obviously to come backstage.

'We'd better ask the bossman if we're wanted for the rest of the day. I rather imagine we're not, don't you, darling?' Ralph took her hand and together they walked to meet Daniel.

They met by the doorway of the Green Room, exchanged a single look, and then Daniel turned to Ralph. 'There'll be no more rehearsals today, Ralph, but I'd like you here at nine o'clock tomorrow morning.'

'So be it,' said Ralph, adding with a sly smile, 'I assume you'll have the lovers' quarrel sorted out by then?'

Daniel smiled ruefully, 'I guess I'll have to.'

'I guess you will, sweetie pie. See you around.' Ralph minced his way off down the corridor.

'Anna?'

'Daniel.'

'Your first twelve hours in New York haven't been that great, have they?'

'I'll survive. To be honest, I'm too tired to care.' Her voice was very quiet and she avoided his eyes.

'Look, Anna, I've an idea. We need to fix up rehearsals for tomorrow morning so I can come along and keep the peace. If I go and sort out Brad, could you have a word with Gerald? I just require his agreement to be here at nine o'clock tomorrow, but I don't want to get involved in a lengthy discussion with him right now. When we've done that, why not come back to my place? We can talk, and I can fix you a drink, and a meal maybe.'

Pride dictated that she should refuse. Pride said, this man moves in a different world from yours, this man must not be trusted, this man is dangerous because he affects you as no one else has ever done . . . but what use is pride in anyone's life?

'All right,' said Anna. 'Shall I meet you front of house in fifteen minutes?'

Chapter Fourteen

'It's good to be back. I'm absolutely bushed, so heaven knows how you feel.'

Anna reluctantly followed Daniel into his apartment. She knew immediately she shouldn't have come, it was too soon after the horrors of the previous evening.

Daniel sensed her reticence. He smiled encouragingly at her. 'Come on, sit down and let me fix you a drink.' He glanced at his watch. 'It's still twenty minutes to go until the cocktail hour, but what the hell, we've had a tough enough day to deserve an early start.'

Anna walked over to the window. 'I think so too,' she agreed wearily.

'How about a gin and tonic then? Would that make you feel more at home?'

For the first time, Anna smiled. 'Yes, it would. That would be lovely, thanks. This is an incredible view, Daniel. I had no idea Central Park was so big – at least it looks big from here.'

'It *is* big, compared with London parks.'

Anna turned round and studied the room properly, for the first time. 'You really do have a lovely home here, Daniel.'

'Home is the wrong word to use. I'm never here enough to call it that and, in any event, I lease it from the Corporation, from my father. The place isn't mine at all really.'

'That sounds very businesslike,' Anna said.

'Oh yeah, everything between my father and myself is very businesslike.'

Anna let the comment go, accepted her drink and the proffered chair. They sat in silence for a moment.

'First, I'd like to say how sorry I am about last night,'

Daniel said, 'but you did over-react, you know.'

'I don't think I did,' Anna said. 'I admit I was wrong to come here. I don't know why I did really. I suppose it was because you didn't reply to my last letter . . .' her voice tailed off, low, uncertain.

'I guess I didn't write because I was piqued, jealous, angry, all that stuff, and I just didn't know how to handle it. I didn't know what to say – I still don't.'

'Don't you think that's rather hypocritical of you, Daniel?'

'Oh come on, Anna. You write and tell me you've been in Gerald's bed, in his arms, that you nearly let him make love to you, that . . .'

'*He* was in my bed,' Anna corrected.

'Does that make it so different?' Daniel's voice was hard and sarcastic.

'Yes, it does,' Anna replied, angrily. 'I never expected things to turn out as they did. In fact what happened came as much of a surprise to me as my letter evidently did to you. How do you think I felt, come to that, when I heard you'd arranged to have your child aborted?'

'If it was *my* child.'

'So far as I'm concerned, it doesn't matter whose child it was,' Anna said. 'Don't forget I was somebody's unwanted pregnancy. It's a touchy subject.'

Daniel hit his forehead with his fist. 'Jesus, Anna, I'm so sorry. Do you know, that never even occurred to me? I just felt I had to tell someone about it and you seemed to be the right person. If I'd remembered . . . shit, what a mindless loony I am sometimes. I'm so wrapped up in myself . . .'

His distress was obviously genuine, but Anna couldn't bring herself to acknowledge it. 'That's what upset me so much about last night,' she said. 'Between you, you and Rosie have needlessly destroyed a life, a life that would have brought a lot of happiness to someone. Yet there you were last night, behaving as though nothing had happened.'

'If you're suggesting what I think you're suggesting, you're quite wrong,' Daniel said. 'I haven't embarked on any sort of affair with Rosie.' He stood up abruptly and began pacing the room. 'Look, Anna, let me at least try and explain. I feel guilty, right? She's too young to have got herself in this mess, and as you correctly say, whether the child is mine or not is of no relevance. It could have been mine – that's the point. Rosie called a couple of days back and asked me out to dinner. She wanted to thank me, would you believe, for having been so kind to her. Anyway, I asked her here instead, and to be honest, I chose the night I knew you'd be arriving at Kennedy.' He stopped pacing and looked at Anna. 'I think, I *think*, I was trying to get back at you, punish you for what happened between you and Gerald. I knew if I had a free evening I'd be tempted to meet you at the airport, so I purposely made sure I was busy. There's another thing too; I thought by now you'd probably be involved with Gerald anyway.'

'Then that's where you thought wrong.'

They'd reached a point of stalemate. They stared at one another, neither knowing what to say next. It was Anna who, at last, broke the silence. 'You know, I've always believed that honesty between people is the most important thing, that you can't have a proper relationship with someone unless you tell them everything. But perhaps I'm wrong, perhaps one can be too honest. Perhaps some parts of a person's life are best kept private. If you hadn't told me about Rosie, if I hadn't told you about Gerald, we wouldn't be winding ourselves up into this state, would we?'

'I guess not,' said Daniel. 'It's the craziest thing, Anna, I've never shared so much of my life with anyone as I have with you. I'm not used to this degree of intimacy, and I don't seem to know how to handle it.'

'Why don't we talk about the play,' Anna said suddenly. 'You never know, it might do us good to talk about something else.'

Daniel smiled, obviously relieved. 'Great idea – let me fix you another drink, while we exchange horror stories. How did you get on with Gerald?'

Anna sighed. 'Gerald will be at the theatre tomorrow morning all right. He'll have an appalling hangover, but he'll be there. How about Brad?'

Daniel handed Anna her drink and came and sat beside her.

'Oh, Brad's no problem. When all's said and done, I employ him. I simply told him to watch his tongue, get his act together and present himself at nine o'clock sharp tomorrow morning.'

'Can't you change directors, Daniel, or at least teach Brad to speak only when he's spoken to?'

'I'm in a difficult position,' Daniel said. 'Actually Brad's a first-class director, for a certain type of show, particularly comedy, but I appreciate he's not ideal for *Sometime* . . . *Never*. The trouble is, he and my father are as thick as thieves. I think my father insisted on our using Brad so that he had a sort of ally in the camp, as it were. You see, in all other respects, this is my production – my father doesn't approve of the play.'

'That's crazy,' said Anna. 'Surely the primary objective must be to find a director who will do the best possible job. OK, that's Martin, and unfortunately he's involved with a TV programme but, heavens above, there must be a director somewhere in this city who doesn't feel it's too demeaning to pander to Gerald's ego a little?' Her tiredness forgotten, Anna stood up and walked restlessly over to the window. 'Gerald Kingdom doesn't need direction in this play. You know it, I know it. I simply don't believe all that stuff about American audiences being different. You bought the play because you liked it as it was.'

'There are pressures here you don't understand,' Daniel said. He swivelled his chair to watch Anna, standing long and graceful, silhouetted against the window.

'That's what people always say when they've run out of arguments,' Anna countered. 'Daniel, you think you've got a lot to lose if this play fails. Brad is already worried about his reputation. This is *my* first big break and if the play fails, it might be my last. But all of us, *all of us*, have far less to lose than Gerald. If *Sometime* . . . *Never* fails on Broadway, Gerald Kingdom is finished. Even if the public were prepared to give him another chance, he wouldn't give himself one. You're not just gambling with a few thousand dollars of Chase Production money, you're gambling with a man's life.'

Daniel stared at her. 'You must be very fond of him.' His

156

voice was flat, empty and Anna caught the insinuation of his words.

'I wondered how long it would take you to get back to that again,' she replied coolly. 'I'm an actress, Daniel, an actress with a small talent, which I'm trying to turn into a bigger one. In Gerald I recognise excellence, perfection in the art form I've chosen to make my life. I just can't bear to see it thrown away, destroyed at the shrine of some brainless idiot like Brad Hotchkiss.' Her voice faltered, fatigue and a whole confusion of emotions proving just too much. Tears came suddenly and unexpectedly to her eyes. She kept her back to Daniel. 'I'm sorry,' she mumbled, 'I didn't mean to preach.'

Daniel was out of his chair in an instant. He placed his hands on her shoulders and turned her around slowly to face him. Her eyes were sparkling with unshed tears, her colour high. Daniel thought she'd never looked more beautiful. 'Anna, tell me how you feel about Gerald now, honestly.' His voice was low and tense.

'I'm not in love with him,' Anna said, carefully, 'but I am attracted to him.'

'Oh Jesus . . .'

'No, wait,' said Anna, 'I don't mean attracted in the obvious physical way. He is a glorious-looking man and I recognise that, of course. What I'm really attracted to though are the complexities of his character. He's such an idiot sometimes, he behaves so badly and yet he's vulnerable too. In a way, I feel sort of protective towards him, and privileged too. He is a great man, Daniel. OK, maybe I sound like some star-struck child, but I do feel very lucky to be able to call him my friend.'

Daniel stared into Anna's upturned face. 'I've never felt like this in my life before,' he said, unsteadily. 'It seems there are a whole lot of emotions I've never really experienced. This relationship of ours hurts, Anna, and yet the pleasure it brings me . . .' he shook his head, bewildered, his hands gripping her shoulders until they hurt.

'I feel the same,' she said shakily. The memory of Rosie the previous evening suddenly flashed into her mind and she flinched.

Daniel seemed to sense her thoughts. 'Look,' he said, 'let's start again, right from the very beginning. No more recriminations, no looking back over our shoulders. I don't understand what's going on between us, Anna, but I do know I don't want to lose it.'

'Nor do I,' Anna whispered.

They gazed at one another, the tension high between them. 'How would you feel if I kissed you?' Daniel asked, quietly.

'No,' Anna said, vehemently, shrinking from him. 'We can't cope with that, not yet, if ever. Friends, remember, that's what we said, that's what we agreed.'

Suddenly, Daniel's face dissolved into a smile, gloriously driving away the tension in a single instant. 'Food is what we need to calm the nerves. Now, here's what we do. You bring your drink into the kitchen and I'm going to cook you the most amazing bouillabaisse you've ever eaten. All you have to do is sit there, make polite conversation, and then eat it with exaggerated relish. After that I'm going to take you back to your hotel so you can get some sleep.'

'That all sounds marvellous.'

'There are two conditions, mind. Firstly, we are not going to talk about *Sometime . . . Never* once, and secondly, you must guarantee to adore my cooking so that I have the necessary excuse to invite you here again.'

Anna smiled, catching his mood. 'You have a deal, Mr Chase.'

'Oh,' Daniel paused, 'we have just one probem – the wine is Californian. Will the mix of cultures worry you?' Anna shook her head. Nothing worries me as much as you do, she thought to herself.

The Algonquin Hotel in many ways reminded Gerald of a London club – the panelled lobby, the cosy elegant bar. The staff had less of the New York brashness than most, and from the doorman to the chambermaid, they never failed to recognise him on arrival and to make a suitable fuss of him thereafter. Somehow though, that particular evening, the Algonquin charm just wasn't working. Gerald sat alone and morose, at a corner table in the bar. He felt on edge, everything seemed out of tune. He'd finished the bottle of Bourbon Anna had brought him. Now he was drinking pure Scottish malt, but the taste was all wrong.

The drink had deadened his anger and he'd already dismissed Brad Hotchkiss from his mind as an unimportant irritant. What plagued him now was Anna. He'd been surprised when she'd gone off with young Chase like that. He hadn't realised that they even knew each other, except professionally. Was there something serious between them? he wondered. Certainly Daniel Chase was a good-looking lad, yet there couldn't be anything going on, *surely* – there hadn't been time for them to meet more than once or twice at the most. Still, he felt insecure. 'Anna keeps me on the rails,' he muttered thickly into his drink. Then downing it, he held his glass high and waved it at the barman.

Before the barman could reach him, a disembodied voice floated into his consciousness.

'Gerald, my darling, darling boy, how perfectly lovely.'

Gerald's semi-focusing eyes swept around the bar and fastened on a frail little figure bearing down on him. He stood up unsteadily and squinted.

The little old lady advancing towards him was vaguely familiar. She had white hair – the true white hair of a former natural blonde, and it was swept up untidily into a small bun on top of her head. Her sweet face, criss-crossed with wrinkles, was smiling kindly at him. She leaned heavily on a stick and was obviously far from well.

She stopped a foot or so from him and regarded him with amused indulgence. 'You old devil,' she said, 'you're drunk. I can forgive you that, but I'm not sure I can forgive you for not knowing who I am.'

Gerald frowned in concentration. 'Of course I . . . do.' He waved his arms expansively.

'No, you don't, you old fraud. But then, darling, why should you, it's been a long time.' She stretched out a tiny bird-like hand and placed it on his arm. 'Bristol Rep – must be thirty-six, thirty-seven years ago – am I ringing any bells yet?'

'Daphne, Daphne Eden!' Gerald's kaleidoscope expression

amused her – fond remembrance, shock at realising that this was the girl he'd once known, followed by horror at the thought that they were contemporaries. Despite the drink, he made a supreme effort to be gallant, and swept her into an embrace. 'Daphne, darling Daphne, how lovely to see you. Sit down, let me get you a drink.'

'I'll sit down,' she said, 'but I won't drink. I'll watch you.'

The barman, who had been hovering behind them wordlessly, topped up Gerald's glass and then left them alone.

Once seated, Daphne took Gerald's hand. 'Now, darling,' she said kindly, 'before we can have a proper talk I need to set your mind at rest. Firstly, you should remember that I am ten years older than you, and secondly, feel my hand.'

'It's trembling,' said Gerald, not understanding.

'Precisely, darling. I have Parkinsons. I've had it for some years. I'm giving it a hell of a run for its money but it's taken its toll. Whereas you, my handsome friend, have barely changed at all.'

Gerald smiled sheepishly. 'Did I look sufficiently horrified that you felt you needed to make that explanation?'

Daphne smiled, 'Yes, darling, you did.'

'I'm sorry, I feel very ashamed.'

'There's no need to be, darling. Now, next question, are you expecting to be joined by some delectable young woman at any moment? Am I keeping you from doing anything?'

'You're certainly not.' Gerald squeezed the little hand in his. 'In fact, I can't tell you how pleased I am to see you, Daphne. Come on, let's have a drink. How about some champagne?' He raised his hand to call the barman.

'No, no,' said Daphne, 'I can't really drink in public – I spill it you see.'

'Then we'll go to my room,' said Gerald. 'I'll order a bottle of champagne, two glasses and a straw.'

'I've never drunk champagne through a straw,' said Daphne, giggling and suddenly looking surprisingly girlish.

'Neither have I, I'll order two straws.'

Gerald Kingdom's education had been privileged and conventional. Prep school at seven, then Rugby, with the promise of a place at Cambridge where his parents intended he should read law. Their only concession to his obviously flamboyant nature was that they saw him possibly becoming a barrister, rather than a solicitor, like his father. It never happened.

The day after Gerald left school, he announced to his astounded family that he was going to become an actor. He offered them a choice – to support him while he did things properly and went through RADA, or to leave him to make his own way, which meant finding a repertory company that would take him. His father refused point blank to support him in such a hare-brained scheme, unable to believe that a son of his could, and had, turned down a place at Trinity College, Cambridge.

In disgrace, and left to his own devices, it took the eighteen-year-old Gerald less than a week to sign himself up with a company touring the west of England. Not for Gerald though, were there the years of obscurity which Anna had endured. He was assistant stage manager for one production only, and then he was *discovered* by the leading lady. First, she insisted he should be given a part in the next production, and then she took him to her bed. He was a virgin. She, ten years older than he, was a liberated woman of considerable experience. During their long passionate nights together, she taught him most of what he needed to know for the years of philandering which lay ahead. Her name was Daphne Eden.

It took them two hours and two bottles of champagne to catch up on each other's news. Then Gerald insisted on providing them with a light meal in his room, despite Daphne's protests. With infinite tenderness, he carefully guided the fork to her mouth so she could eat, and she relaxed under his ministrations. They exchanged gossip concerning old friends, discussed details of their amorous adventures. He paid her extravagant compliments and made her laugh a great deal. The evening was a huge success and achieved two things – by the end of it, Gerald was a great deal less drunk than he would otherwise have been, and Daphne felt more cherished than she'd felt in a long time.

'So why are you living out in America, darling?' Gerald asked. 'You've never worked over here much, have you?'

Daphne shook her head. 'No, I wouldn't be in America from choice, to be honest, but my son works here, you see.' She leaned conspiratorily towards Gerald. 'I love him, of course, but he's a bit of a stuffed shirt. He and his wife and two children live in Kentucky. Bob's a banker, and he's so . . .' she groped for the word '. . . boring. He and his wife are so concerned with status. They're always giving me lectures about how much gin I drink and how I must clean up my language.'

'Darling, it sounds terrible,' said Gerald. 'Why do you stick it?'

'I'm old, I'm alone and I'm sick,' said Daphne, without rancour. 'I'm not sorry for myself, mind, but I am practical. I simply can't manage on my own – I never made much money you know.' She winked, 'I still have one claim to fame though – I launched the great Gerald Kingdom on his way, didn't I?'

'You certainly did, darling,' said Gerald, taking her hand and kissing it, 'and in some style. Do you realise that, without you, I'd probably still be playing the boards in Bolton.'

'Not you, my sweet, you were always destined for great things. If it hadn't been me, someone else would have helped you.'

'Funnily enough,' said Gerald, 'I was thinking about you the other day. I've taken a young actress under my wing, given her a chance. Her name's Anna Wetherby, she's in *Sometime . . . Never* with me. The part's small but it's a lovely little cameo and she plays it to perfection.' He grinned, 'It's such a gamble, our business, and it's been a great source of pleasure to me to make this opportunity available to her.'

'You know, Gerald, for a brief moment there I almost believed you were being altruistic.' Daphne smiled naughtily. 'But I haven't quite lost touch with reality, and I must remember you're a great actor. So . . . no doubt this young lady is providing you with a few creature comforts.'

'No,' said Gerald, 'no, she's not.'

'Scout's honour?' Gerald nodded. 'Dear, dear.' Daphne eyed him quizzically.

'What's that supposed to mean?' Gerald said, a little aggressively.

'Don't be touchy, darling, I was just toying with the possibility of your actually being in love. I suppose it had to happen sometime – even you couldn't play Peter Pan for ever.'

'I have a feeling, Daphne darling, you're taking the piss,' Gerald said reprovingly.

'Certainly not,' she replied. 'After all that champagne and such a delicious meal, I wouldn't dream of being so ill-mannered. I just seem to be subject to some conflicting emotions at present.'

Gerald frowned. 'Like what?'

'On the one hand, bearing in mind all the hearts you've broken over the years, it would serve you right if this girl broke yours. On the other hand, I like my rogues as they are. I think the concept of your developing finer feelings might be too much of a culture shock.'

'You're a very naughty lady,' Gerald said.

'I've had my moments,' Daphne agreed.

Daphne, too, was staying at the Algonquin and shortly after midnight, Gerald took her in the elevator to her floor, and escorted her to her bedroom door.

'How much longer are you in New York?' Gerald asked.

'Just until tomorrow morning. My son is here on business. He's fetching me first thing and then we're going home. I wanted to come and see New York again, just once more – I've always had a soft spot for it.' She spoke the words quite naturally, her expression composed – there was little sadness in her.

'Let me write down your address,' said Gerald, taking out his pocket book. She gave it to him and then he embraced her. 'Goodbye, darling,' he said, 'it's been so lovely to see you.'

'Thank you for a wonderful evening – I haven't enjoyed myself so much in years,' Daphne said.

'I'll come and see you in Kentucky in a month or two,' Gerald assured her – but they both knew he never would.

Gerald considered Daphne's words as he wandered back through the corridors towards his room. What *were* his true motives concerning Anna? He was damned if he knew. He recognised among his feelings for her the strong desire to give rather than take, but give what – his time, his influence, himself? His emotions were complex, unfamiliar . . . and they worried him.

The following morning, after a short, sharp lecture from Daniel, Gerald and Brad agreed to make up their differences. Gerald was to be allowed to rehearse the play in whatever order he considered most appropriate, but only on condition he listened closely to Brad's instructions – particularly where the director felt the emphasis should be changed to reflect the American audience.

The day dragged on. Certainly there were no more scenes, but both men prowled around one another with the result that Gerald's performance was far from good, and by mid-day, despite all Anna's efforts, he was drunk again. At two o'clock Brad abandoned rehearsals for the day and Anna had to admit he was right to do so. Nothing more could be done with Gerald in his current state.

As Anna wandered through the streets on the way back to her hotel, she felt very much alone and oddly responsible for the fate of *Sometime . . . Never*. Daniel had been tied up on other Chase Productions business during the day and had not seen the way the rehearsals had gone. Brad, having called rehearsals for ten o'clock the following morning, had disappeared without a word to anyone. Clearly he had made up his mind that the play was going to be a disaster. He was simply following Daniel's instructions to the letter, but making no special effort to put things right. Anna almost felt he wanted the play to be a failure, just to prove his point.

Anna's major concern, though, was Gerald. She had been quite unable to reach him – he simply would not talk to her. She'd never seen him like this before, locked in his own particular hell, refusing to communicate with anyone. When rehearsals ended, he'd simply ordered a cab to take him back to the Algonquin, where, she had no doubt, there would be a lot more whisky consumed before the end of the day.

If there was only someone she could talk to, like Martin or Richard. She toyed with the idea of going herself to the Algonquin, but after what had passed between them in

Oxford, the idea of visiting Gerald's room seemed awkward, and possibly subject to being misunderstood.

Anna reached the entrance of her hotel and realised that she'd walked the whole distance from the theatre without even noticing the bodies strewn about the pavement. That's what two days in New York has done for me, she thought – it did indeed seem a lifetime since she'd boarded the plane at Heathrow.

Gerald arrived at the theatre the following morning completely sober, and probably would have remained so had rehearsals begun right away. Instead, the carpenters who had been working through the night to complete the set still needed two more hours to finish the job.

'It's not worth finding rehearsal rooms for a couple of hours,' Brad announced to the company. 'You guys just hang loose round the theatre and don't go wandering off anywhere. We may get use of the stage quicker than we think.'

'May I just remind you that we have a preview performance tonight,' Gerald said. 'I trust we will have a set by then.'

'I haven't lost sight of that, buddy – I think we all agree that the play is going to look one hell of a lot better with a set.'

'Blueberry Daiquiris in my dressing room,' Ralph whispered, as soon as Brad was out of earshot. He smiled at Gerald. 'They'll match your eyes, sweetheart.'

'My dear fellow,' said Gerald, 'how perfectly splendid you are. Lead the way.'

Anna shot Ralph a warning look. 'It's OK, sweetie pie,' he said, tickling her under the chin, 'Uncle Ralphie will make them nice and weak.'

'Uncle Ralphie will get a kick up the arse if he does that,' Gerald said.

'Ooh whoopee!' Ralph scampered off with cries of delight leaving Gerald and Anna laughing helplessly.

The Daiquiris were excellent. 'The trouble is,' said Anna, 'they're like Pimms, they slip down so easily.'

'Wonderful, aren't they? Have another, darling child.'

After a while, they began to play cards, then, bored with that, they spent a happy half hour conducting the character assassination of Brad Hotchkiss.

'Full dress rehearsal in fifteen minutes.' The call over the tannoy made them all jump.

'A dress rehearsal!' said Gerald. 'Why in God's name haven't we been told about this before? It's hardly necessary, surely – that man enjoys cracking the whip.'

'I did hear the money bags were coming this morning,' Ralph said, 'perhaps that's why.'

'Heavens, Ralph,' said Anna, 'you might have mentioned it instead of filling us full of drink.'

'Sorry, sweetie, I've only just remembered.'

'Angels or no, I still think a dress rehearsal is asking too much,' grumbled Gerald. 'Anna, kindly lead me to my dressing room, I can't remember where it is. Amy! Someone find me Amy – I'll never be able to get into that suit otherwise.'

Whether it was the effect of several days' drinking, or whether Gerald followed the Daiquiris with whisky, no one ever knew, but as he took his position centre stage for the first scene, Anna was the first to realise what was wrong. 'He's drunk, I mean really spaced out,' she whispered to Ralph in horror.

For the first time since she'd known him, Ralph looked serious. 'Are you sure, darling? I didn't mix those drinks strong, honest. Do you feel OK?'

'Yes, I feel fine,' she said, 'and I didn't even have any breakfast.'

'Oh Jesus, the old bastard, he must have been knocking them back while he was getting dressed.'

'Are the backers really out front?' Anna asked.

Ralph shrugged his shoulders, 'I don't know, but I guess they are. Why else a full dress rehearsal?'

'Why don't you two guys just shut up.' Brad appeared behind them. 'And if it will satisfy your curiosity, yes, the backer is out front, so your arses are really on the line.'

Anna stood in the wings, watching the figure on the stage, swaying slightly, with terror in her heart. As the curtain rose, a little unsteadily Gerald stepped forward to speak. His speech was slurred – about one word in three was totally unintelligible, and all Anna could do was stand in agony watching him.

166

They let him well and truly hang himself. He dragged his way, for over five minutes, through his opening speech without any interruption. Then, from the back of the auditorium a voice boomed out, 'Right, that's it, that's enough, I don't want to hear another goddam word.'

Gerald stopped in mid-sentence, blinking in the blinding brightness of the footlights. 'And who, pray sir, may you be?' he said.

A small, burly figure could just be made out thundering down the centre aisle. 'I am Walter Chase, Walter B Chase of Chase Productions. I *was* the guy talked into putting my money, my own personal money that is, into this show. Not any more. This show will never run, not under the Chase Productions' banner, not with my money, not in this theatre, and not, by Christ, on Broadway.'

Chapter Fifteen

A long silence followed Walter's announcement. Gerald stood alone on the stage, bewildered and speechless. Anna and Ralph, in the wings, simply stared at one another.

Suddenly the house lights came on and Anna hurried to join Gerald on stage, feeling that perhaps her presence might at least provide some sort of moral support.

Daniel came striding down the aisle to join his father. 'What the hell are you talking about?' he shouted.

Walter turned, stabbing a short, fat finger at his son. 'Just what sort of a schmuck are you? Jesus, Daniel, how can you ask that question and be a son of mine?' Walter shook his head despairingly. 'Look, boy, let me spell it out for you since obviously you're too dumb to figure it out for yourself. There's no way we're running this show – we'd be a laughing stock. Holy shit, I must have been out of my mind to agree to it in the first place. Christ knows what came over me, but for one crazy moment, just one crazy moment, I actually thought you might be on to something, might even be displaying a little skill. God help us, how can a guy be *this* wrong.'

'I'm not wrong.'

'Not wrong?' Walter turned, appealing to the growing audience, as the company gathered round him. 'The boy says he's not wrong. Would any of you guys put your money into a show where you had to listen to some drunken old bum rambling on for a couple of hours? What were you doing just now, Dan, looking up your own arse? Jesus, did you hear him? Shit, just look at him now, *look at him* – he can hardly stand, let alone act.'

Everyone turned and stared at Gerald – criticism, mockery

and anger were in the air. Suddenly, it was as though something burst inside Anna's head. 'Don't you dare speak about Gerald Kingdom like that.' She strode to the front of the stage. 'The only reason he was drunk this morning was because Chase Productions couldn't provide a director worthy of him. There's only one thing wrong with *Sometime . . . Never* running in the Chase Theatre – Chase Productions doesn't deserve to have such a good play.'

'I don't know who you are, young lady,' Walter replied, 'but you're right about that – Chase Productions doesn't deserve *Sometime . . . Never* and, thank God, we've still time to pull out.' He smacked his forehead. 'To think I nearly skipped this rehearsal, too.' He gestured to everyone. 'OK, the show's over. There'll be two weeks' money for everyone involved. Come and see the company manager here at ten o'clock tomorrow morning and you'll get paid.'

'Some of us have contracts.' Gerald spoke for the first time. His face was composed, but his voice was shaking slightly and he looked very pale.

'Contracts are there to be broken,' Walter replied dismissively.

'You can't do this.' Daniel's voice rang out into the tense atmosphere.

'I can, and I will, if not to protect my dough, at least to stop you making an arsehole of yourself, or rather, any more of an arsehole of yourself than you already have.'

'I am going to see *Sometime . . . Never* run on Broadway, with or without you.' There was conviction in Daniel's voice. People who'd been starting to disperse, stopped in their tracks, suddenly conscious of a new development in the crisis.

'Oh you are, are you? And how do you propose to do that without the backing of Chase Productions?'

'I'll find a way,' said Daniel.

'Well, you can't find a way in my time. You work for Chase Productions and don't you forget it. Any play you put on, which isn't backed by the Corporation, is a rival – even a crummy play like this.'

'Then I'll stop working for Chase Productions.' Daniel's voice was calm. He wasn't angry, Anna realised – he was making this stand because of his commitment to the play, not through a fit of pique. She felt her heart leap for him, sensing this was probably the first time he'd ever really stood up to his father.

'Oh yeah?' Walter smirked. 'May I just remind you what that would mean before you start playing the smart-arse – no wages, no office, no apartment, no theatre and no cash.'

'I'll manage,' said Daniel, 'this play *will* run on Broadway, and I'm going to see it gets there.'

Walter was losing his temper. 'You crass idiot. I don't mind you being stubborn, I don't mind you arguing the toss – I wish the hell you'd do it more often – but not over a deal like this. What's with you, Daniel, why are you so dumb?'

'The play is a no-no, Dan,' said Brad, who was standing close beside Walter. 'I told you that from the start, it just doesn't feel right.'

'Yeah,' said Daniel, 'and so you made darn sure it wouldn't work. If you'd treated me like you've treated Gerald Kingdom, I'd have taken to the booze, too.' Ignoring both his father and Brad, Daniel turned and addressed the company. 'I'm sorry, guys, that the play has ended like this for you all, and I'd like to thank you for the hard work you've put into it. *Sometime . . . Never* will run . . . and soon. Now I have a lot of preparations to make – Gerald, Anna and Ralph, could the four of us meet at the Algonquin at, say, five this evening? I'll be able to advise you then about future plans.'

Without waiting for further comment, Daniel walked away up the auditorium, a lonely figure but a determined one. Anna, reeling with shock at what had just taken place, nonetheless felt a stab of pride.

It was a subdued little group that met in the bar of the Algonquin that afternoon. Daniel, quick to sense their mood, came straight to the point. 'I've been round the theatres since this morning's roughhouse, and I'm pleased to be able to tell you I've managed to secure the Barrymore on 47th.'

Ralph frowned. 'Isn't something running there at the moment?'

'Yeah,' said Daniel, 'but it comes off at the end of next

week. I reckon it like this – the current show closes Saturday week. I'll get the carpenters in over the weekend to build the set, we can rehearse Monday and Tuesday, and we'll open Wednesday night.'

'With a preview?' Gerald asked.

'No, we haven't time for that, I don't think the publicity will stand it. We're going to need some good reviews fast to counter the inevitable bad publicity which will arise from Chase pulling out of the show.' Daniel grimaced. 'So, I've got the theatre. Now all I have to do is find the money.'

'All!' Anna burst out, 'you've only got just over a week – surely it's going to be very difficult to raise the money in such a short time.'

'Not easy, I agree,' said Daniel, 'but I'll do it, don't worry.'

'But I do worry,' said Anna. She paused for a moment trying to arrange her thoughts. 'Look, I know you all have a great deal more experience of the theatre than I do, but it seems we're moving from one shambles to another. It's such a tragedy. In London, we were playing to packed houses every night. The production was running smoothly under an excellent director and we had everything going for us. OK, I know I was just an understudy, but at least I had a job. We could have sat tight in London . . . for a year, two probably. But no, we threw it all up to come here and just look what's happened. Heavens above, I haven't been in New York a couple of days yet, and already this so-called chance of stardom is in tatters around me.'

'Calm down, Anna,' said Gerald. 'Young Chase knows what he's doing.'

'Calm down, *calm down*, how can you of all people say that to me?' Anna said. 'I've spent five months struggling to get you on stage sober every night, and for what? You spun me this tale of how *Sometime . . . Never* would be my big break, of how you wanted me to be a success, and then, at the first possible opportunity, you blow the whole thing.'

Gerald's face was tight with anger. 'All right, so I drank a little too much this morning, but nobody could be expected to work with that man. He was impossible, quite impossible.'

'If you felt so strongly about who should direct you, why

171

didn't you discuss it with Daniel beforehand?' Anna replied. 'It's a bit late to start moaning about the director now you're here, when we're just a few days away from opening. It's . . . it's all right for you to throw away this play, I'm sure there are always plenty of opportunities around for Gerald Kingdom. But this was my chance – I'll probably never have another – and you've ruined it.'

'You're a silly, ungrateful child,' Gerald bit back. 'Just remember who secured this job for you in the first place.'

The truth of his words silenced her for a moment. To cover her discomfort, Anna turned to Daniel. 'Even if you can find the money, surely the adverse publicity is going to kill the play before it can open. Once the critics know that your father pulled out because of Gerald's drinking, the play is just going to be a joke.'

'Yes,' said Gerald, 'what about the publicity? There's supposed to be a preview tonight, how are you going to handle that?'

'I've thought about it, obviously,' said Daniel. He hesitated and then looked directly at Gerald. 'My father isn't going to mince his words, Gerald. He's bound to say that he reckons you're a has-been, a drunken old bum who won't make it. Knowing him, he'll describe in graphic detail your performance this morning.' He shrugged his shoulders. 'The fact is though, the human race isn't a particularly pretty bunch and people will be attracted to the show *because* they think you're going to make a fool of yourself. Remember Peter O'Toole in *Macbeth*? The critics slayed that show, yet it was a box office dream. It was simply because so many critics said it was bad that people flocked to see it. Bad publicity is better than none at all and sometimes, just sometimes, it's better than good publicity.'

'I hope you're not suggesting I play it drunk every night just to satisfy the audience's lust for blood?' Gerald frowned.

'No, of course I'm not. When the audience gets there I want you to wow them, wow them like you did in London. My job is to make sure you have an audience to play to, and I have a feeling that isn't going to be as difficult as one might imagine.'

'I can see what you're getting at,' Ralph said slowly.

'I can't,' said Anna. 'If you're saying the critics' opinion doesn't matter, then why does everybody get in such a state about reviews?'

'I'm not saying the critics' opinion doesn't matter,' Daniel said impatiently. 'I'm simply saying that the bad publicity may not drive the audiences away.'

'*May not, may not*, that's the point, isn't it? We just don't know.'

'Anna, will you quit grousing for a moment?' Daniel looked tired and strained but his voice carried surprising authority. 'If you're looking for a gilt-edged future you're in the wrong business. I've known plays where all the ingredients have been right, plays brought over from London with stars and directors intact, plays where the production has gone without a hitch . . . and yet what's happened? They've flopped – flopped for no reason that any of us can define. Theatre-going audiences are fickle, volatile, unpredictable. If you don't like to gamble, Anna, it's time you took a course in shorthand typing.' His words hit hard and Anna visibly crumbled.

It was Gerald who, surprisingly, came to her aid. 'Daniel, I understand what you're saying, but Anna is right up to a point. At the moment we certainly don't seem to have a lot going for us. I'm also painfully aware that, on our behalf, you've broken with your father, given up your job and goodness knows what else besides. Look . . . I haven't a great deal of money, but what I have is yours, should you need it to help finance the play.'

'Thanks,' said Daniel, 'I may need to take you up on that. It's with regard to finance that I'm particularly anxious about the publicity. My chief concern is that the story shouldn't make the papers tomorrow, not in a big way anyway. I want to get my version round the banks before the press start raking the dirt.' He paused for a moment. 'This brings me to a tricky subject – your wages and expenses. Money is going to be tight, and I certainly won't be able to start paying you anything until Monday week. Having said that, of course, Chase Productions will be covering you for the next two weeks, so you won't be out of pocket. Is that OK?'

'No problem,' Gerald said swiftly, and Ralph nodded.

'Anna?' Daniel asked.

'I suppose so,' she said quietly.

'And now,' Daniel continued, 'there's the question of accommodation. Cutting myself off from my father has left me in a difficult position at the moment. I don't even have anywhere to live myself. I've never had any capital of my own worth mentioning, and I've suddenly realised that Daniel Chase, without Chase Productions, amounts to very little more than the suit I stand up in.'

'If you don't mind my saying so, dear boy,' said Gerald, 'you should never have put yourself in that position. How many years have you worked for your father?'

'Since I left college – ten, maybe eleven years.'

'If you weren't his son, as chief executive in a corporation the size of Chase Productions, you should have been stacking it away by now.'

'That's right, sweetie,' Ralph agreed. 'A beach house in Miami, a permanent suite in Claridges, an apartment overlooking the Seine . . .'

'Oh shut up, Ralph, there's a good chap,' said Gerald. He turned to Daniel. 'So, what are you proposing?'

'Well, I guess what I'm really trying to say is that I can't go on paying your hotel bills at present, not until the play opens and I get some revenue. What money I have, I've already needed to commit as a down payment on the theatre. I guess I'm entitled to money in lieu of notice, but frankly I'm not going to have the time to argue the toss with my father. Nor, I must admit, do I have the inclination.'

'Oh, that's wonderful,' said Anna, 'so now we have nowhere to live. What do you want us to do? Camp out on the streets?'

'There's no need for that, sugar pie,' Ralph said. 'I have my own little place in Greenwich Village. It's small – it would be a squash, but you're all very welcome. Sounds fun, eh?'

'I have a better idea,' said Gerald. 'Anna and I will go and stay with Marcus Bradbury.'

Daniel gave him a quick look. 'Marcus Bradbury, the agent?'

'That's right,' said Gerald. 'He's an old friend of mine. In fact, when I first came to New York he was very good to me. He's retired now, you know, but we keep in touch, and he has a big apartment in United Nations Plaza. There'll be plenty of room for Anna and I, and we can certainly stay there until the play opens.'

'OK,' said Daniel, a little reluctantly, 'but if there's any problem, I can easily sort something out for Anna.'

'It sounds to me as though it would be a lot easier for everyone if you simply put me on a plane home,' Anna said.

'Do you know, I'm sorely tempted to do just that.' Shocked, Anna's eyes met Daniel's. In the silence that followed his words, tension raged backwards and forwards between them. Mercifully, before either of them could speak, there was an interruption. 'Mr Chase?' A bell boy stood, tray in hand, looking at the group enquiringly.

'That's me,' said Daniel.

'There's a telegram for you, sir.'

Daniel took the message from the tray, his heart pounding. Upon this single piece of paper, he knew, instinctively, his destiny hung. He opened it and read the message carefully, watched intently by three sets of eyes. Then, he raised his head and smiled. 'The first thing I did on leaving the theatre this morning,' he said, 'was to cable Martin Peters. It occurred to me that as the play was being delayed by almost two weeks, it could just be that Martin would be able to finish his TV documentary in time to join us.' Daniel tossed the telegram to Gerald. 'That's his reply.'

Gerald scooped up the paper and he and Anna pored over it. 'Wild horses wouldn't keep me away – Martin' it read. They both looked up at Daniel. Anna was openly crying and Gerald was close to it. Daniel grinned. Actors . . . what a bunch, he thought indulgently. Perhaps if I work in this business for another thirty years I might even get to understand them. He was closer than he knew.

Chapter Sixteen

Manufacturers Hanover Trust on Wall Street, affectionately known as 'Manny Hanny', had been the bankers for Chase Productions since before Daniel was born. Waiting in the reception hall for his appointment, Daniel had a sense of confidence and well-being. He was on familiar ground. He had been coming to this bank since he'd first joined Chase Productions. The clerks all knew him, greeting him with deference as they hurried by. He felt both comfortable and relaxed. Too relaxed.

'Daniel, good morning, how are you?' Vice President Mark Price called to him across the hall.

'Hello Mark.' The two men shook hands warmly.

'How is your father?'

'Fine,' said Daniel.

'I'm so looking forward to seeing *Emma*. Irene and I have tickets for the first night, your father sent them through yesterday. I just know we'll love it.' He gushed enthusiastically, and Daniel felt his first thrill of disquiet. He hadn't realised that his father's passion for big splashy musicals was shared by his banker. Knowing Walter, it was certain to be more than just a happy coincidence.

'Yes, I'm sure it will be a great success,' Daniel said.

The two men seated themselves in comfortable chairs in Mark's sumptuous office. Having refused coffee, Daniel launched straight in. 'Actually Mark, I – I'm here on rather a delicate matter and I've come to you because you're someone I can trust. What I have to tell you I don't particularly want to share with anyone else.'

Mark Price's face assumed a suitably serious expression.

'My father and I have had something of a punch-up. He has probably mentioned to you that we had decided to back the transfer to Broadway of the London smash-hit *Sometime . . . Never*. It stars Gerald Kingdom and has played to packed houses for weeks in the UK.'

'Yes, yes,' said Mark. 'Your father has taken the view that as it is a rather uncertain project, very generously, I thought, he is going to fund it himself, from his own personal finances rather than involve Chase Productions' capital.'

'That's right,' said Daniel uneasily. 'We issued contracts, brought the actors over here, and were scheduled to open with a gypsy run last night. However, my father has now decided he doesn't want to proceed with the production.'

'I see . . .' said Mark.

'Well, no, I reckon you don't see. The thing is, Mark, I do wish to proceed, and so I'd like to arrange alternative financing.'

'I see . . .' said Mark again, 'so what you're saying is that Chase Productions will be funding it after all.'

'No,' said Daniel, 'no, that's not what I'm saying at all. I'm saying that *I* will be financing it – at least I will, with your help.'

Mark frowned. 'Let me get this straight. Your father has pulled out, but you are wanting to finance the play on your own behalf. Forgive me, Dan, but doesn't that conflict with your position within Chase Productions?'

'I'm no longer working for Chase Productions,' said Daniel. 'I'm on my own now and I'm asking you to back me, Mark.'

'Collateral?'

'None, other than my experience,' said Daniel, 'which, I think you will agree, is considerable.'

Mark shrugged. 'Well, I don't know about that. As far as I'm concerned, and I speak for the bank here, your father has always been at the helm. You and I have met, of course, many times on and off over the years, but I can't really gauge your role within Chase Productions other than to acknowledge that, obviously, you have trained under a master.'

'A master who's had his day.' As soon as he said the words, Daniel knew he'd made a terrible error.

'Dan, you just have to be wrong about that. Your father is at his peak. All his years of experience are really making themselves felt now – it's consolidation time. Tell me this, when did he last have a real box office disaster?' Daniel shrugged. 'Well, I'll tell you then – it was eleven years ago – *eleven years*, Dan, in your line of business. It's incredible! I trust his judgement implicitly. So must you.'

The conversation was not going right. 'No, I don't trust him – not blindly, anyway,' said Daniel. 'Success in any form of business depends upon the ability of those in charge to move with the times, to anticipate trends. I'll grant you, my father has always done this in the past, but he's been trapped in a kind of time warp recently. He can't look beyond the big, the spectacular – he just can't recognise that there is any other type of theatre.'

'He may recognise other types of theatre,' Mark said, 'but he may not believe them to be so profitable. Had that thought occurred to you?'

'Of course it has,' said Daniel, 'but you know what it costs to put on these shows of his. Granted, a more modest production might not bring in as big a box office, but what interests me, and you too, is the bottom line. I'm talking about profit, Mark, which should be our main concern here.' Daniel gained a little ground, he could feel it, and he pushed home the advantage. '*Sometime . . . Never* is a low budget production which will run, and run some more. I'm asking you to back me in a sure-fire winner. Is that such a big deal?'

'It is a big deal when we're talking about something Chase won't touch. Dan, I'm going to level with you. There are two reasons why I can't help you. The first is this. Consistently over the years, Walter Chase has made money for himself and the shareholders of this bank. If Walter Chase says *Sometime . . . Never* won't work, in the bank's interests I *must* back his judgement. Secondly, there's a question of ethics. Let us forget your lack of security and management experience, and consider the moral issue at stake. If at this branch we were bankers for the Coca Cola Corporation and Pepsi Cola approached us for banking facilities, I would turn them down. Now, I think you will agree, Dan, that the Pepsi Cola

178

Corporation suggests itself as being a more tangible asset to this bank than anything at the moment Daniel Chase can offer us. The argument, however, remains the same. A client at this bank must feel that he can speak his mind, that he can have complete confidence in myself, in my staff, and that at all times, the bank has his best interests at heart. No more can I enter into the Chase war, than I can enter into the Cola war. I wish you luck, Dan, but you have to go and find your finance elsewhere.'

Whether it was true or not, it seemed to Daniel that the word had gone up and down Wall Street by the time he stepped onto the sidewalk outside the Manny Hanny Bank. He tried everyone, every different approach, but each time he received the same answer. He even visited the National Westminster Bank, thinking that British banks might be more susceptible to backing what, after all, was essentially a British play. The answer everywhere was the same. His personal track record was non-existent – he stood in his father's shadow – his collateral was nil and the play automatically carried the stigma that Walter B Chase wouldn't back it.

Lunchtime found him in a burger bar. He ate hungrily, having missed dinner the night before. Next, he took a clean paper napkin and, in an effort to reassure himself, he began to write down the pros and cons. He had actors, a director, a theatre and above all . . . a play with a proven track record. He had no cash, no office and nowhere to live. 'Hell,' he said out loud, 'I've got more pros than cons. How can I fail?'

He decided after such a harrowing morning that he would spend the afternoon on his easiest problem. By four o'clock he had an apartment just round the corner from the Barrymore Theatre. It wasn't great, in fact it was downright gruesome – two rooms, with bathroom and toilet, on the 9th floor of a dilapidated building, heavily populated by hookers and drug pushers. Still it had a bed, a desk, and above all, a telephone.

His first phone call was to Scarsdale. 'Penny, is that you?'

'Dan, how are you?'

'OK, just. Look Penny, I've got some problems. I need to

talk them out with you and Jim. How do you feel about my coming for the weekend?'

'Hey, that would be great,' said Penny.

'Can I come out tomorrow?'

'Of course, come in time for lunch.'

Dan hesitated. 'And would it be OK if I brought someone?'

'Of course. Male or female?'

'Female,' Dan said.

'Two rooms or one?'

'Two.'

'Daniel Chase, I never thought I'd hear the day when you'd say that! What's happened to you, has she got two heads or something?'

'No,' said Daniel, laughing, 'she's beautiful.'

'Then hell, this has to be serious. What's she like?'

'Never you mind and, Penny, please don't go to any trouble,' said Dan. 'She may not even come, I haven't asked her yet.'

'Stop it,' said Penny. 'I'm positively reeling. You mean she might turn you down?'

'More likely than not,' Daniel confirmed.

'Wow, that is something! Hey, I can't stay talking to you, I have to go out and kill a fatted calf.'

Daniel took a cab back to the Algonquin, where he'd stayed the previous night, in order to collect his few belongings. The cab journey was slow. It was the wrong time of day to be travelling in New York, and it gave Daniel the first opportunity he'd had to really take stock of what had happened during the previous twenty-four hours. For the first time he had serious doubts. A lot of people were relying on him now and the question was, could he come up with the goods?

His visit to Scarsdale had an ulterior motive. Jim's family business was doing very well and Jim, the sole proprietor now, was not short of a few bucks. But was he right to even consider asking for his friend's help? Was Wall Street perhaps right to refuse his application for finance? Was indeed his father right about *Sometime . . . Never*? Gerald had been very contrite and Daniel felt sure that now he would do his best, if the new production got off the ground. The fact remained though, that as far as Daniel could tell, Gerald Kingdom had been drunk almost from the moment he'd arrived in New York. Was a new producer and a new director going to make the difference? Would the magic that had worked in London work in New York? Could they overcome the inevitable bad publicity? Daniel's mind was in a whirl as he paid off the cab and walked through the doors of the Algonquin Hotel.

A familiar figure sitting upright and alert was waiting for him just inside the door.

'Mattie!'

'Hello Dan. How are you doing?'

'Not so good.'

'No kidding, that doesn't sound like my guy.'

She sounded so surprised that for a moment Daniel wondered whether she'd heard the news. He hadn't been back to the office since the confrontation with his father.

'Well, you may be feeling lousy,' Mattie continued, 'but I feel great. I've got this fantastic new job.'

Daniel felt a pang of hurt. Already their partnership, which had spanned so many years, was a thing of the past. 'You have?' he said. 'With whom?'

'This brand new Broadway producer. He's got one hell of a future. The pay's lousy and I expect the conditions are worse, but I'm as excited as hell about it.'

There was the slow dawning of understanding as Daniel listened. 'Mattie, what are you saying exactly?' he said.

'What do you think I'm saying, you great dope? I'm coming to work for you, blockhead.'

Daniel stared at her, dumbfounded. 'But Mattie, you can't. I can't pay you anything like as much as Chase Productions, and what about your pension rights? You can't do it, you mustn't do it.'

'Dan, sweetheart, it's too late to holler at me, I've already done it. As for my pension rights, I'd have willingly given up three times as much for the wonderful sight I had of Walter's face when I told him I was quitting.' She threw back her head and laughed. 'Boy, was he mad. Mad . . . he was insane. I so enjoyed it.'

'Jesus, Mattie, if anyone's mad round here it's you. I just have two small rooms in which to work and live. I do have actors and a theatre, but I've no cash – yet, anyway.'

'Two rooms is dandy,' said Mattie. 'As it's going to be a round-the-clock job, you take the bedroom and I'll sleep on the couch in the sitting room. There is a couch, I take it?'

'There is,' Dan agreed, 'but I'll sleep there and you can have the bedroom.'

'Oh Jesus, Daniel, don't start griping. You need your beauty sleep because you have to look great. Who knows, we may have to resort to your casting couch charm if all else fails.'

'That, Mattie, was below the belt, so to speak.'

'And, my dear, was no more nor less than you deserved.' They started to laugh.

The lobby of the Algonquin has seen many strange sights over the years. The handsome young man clasping in his arms a plain, middle-aged woman, whilst they both alternately laughed and cried, was perhaps one of the more bizarre.

As Daniel Chase drove across town with Mattie half an hour later, he couldn't have known that the circumstances of his first production were now in many ways a carbon copy of his father's – more than forty years before.

Chapter Seventeen

Anna, meanwhile, was having a most entertaining and relaxing time, in stark contrast to her first two days in New York. The thought of Martin coming out to join them somehow changed everything. She felt no longer alone and, accordingly, her spirits rose. She had arranged with Gerald to check out of her hotel and take a cab to the Algonquin. From there, together, they would go to Marcus Bradbury's apartment.

Gerald was also in high spirits as the cab took them across town towards the East River. He quite clearly bore no grudge about what she had said the previous evening. Anna was tempted to mention their differences, but somehow Gerald's mood made the gesture unnecessary.

'This is awfully kind of your friend,' Anna said. 'Are you sure he doesn't mind putting up with me too?'

'He doesn't know either of us are staying with him yet, darling.'

Anna looked at Gerald, horrified. 'But we're going to be landing on his doorstep with all this luggage.' Anna had thought herself rather excessive with three cases, but Gerald was incapable of travelling light. They'd barely managed to squeeze all his luggage into the cab.

'Darling,' Gerald slipped an arm round Anna, 'relax. I have a secret formula, a commodity so vital to Marcus's well-being, that it will buy our way into his apartment without a shadow of doubt.'

'Good heavens, what?' said Anna. Visions of cocaine, of hashish sprang into her mind. She wondered idly if the New York police cells were as bad in reality as they appeared on TV.

'It would spoil the surprise if I told you in advance, darling,' said Gerald. 'I'll give you a tiny clue though. Old Marcus has spent almost his entire working life in New York, but he's still a tremendous anglophile at heart.'

Anna relaxed a little but was still somewhat apprehensive as the cab stopped outside a modern apartment building.

'This is East 47th Street,' said Gerald, 'and that's Second Avenue. Over there is the United Nations Building and right around the corner is Dag Hammarskjold Plaza. Marcus's apartment has a superb view of the East River, including the Pepsi Cola bottling plant. How about that?'

'Fantastic,' said Anna nervously.

'Come,' Gerald commanded, running up the steps. After an altercation with the porter who wanted to announce them, they took the elevator to the tenth floor.

'You were rude to that porter, Gerald,' Anna said. 'It will serve you right if Marcus isn't in.'

'Darling girl, it's eleven o'clock in the morning. Marcus will hardly be out of bed.' Gerald rang the bell, keeping his finger on it for some time.

'That's rude too,' said Anna reprovingly.

'It's practical, he's probably in the bath.'

A few moments later, the door opened. Marcus Bradbury cut a very dashing figure. Although, Anna realised, he must have been in his seventies, he had retained most of his iron-grey hair. His face was pink-cheeked like a child's, he was tall and slender, dressed in cavalry-twill trousers and a rather dashing cashmere sweater. In his hand he held a champagne glass of what appeared to be orange juice.

Marcus looked Gerald up and down. Then he turned his attention to Anna, whom he studied carefully, and then returned his enigmatic gaze to Gerald. 'Dear boy, what an extraordinary ability you have for sensing the popping of a champagne cork. I'm just indulging in a little Bucks Fizz to perk me up. What *are* you doing here so terribly early?'

'Anna and I need to take advantage of your hospitality for a few days, possibly even a week or two. We need a bed – one each, sadly – and our luggage is waiting in a cab downstairs.'

'Ah, I see. Then I trust, my friend, you've remembered to bring it?'

Gerald produced a small package from his jacket pocket and handed it over.

'You did, how perfectly splendid. Then, naturally, my apartment is at your disposal, and that of your charming friend.'

Anna stood watching this exchange with fascination. 'It's no good,' she burst out, 'I simply have to know what's in that package.'

'Good heavens,' said Marcus, 'didn't he tell you? Why, it's Gentleman's Relish, of course. I'll do absolutely anything for a pot of Gentleman's Relish.'

Marcus's apartment was as elegant as its owner. The rooms were large with high ceilings. There were four bedrooms in all, so there was plenty of room for all three of them.

It was easy to understand why the two men were such friends. In many ways they were very alike. Marcus was simply an older version of Gerald, without the talent. Because he didn't possess the talent, he didn't have the accompanying torment either, Anna mused, as she listened to their reminiscences. Far from feeling left out, she loved to hear them talk. The names of the rich, famous and influential of the world fell naturally, and without pretension, from their lips. It made Anna speculate, not for the first time, on the curious world of the actor.

If an actor is very successful he makes money, a great deal of it sometimes. His success often leads him to move in all the top international circles in the world, as Gerald had done. Yet his actual working life, the method by which he earns his money, contrasts so drastically with that life style – dreary dressing rooms, long hours of slog, endless rehearsals. There was another point too. A successful businessman, once his business is established, can, up to a point, rely on others to make money for him. Not so with the actor. Every penny he earns must be literally that – earned by his own sweat and no one else's. It's surprising any actor stays sane, thought Anna.

The three of them had lunch at an oyster bar, accompanied by seemingly endless bottles of Muscadet. Then they returned to the apartment and went to their respective rooms, to sleep off the effects of the meal.

When Anna woke it was quite dark, and looking at her watch she found it was eight o'clock. There was no sound coming from the rest of the apartment, so she got up and had a long, leisurely bath. Then slipping on jeans and a T-shirt, she wandered through into the sitting room.

Gerald was sitting by the window, in semi darkness. 'Hello, darling,' he said, as Anna came in. 'Come and look at the view.' She leaned on the back of his chair and gazed with him out of the window. 'That's the tip of Roosevelt Island over there. There's a fountain – you can't see it in the dark but it shoots the water four hundred feet into the air, amazing isn't it? And see what I meant about the Pepsi Cola plant?' A huge red neon light lit up the whole area.

'Yes,' said Anna, thoughtfully. 'It's an odd part of the city somehow, though quite spectacular in its way, I suppose.'

'Yes, I know what you mean. Perhaps it's a lingering atmosphere – all this area housed one of the more unpleasant sides of so-called civilisation, once.'

'What's that?' Anna asked.

'This is where all the slaughter houses were, years ago.'

'Poor beasts, it's enough to make one a vegetarian,' said Anna, straightening up.

'On the subject of food, Marcus has gone out to some dinner party. He says there is a bottle of champagne and some pâté in the fridge. He's invited us to help ourselves and I suggest, darling girl, we do just that.'

'I'm not sure I could eat or drink another thing,' said Anna.

'Don't be wet, darling, you're supposed to be on holiday.'

They picnicked in front of the big window, laughing and talking companionably.

'You know,' said Gerald, 'I was thinking, while you were asleep, what fun it would be over the next few days, if you would let me show you New York. I've been coming here so long, I'm afraid I'm totally oblivious to the city's charms, but seen through new eyes, it could prove quite refreshing.' He turned to look at her, his craggy good looks enhanced by the shadows. 'What do you say?'

'I'd love it,' said Anna, 'but won't we be mobbed by your fans everywhere we go?'

Gerald shook his head. 'Not in New York – they're used to celebrities. Besides which, if it gets us a little preferential treatment, why not? We could start tomorrow – there's such a lot to see.'

They sat in silence for a while, lost in their own thoughts. Gerald broke the silence at last. 'Do you remember the black swans?' he said, suddenly. 'I was thinking about them tonight, too.'

'The black swans of Blenheim we saw in the Parks?' Anna smiled at the memory. 'Yes, I do. Weren't they lovely?'

Gerald stared at her with a strange intensity. 'Yes, they were and that was a lovely day.'

'Yes, it was,' Anna agreed. Up until that moment, the dramas of the night that followed had obliterated the day from her mind. Now, for the first time she remembered it with pleasure. 'It seems so long ago,' she said, almost to herself, 'light years away, in fact.'

Her reverie was interrupted by the ringing of the telephone. 'I'll take it,' said Gerald. 'If it's not for Marcus it will probably be Daniel Chase. He said he'd ring to let us know how he faired with the banks.'

At the mention of Daniel's name, Anna felt her stomach churn. Since their meeting at the Algonquin, Anna had been beset by a growing feeling of remorsefulness. She knew she'd behaved badly yet could see no way of making amends without losing face.

The call obviously was from Daniel and by all accounts, Anna judged, the news was not too good.

'Well,' said Gerald, having listened for some time, 'remember my offer, Daniel, for what it's worth. At a rough guess I could let you have thirty maybe forty thousand dollars, but no more.' There was another silence while Gerald listened. 'OK, I'll see you next week. Yes, I'll fetch her, she's just here.'

Gerald walked across the room. 'It *is* Daniel Chase and he wants to have a word with you.'

'Has he had any luck?' Anna asked.

'Not a lot,' Gerald sounded less than happy.

Anna took the phone. 'Hello, Daniel.'

'Anna, how are you? Are you feeling any better?'

'Yes, I'm fine now,' she said, 'and Daniel, I'm sorry about yesterday . . .'

'Forget it. I guess we were all a little jumpy. Tell me, is the apartment OK?'

'It's fine, in fact I have to admit, it's a great deal nicer than the Wentworth.'

'Fair comment. Actually I'm just round the corner from your old hotel,' he said.

'You're not! You mean you've really given up your lovely apartment?'

'I didn't have any choice, did I?' Strangely enough, his voice held no trace of bitterness.

Anna thought about his beautiful apartment overlooking Central Park. 'Daniel, you don't even sound as though you're sad about it,' she said incredulously.

'No,' Daniel agreed, 'but then it wasn't really mine, was it? Do you know, I believe I've learnt more in the last twenty-four hours than I have in the last ten years and, strangely enough, I feel good about things. Hey, listen, I mustn't hold you up. The reason I called you was to ask whether you'd come away for the weekend with me.'

'Well I . . .' Anna began.

'No, wait, let me explain,' said Daniel, 'this is a legitimate, all-above-board working weekend. I have these friends in Scarsdale and I'm going to see if they can help me with the finance of *Sometime . . . Never*. I'd like you to meet them anyway, they're a lovely couple . . .'

'Look, Daniel, before you say any more,' Anna interrupted, 'I'm sort of committed this weekend. Gerald said he'd show me New York.'

'Hell, Anna, he can show you New York all next week. Martin won't be joining us until the weekend so there'll be no rehearsals, and I'll be tied up completely. Besides which, I really need you there, *genuinely*. You were part of the show in the West End, you can explain to them how the audience was, how the critics felt.'

'Gerald would do that far better than me,' Anna said.

'Anna, I can't take the risk. Supposing he hits the bottle again? Gerald's great, but I daren't wheel him in front of a banker, just in case I catch him at the wrong moment.'

The offer was tempting. The thought of spending several days with Daniel was enough in itself, but it also proved he was bearing no grudge about her outburst of the previous day. 'Hang on a moment,' she said, 'I'll see what Gerald says.'

'I get the gist,' Gerald called from across the room. 'Young Chase wants to spirit you off somewhere for the weekend.'

Anna put her hand over the mouthpiece. 'Gerald, he's trying to get some backers interested in *Sometime . . . Never*, and wants me to go along to tell them how the play went in the West End. As he says, we do have all next week to see New York, when he'll be tied up.'

Gerald let out a sigh. 'OK, darling, you accept, but on one condition.'

'What's that?' Anna asked.

'Don't go with the illusion that he wants your help in any way. In my view, he has quite other ideas where you are concerned.'

Anna turned away, embarrassed. It was not the moment to start an argument. 'OK, Daniel, I can come,' she said.

'Great. I'll pick you up, what, about half past ten tomorrow morning?'

'That would be fine,' said Anna.

'And we'll be away until early afternoon Monday, I should think. Will that be OK?'

Anna put down the telephone with mixed feelings. Gerald was standing by the window again, gazing out of it, moodily.

'Gerald, you don't really mind, do you?'

'Don't be tiresome, Anna. The decision is made, the subject is closed,' he replied testily.

'You will show me New York next week though, won't you?'

'You're a lady who likes to have her cake and eat it, aren't you?' He turned and looked at her, his expression cold. Then he relented a little. 'I expect so,' he said, wearily. 'Now, I'm rather tired. If you'll excuse me, I'm going to bed.'

Anna watched his departing back, with a mixture of irritation and sorrow.

* * *

The journey to Scarsdale was fun. After a good night's sleep and a busy morning spent handing out instructions to Matilda, Daniel's humour was completely restored.

'Tell me about Jim and Penny,' Anna said, once they had negotiated the worst of the New York traffic.

Daniel leaned back comfortably in his seat. 'Are you sure you want to hear the whole story?'

'Yes, please,' said Anna, 'every last detail.'

'Here we go then. Jim Henderson and I were at school together. We were very close, more like brothers, partly because of our home lives.' Daniel paused.'

'Go on,' said Anna.

'Well, as you know, I never knew my mother, and my father was always working.' Daniel smiled. 'Even then, I guess, my father and I didn't really see eye to eye. Jim's family were in theory quite the reverse and yet oddly the same. Jim was an only child too, but whilst I was very alone, he was over-protected. His father was in construction – successfully too. Harry Henderson had come up the tough way which was why he wanted his son to have everything – and that's where the similarity lay. In fairness, my father appeared to feel the same. It was just our family lives which were very different. Jim's mother, Maria, is a lovely lady, very warm, and as her name suggests, of Italian extraction. And what a cook, wow!' Daniel rolled his eyes. 'Not just pasta either, she can cook apple pie better than any American.'

'So you spent a lot of time with the Hendersons?'

'Yes, I did – holidays, weekends, that sort of thing. Anyway, I guess Jim and I weren't too stupid. We worked hard and both managed to get to Harvard. I read economics and business studies, and he read architecture.' Daniel laughed. 'Jim's dad reckoned architects had the easy life. Harry was always saying that he did the work while the architects drew pretty pictures and earned three times as much . . . so he reckoned it was a smart trade for his son. Jim and I lived together at college then, during the last half of the second summer term, everything changed.'

'How was that?' Anna asked.

'Jim's dad died. He had some kind of accident at work. He

was rushed to hospital and the shock, I guess, caused him to have a heart attack. He never regained consciousness.'

'How awful,' said Anna. 'So what happened?'

'Well, in theory there was enough money in the kitty for Jim to finish college, but he was worried it might leave his mom short. There was also the problem of his dad's business which needed running.' Dan grimaced. 'So Jim never qualified. Instead, he dropped out of college and got cracking on running his father's business.'

'That was a brave decision,' said Anna. 'It can't have been easy for him.'

'I tell you this,' said Dan, 'it was the best decision he ever made. That guy is worth so much money now . . .' He shook his head in disbelief.

'How? From building?' said Anna.

'No, not exactly – real estate. He used his father's business as a base and started negotiating bigger and better contracts. Now he constructs condominiums, shopping malls, that sort of stuff, and he buys and sells too. The smartest thing Jim's pop ever did was *not* teach his son which end of the shovel was which. Jim spends all his time in the office, working out ways of making enough money so he doesn't have to go on a building site and show his ignorance.' Anna laughed. 'The crazy thing is,' said Dan, 'he manages to be so nice. I can honestly say, I've known the guy since he was nine years old and he hasn't changed one bit. He goes on doing deals, making pots of money, and staying Mr Nice Guy. It makes you sick.'

'How about Penny?' Anna asked.

'Oh, we were at college with Penny. She's a really bright lady. She read law, could have had a fantastic career, but she threw up college when Jim did. They married and she worked as a legal secretary to support them both until the business really started to pay.'

'She must have loved him very much,' Anna said quietly.

'Yeah, and that's another amazing thing. That couple seem more in love every year. They do a lot to restore one's faith in human nature. I envy them.'

There was a wistful note in Dan's voice, which Anna couldn't fail to notice. She looked at his profile as he drove.

What a strange, complex person he was, and such a creature of extremes – one minute so tough, and the next, almost a romantic.

Daniel caught her watching him. 'Hey, what are you looking at?'

'I was just wondering about you,' said Anna. 'You're an odd mixture, Daniel.'

Dan pulled a ghastly face. 'It's the life I lead,' he said.

Anna nodded. 'I think it is.'

'OK, enough serious stuff. This will really blow your mind. Take a look in that bag on the back seat.'

A huge brown paper parcel occupied most of the back. 'I can't move it,' said Anna. 'What is it?'

'It's an elephant,' said Daniel. 'It's really great, I fell in love with it – grey velvet, really cuddly.'

Anna looked at him, amazed. 'Now I really know you're cracked.'

'I haven't mentioned the third member of the family, have I?' said Daniel. 'Jim and Penny have a son, Chuck. He was two last week and he's my godson. The elephant is his birthday present, if I can bear to part with it.'

'Well, that's a relief,' said Anna, 'I'm glad at least you have an excuse for buying a toy elephant.'

'Fact is,' said Dan, 'I'm really nervous about all this. You see, I'm going to ask Jim to put up fifty per cent of the money for *Sometime . . . Never*. He's got it, he can spare it, but he can't afford to lose it. Because he's such a regular guy, the banks respect him enormously, and I reckon if he backs the play fifty per cent, one of his banking contacts will put up the other fifty. Even if they only put up forty, there is always Gerald's money to close the gap.'

'So where's the problem?' said Anna. 'There is one, I take it?'

Daniel nodded. 'If Jim wasn't a friend, then I'd feel less sense of responsibility. It would be simply a straightforward business deal – he'd either think it was worth the risk, or not. Supposing I have judged this whole thing wrong, Anna – supposing the play does fold – I'll have taken one hell of an advantage of a friendship.'

'In similar circumstances, if Jim came to you, would you lend him the money?'

'Yes, of course,' said Daniel.

'To do anything?'

'Absolutely anything.'

'Then you haven't a problem.'

'But if it fails . . .'

'Daniel, it can't fail,' said Anna, 'not after all this, not after having broken with your father, not with all you're putting into it.'

'Being stubborn isn't sufficient a recipe for guaranteed success,' Daniel said. 'My father could be right, and then . . . there's Gerald. Do you really think once Martin is here and everything's underway, he'll stabilise on his boozing?'

'If he had enough encouragement, yes,' said Anna, '*and* if we keep him sweet. Look, don't jump down my throat, Daniel, but he wasn't pleased about this weekend. He was all set with ideas for showing me around New York. I think we were wrong not to go along with his plans.'

'He's got no right to monopolise your time like that,' Dan said angrily.

'Daniel, you're . . . you're going to have to sort out your mind over Gerald and me,' Anna said. 'You're putting me in an impossible position. On the one hand, you keep asking my advice, actually expecting me to nursemaid him – but when I do, you don't like it.'

'I'm sorry.' Daniel took his hand off the steering wheel, and taking one of Anna's in his, he squeezed it gently.

Anna looked down at his hand lying in her lap – brown, young, strong, with a thin dusting of golden hairs. She shivered involuntarily.

'Are you OK?' Daniel said anxiously.

'Yes, I'm fine, but . . . Daniel, if Jim is going to lend you this money anyway, you didn't really need me down here this weekend. I *could* have stayed with Gerald.'

Daniel squeezed her hand again. 'I need you with me, Anna. Just accept, I need you.'

* * *

The toy elephant caused a riot. It was big enough for Chuck to ride on and he had to be given his lunch on board, since no one could prise him off it.

'Daniel Chase,' said Penny, 'why is it that every time you come here, you take our well-ordered life and reduce it to a state of anarchy?'

'OK,' said Daniel helplessly, 'I agree the elephant's a liability, but Anna's an asset.'

'I'll say,' Jim agreed.

Anna warmed to Jim and Penny immediately. Jim was not a good-looking man – shortish and stocky, with a thatch of sandy hair – but his smile split his face in half and crinkled the corners of his eyes. Even without being told Anna knew, instinctively, that here was a nice man.

Penny was as tall as Jim, slim as a wand, with a thick, dark curtain of hair stretching down her back. She was the very epitome of all that is best in American hospitality – warm, friendly and interested. Within seconds Anna felt completely at home, and wondered how Daniel ever managed to tear himself away from this charming couple.

Lunch over, Chuck despatched to bed, the four of them sat with coffee in the lounge. The house was surprisingly modest, considering Jim's trade, but it was comfortable – a real family home.

It was while they all sat drinking their coffee that Daniel talked Jim and Penny through his proposal. He told the story of *Sometime . . . Never*, well but honestly, balancing Gerald's unpredictability against his brilliance and box office appeal. Then, opening his briefcase, Daniel drew out a pile of newspapers. 'It's only fair to show you these,' he said solemnly. 'The split with my father is fairly well documented in all the New York press today. One has to say that Chase Productions come out of it smelling like roses, but not so Daniel Chase.'

Anna was horrified. 'I didn't realise the story had hit the papers already.'

'I hid them purposely so you wouldn't see them on the way here,' Daniel said, smiling. 'I didn't want to spoil your journey.'

The four of them pored over the newspapers in silence for

a few minutes. The story was roughly the same in every paper. Walter Chase came across as the wise old impresario, Daniel was the spoilt brat, Gerald was the drunken has-been and *Sometime . . . Never* was a joke.

'Oh Daniel, this is awful,' said Anna.

Daniel shrugged his shoulders. 'It's publicity. Bad publicity can be just as useful as good, as I said to you the other day. What's important now is that the story doesn't drop. Matilda, my secretary, is trying to fix up interviews for us all. We must keep the story alive until we can open the play. I don't care what the newspapers say, so long as they keep printing.'

'That makes sense,' said Jim. 'Come on then, pal, let's go into the study and put some figures down on paper. We'll get a proposal knocked together this afternoon and I'll ring my pet banker at home this evening. We'll go and see him first thing on Monday morning.'

'Oh yeah,' said Penny, with a grin, 'and who's going to have to spend part of her weekend typing up the proposal?'

Jim bent down and kissed her. 'Don't ask silly questions, sweetheart.'

As soon as the men had left the room, Anna turned to Penny. 'How . . . how do *you* feel about all this? It's an awful lot of money.'

Penny shrugged. 'Dan's our friend. There's nothing in the world we wouldn't do for him, and he believes in this play. To be honest, if the play's a flop, things will be difficult for us, but the big news of today is that he's split with his Dad. That man just ate away at Dan's soul.'

'But Daniel's not a child any more,' Anna said.

'True, but you know what parents are like. It doesn't matter how old you are, you still feel like a kid. They can always get you where it hurts in a way no one else ever can. Walter Chase is a great businessman, but he's a swine of a human being. Perhaps if his wife had lived . . .' She shook her head, 'All I know is he's made his son suffer every day of his life for being the unwitting cause of his mother's death.'

Anna was appalled. 'Do you really believe that?'

'I know it,' said Penny. 'Remember I've known Dan since he was eighteen and, of course, Jim and Dan have been friends a lot longer than that.' Anna digested this piece of information. 'You know,' said Penny, 'the other real piece of good news is that he's brought you here. He very rarely brings his girls to see us.' Penny grimaced, 'Hey, perhaps I shouldn't say that, but with his looks, his position and all that access to would-be starlets, I'm sure you'll appreciate . . .'

'Say no more,' said Anna, immediately thinking of Rosie and the abortion.

'Hey, don't look like that, you're very special to him. I know that already,' said Penny.

'I'm not,' said Anna emphatically. 'There's nothing between us, honestly. We wrote to each other a little whilst I was still in London, but that's all.'

'Daniel wrote letters?' Anna nodded. 'Jesus!' Penny was clearly impressed.

'Penny, I can't cope with him and the way he lives,' Anna said, for the first time expressing her secret fears. 'All his glamorous women – I just can't compete. I have two outfits, my new jeans and my old jeans. I've existed on a wage below the poverty line for so many years, I wouldn't know how to look glamorous if I tried.'

'Anna, my darling girl, you *are* glamorous,' said Penny. 'That hair, those eyes, that skin, those legs – boy, you are so lucky.'

'Am I?' said Anna, genuinely surprised at Penny's reaction.

'Yes, you are . . . only you need to start thinking straight. By the time Daniel Chase finishes with *Sometime . . . Never*, you're going to be a star, and it's high time you started behaving like one. Hey, I've got a fantastic idea. You say you were being paid money in lieu of notice by Chase Productions. Let's go and spend it all on clothes.'

'But what if *Sometime . . . Never* flops?' said Anna in a panic. In every actor is borne the built-in knowledge that a period of employment usually precedes abject poverty. The uncertainty, so bred, always causes a degree of caution where money is concerned.

'Then you come and stay with us, lick your wounds and decide what to do next. Look, Anna, you never have to worry about where the next meal is coming from while you're in New York State. OK?'

'That's terribly kind of you,' Anna said, 'but why – we've only just met?'

'Because you're the best thing that's ever happened to Daniel Chase, that's why. Now, come on, say yes. Which day shall we go mad? I'll come into the city and we'll do it together. I'll take you to all the really great places – I could really do with some more clothes myself. What do you say?'

'Yes,' said Anna firmly.

The rest of Saturday and Sunday had a magical quality so far as Anna was concerned. Daniel was a different person – relaxed and approachable. He positively blossomed under Jim and Penny's influence, and Anna felt herself doing the same thing. It was not that they went anywhere or did anything particularly riveting; they just enjoyed each other's company.

On Saturday night, Anna bathed Chuck. She'd had very little experience of small children and she found playing with the soapy little boy oddly touching. They all ate and drank a lot, talked endlessly, played backgammon, dug the garden and by Sunday afternoon Anna felt more relaxed and confident than she'd felt in months – if ever.

They were all drinking coffee in the kitchen on Sunday evening when Penny said, 'Hey, you two, we've got a real favour to ask you. We've been invited by some neighbours, the Reynolds, to go for supper tonight. They haven't a very large place and I don't think it would be fair to expect them to invite our house-guests to their party. Would you mind if we went and you baby-sat Chuck?'

Jim looked suitably bemused but said nothing.

'No,' said Daniel, 'that would be fine. Anna is now extremely adept at child-care, following her experiences of last night.'

'I'll certainly do my best,' said Anna, smiling.

'OK, that's fine,' said Penny. 'Thanks a lot. There's wine in the fridge, plenty of food in the freezer, just help yourselves. Come on, sweetheart, we must go and change.'

In the car, a quarter of an hour later, Jim was even more confused. 'Why are you sending me this way? This highway doesn't take us to the Reynolds.'

'Do you know, for a bright man you can be so dumb,' said Penny. 'Of course the Reynolds haven't asked us out, I'd have told you before if they had.'

'So what are we doing?' said Jim.

'We're leaving those two alone, of course.'

'Why?'

'Jim . . . stop the car a moment.' Jim obliged. Leaning over, Penny slipped her arms round him and kissed him, long and hard on the lips. 'How does that feel?' she asked.

'It feels great,' said Jim. 'Can I have another one?' Penny obliged. 'Jesus,' said Jim, 'you're making me feel very horny, sweetheart.'

'Good,' said Penny. 'Shall we go to a motel first and then have dinner, or the other way round?'

'A motel?'

'Jim, my love,' she said, 'we're not going back to our home until at least one o'clock in the morning. We have to give them a chance.'

'You mean . . . Anna and Daniel?'

'Yeah, I mean Anna and Daniel,' said Penny.

'Ah,' said Jim, 'and because of them I have to make love to my wife in a motel, right?'

'Right,' said Penny.

'In that case,' said Jim, grinning, 'I'll take the motel first and the dinner second. OK with you?'

'It certainly is,' said Penny. 'You know, it's really great the way you cotton on so fast.'

'One more word out of you and I'll come and ride your elephant,' Daniel shouted as he came down the stairs.

'Are you winning?' asked Anna, smiling as he came into the kitchen.

'I guess so, he looks real sleepy. I don't think it will be long. Hey, that smells good, what is it?'

'Spare ribs,' said Anna. 'Sweet and sour sauce is one of the few things I can cook properly – though, you should know

198

somebody really well before you eat spare ribs in front of them
– the mess!'

'Is that an invitation?' said Dan, making a mock lunge
towards her.

'No, it isn't,' said Anna firmly.

'Hell, I'll just have to pour some wine to drown my sorrows. Anna, this *is* nice, I'm glad they've gone out.'

'That's no way to speak about your best friends and future
backers.'

'I know, I know,' said Dan. 'They are great, aren't they?'

'I've been having a lot of lectures about you from Penny
over the last couple of days,' said Anna.

'Have you now?' said Dan. 'That's interesting, because
I've been subjected to the same thing – not that she's told me
anything I didn't already know.'

'Know all!' said Anna, laughing. 'There is one thing,
though, which Penny hasn't mentioned but which *I* can't
help noticing, and that's how different you are here.'

'I am?' said Daniel.

'Very. You're more easy-going, relaxed, oh, I don't
know – just different.'

'It helps having finally made the break with my father, I
think,' said Daniel. 'I can't tell you how much better I feel
about that.'

'Try,' said Anna, lifting the sauce off the stove.

'Well, I guess I just feel as though I'm being myself for the
first time. The odd thing is I don't feel resentful or angry with
my father for quitting on the play. Quite the contrary – in an
odd sort of way, I'm grateful to him. I just wish the hell I'd
done this years ago. You see, things have always been too easy
for me, haven't they?'

'On some levels, I suppose so,' said Anna. 'Certainly
you've had plenty of material advantages, yes. What your
father hasn't done though, is to allow you to develop skills of
your own – he should have given you responsibilities so you
could gauge your own worth.'

'We're sure as hell going to see what I'm worth in the next
couple of weeks,' said Daniel. 'Hell, let's stop talking about
work. Can we eat now?'

After dinner they made coffee and went through to the sitting room. During the meal there had been a gathering restraint between them – the effects of being alone together. An uneasy silence established itself as they sipped their coffee.

Daniel let out a sigh. 'The last time I felt like this – not precisely like this – but something close, was about eighteen years ago.'

Anna looked up, grateful for the diversion. 'That makes you about fifteen.'

Daniel nodded. 'I was at this girl's house. She was sitting at one end of the sofa and I was at the other. It was my first date and I was nervous as hell.'

'What did you do?' asked Anna, genuinely interested.

'I asked her if she'd like a hot dog, and she said she would. We went downtown and there we met a bunch of other kids, and so I didn't have to worry about what to do next because we weren't alone again that evening.' Daniel set down his coffee cup and looked at Anna. 'But that was eighteen years ago.' Their eyes held.

'And I don't want a hot dog,' Anna said, her voice barely audible.

'I know,' said Daniel.

There was nothing else to say. The conversation was at an end. Over the past months, they had said all they could say to one another. It was as though everything that had happened had been leading them to this point, this moment. Now the talking was over.

Daniel crossed the small space between them and sat down on the sofa beside Anna, not touching her, but close. The tension between them was unbearable. Anna was trembling, her mouth dry, her heart beating so fast, so strongly, she wondered if she was going to faint . . . and he hadn't even touched her.

She raised her eyes to his. 'I'm frightened,' she whispered.

He came to her then, folding her in his big arms, holding her close to his chest so that she could hear the ferocious drumbeat of his heart matching her own. He felt clumsy, shy – this man with so much experience of women.

Tears fell soundlessly from Anna's eyes. Daniel gently brushed them away, aware of being near to tears himself. Then he gathered her closer to him so that his body seemed to envelop hers, and leaning forward, their lips met as they kissed for the first time.

Anna gasped at the joy of it. Her hands flew to his face, gently running her hands over the hard planes of his features, ruffling the hair at the back of his neck, covering his face with fierce little kisses. Daniel held her close, shocked by his own reticence. He wanted her so badly, yet he was terrified of making the wrong move.

It was Anna who drew away at last, Anna who stood up, Anna who took his hand and led him upstairs to her bedroom.

It was almost dark outside. Daniel drew the curtains and switched on the bedside light. Only then did he look at her properly. The light had turned her skin to a soft apricot, her hair tumbled richly onto her shoulders, her eyes were bright with tears. It was in her eyes he saw the uncertainty. He wanted to tell her he loved her, he wanted to reassure her, but no words came.

He moved towards her unsteadily, still unsure. When he reached her, he realised he was trembling. Slowly, he began to unbutton her blouse. His hands fumbled with the buttons, he felt unco-ordinated, incompetent, his nerves jangling dangerously.

They helped each other undress, neither could have managed the task alone. Naked at last, they lay down on the big bed and as they came into each other's arms, in one voice they let out a sigh of pure relief. They lay thus for some time, feeling the length of their bodies against one another while passion gathered and swirled around them like a beautiful mist.

At last Daniel drew away a little. In contrast to his deep tan, Anna's body beside his own was almost luminous white. He thought he had never seen anything so beautiful – the small firm breasts, the long smooth thighs. The sight of her seemed to touch some secret core of his soul. She was wholesome, so pure and yet so incredibly sensuous.

He stroked her breasts and she shuddered at his touch. 'Anna . . .' he began.

She put a finger to his lips. 'Shhhh, not now.' She pulled his head down to hers, and as their lips met it was as if a dam burst between them.

Their mutual need took over, and suddenly Daniel was the leader, Anna joyously following wherever he chose to take her. He entered her quickly, simply, and as he thrust deep inside her, he felt her body leap to meet his with an urgency that matched his own . . . as, for that brief moment that is allowed, they became one flesh.

It was as though they invented lovemaking during that long night. To Daniel, so experienced in the art, he was mesmerised by the realisation that Anna had created a brand new experience for him. His tired mind tried to analyse this wonderful new depth of feeling, but he had never been in love before, and so could not put a name to the emotion that assailed him as he held her in his arms.

Anna's experience was limited to two uninspired, and mercifully short, liaisons which had been more experimental than anything else – borne of curiosity rather than passion. Lying awake in the early hours of the morning, watching Daniel sleep, she was aware that at last she understood why love had so dominated the hearts, minds and bodies of men and women over the centuries. She felt truly alive for the first time.

As if sensing her gaze, Daniel opened his eyes. He smiled, gently. 'I love you, Anna Wetherby.' He spoke slowly, carefully, savouring the knowledge that at last there was truth behind the well-worn words.

'I love you, Daniel,' Anna whispered, 'but . . .'

'No buts,' Daniel said. 'I don't know where we go from here, darling, but I'm not going to lose you – not now, not now I've found you.'

They came into each other's arms again and clung together.

Anna's mind was suddenly awash with all the problems they had to face – the play, the finance, Gerald, the publicity. She squeezed her eyes tight shut to stop the tears, she buried her face in Daniel's chest and wrapped her legs around his . . . as if to protect herself from being snatched away from him.

Chapter Eighteen

'Fuckin' hell, Martin, do you have to walk so quickly?'

'Sophie, I'm going to miss this flight in a minute.'

'So what, there'll be another.'

'Sophie, this is the one I'm booked on.'

'OK, OK, don't get ratty. You know, Martin, you're getting an awfully boring old sod. Spending half a day with you feels like walking through thick mud. Where's your sense of humour? Where's your *joie de vivre*?'

Martin frowned, concentrating on the difficult task of trying to park his luggage trolley by the queue at the British Airways desk. 'Sophie darling,' he said, 'my *joie de vivre* has been fairly consistently drained from me, inch by inch, over the last . . . how many – eight hours?'

Sophie grinned. 'Something like that, lover. Fun, wasn't it?'

Martin's expression softened. 'Yes, yes, it was.'

'It will be interesting, won't it?' Sophie said brightly.

'What will?'

'Seeing what's happened to Gerald and Anna. I bet they're in the middle of the most turgid affair. You'll probably have to prise them apart every time you want to get them on stage.' The woman in the queue ahead of them turned round and glared at Sophie.

'Sophie,' said Martin, warningly, 'shut up.'

'I bet you will, though. That Anna, God – I bet she's got some tales to tell.'

'If it was you in her position, I'm sure you're right,' said Martin evenly, 'but knowing Anna, I'm equally sure she's been doing all sorts of worthy things like visiting the Empire

State Building and gazing at the Statue of Liberty.'

'You're turning into a prude,' said Sophie, accusingly, 'that's obviously what you think she ought to be doing.'

Martin lowered his voice to a whisper. 'I don't honestly see that you have any justification for calling me a prude, bearing in mind how we've spent the last few hours.'

Sophie winked at him. 'Hey, do you think they have a rest room here?'

'A rest room? I should think so. Why?'

'Well, what about a quick . . .' she whispered into his ear. 'After all,' she continued, 'everyone round here looks half dead, they wouldn't even notice.'

'You know,' said Martin, 'when the good Lord was doling out sexual appetite, he must have gone to sleep over you and forgotten to turn off the machine.'

The woman in front of them turned round. 'I'd be grateful if you two wouldn't discuss your private life in front of us all. It's extremely embarrassing.'

'Madam,' said Martin, 'I am this young lady's psychiatrist. Unfortunately, due to pressure of work, I am having to take a flight to New York, leaving her in a most distraught emotional state. I must do everything I can to reassure her before I'm forced to leave, otherwise heaven knows what she might do.'

The woman stared at him, torn between anger and disbelief, clearly worried that however she reacted, she'd make a fool of herself.

'Don't take any notice of him, dear,' said Sophie. 'He's the one that ought to be certified.' The woman turned away in confusion.

Martin had hardly collected his boarding card before the flight was called. He and Sophie stood briefly at the entrance to passport control. 'Take care, Sophie, thanks for everything,' said Martin quietly.

'See you around, sunshine,' said Sophie, cheerfully. 'You know, you're not so bad, particularly bearing in mind you're knocking on a bit.'

Three hours later, Sophie lay in the arms of a sleeping friend, a man she'd met at a party a few weeks earlier. He was a better lover than Martin – more inventive, younger, good looking . . . so why am I crying? she thought angrily.

Thirty thousand feet over the Atlantic, Martin drained his third double brandy. As he had done, so many times before, he went over the same old ground in his mind, looking for some avenue, some way in which he could justify any sort of future with Sophie. There was none. He knew, as she did, that they would never meet again.

'Miss Wetherby, you'll be on in approximately fifteen minutes' time. Would you like to come down to Make-up?'

'Yes, fine,' said Anna.

'It's a bit tatty in here,' the girl said, opening the door to a large make-up room with several well-lit mirrors.

'Believe me,' said Anna, 'compared with the average backstage dressing room, this is the height of luxury.'

The make-up girl came forward and smiled. 'Are you an actress then?' Anna nodded. 'So you probably don't want any help with your make-up?'

'No thanks,' said Anna. She sat down at one of the tables and stared at her reflection. She was in the studios of CBS, due to go out live on their breakfast show, Good Morning America. She was frankly terrified.

During the course of her career, Anna had been involved in several TV commercials and far from giving her confidence in front of a television camera, they had made her only too aware of how easily things could go wrong. There was that worry and the knowledge, as Daniel had warned her, that the interviewer could well be hostile. It was also far too early in the morning. Anna took a deep breath to calm herself and then began applying her make-up.

It was Friday and it had been quite a week, one way and another. Being in love, Anna had discovered, was exhausting. She and Daniel had only met once during the week, and then for a hurried lunch between his appointments, but at some time during every day, he'd rung her. The telephone had become her greatest friend. She watched it surreptitiously, waiting for it to link her with Daniel for those few precious minutes, when just the sound of his voice sent her pulses racing and brought colour to her cheeks. Being in love meant everything was more extreme she discovered. When she was happy, she was happier than she'd ever been in her life. When she was sad, she was inconsolable. The sunshine was brighter, the rain wetter, everything looked different, felt different, and then . . . and then, there was Gerald.

Daniel had dropped her outside Marcus' apartment on Monday evening. The meeting on Monday morning with Jim's tame banker had been a success. *Sometime . . . Never* had the finance and this piece of news, Anna felt, would carry her through the inquisition she felt sure was coming.

Gerald was at home, alone, and moderately drunk. 'Darling,' he said, 'how lovely to see you. How are you?'

Anna wasn't fooled by his greeting. There was a malevolent look in his eye. 'I'm fine thank you, Gerald.' She walked over to where he sat and kissed him on the cheek.

'How was young Mr Chase, then?' Gerald stood up and studied Anna in silence for a moment.

'Fine,' Anna answered casually.

'Did he behave himself? No, no I can see he didn't.'

Anna felt the beginnings of a blush. 'Actually he did behave himself,' she said hurriedly, 'and what's more important, he has secured the finance for *Sometime . . . Never.*'

'Oh good,' said Gerald, walking over to the drinks table for a refill.

'Gerald, did you hear what I said?'

'I heard.'

'Aren't you pleased?'

'Pleased yes, but not surprised.' He turned round and glowered at Anna. 'Frankly, darling, do you think I'd really still be hanging round this godforsaken city if I'd thought for one moment the boy wasn't going to pull it off?'

'No, I suppose not.' Anna looked crestfallen. She'd hoped Gerald would be as excited as she was by Daniel's success. Suddenly she brightened. 'Gerald, you haven't forgotten you're showing me New York this week, have you?'

'Are you still sure you're not going to be too busy with invitations from young Daniel?'

'Heavens no,' said Anna, 'he'll be totally involved each and every day, putting the production together.'

Gerald sipped his drink in silence for a moment. 'We're both liable to have a number of publicity commitments.'

'Yes,' agreed Anna, 'but there'll be lots of time in between. Please, Gerald, don't be an old grouse.' She walked over to him and slipped an arm through his. 'Please . . .'

Gerald looked into her big brown eyes, alive now with warmth and mischief. She was an extraordinarily attractive girl. He set down his drink and smiled slightly. 'If you give the Old Man a hug, I just might.'

She came readily into his arms and hugged him tight. Then, slipping out of his embrace, she said, 'I'm just going to have a bath and then I'll cook you some supper. I'll be about half an hour – will that be OK?'

He nodded, watching her walk across the room with her long-legged stride. Her embrace had been warm, loving, full of youthful exuberance, but without any form of sexual connotation. For Anna, it had been like hugging her favourite teddy bear, Gerald realised with shock. She'd changed. He frowned – in one weekend, she'd changed irrevocably. She was more confident, more aware of her attractions. Why, just then, she'd openly flirted with him – she'd never done that before.

He went over to the window and gazed out across the East River. The boy must have had her, there could be no doubt of that, and the impact on her had been considerable. He felt a sudden stab of jealousy, an emotion he wasn't used to, and one he couldn't handle. All he knew was that he felt ashamed of the feeling, that at all costs it had to be suppressed.

'Would you like me to come and scrub your back, darling?' he called through to the bathroom.

'No, I would not,' Anna called back, laughing.

'Buck up then, I'm starving.' His voice, even to himself, sounded carefree and relaxed. That's better, he thought.

With a shaking hand, Anna began to apply her eyeliner. Yes, she and Gerald had enjoyed their week of sightseeing. Good as his word, he'd been very thorough. They'd been up the Empire State Building, they'd taken the Circle Line Ferry round Manhattan Island, they'd done the Metropolitan Museum, driven round Central Park in a horse-drawn cab. They'd been to Chinatown, Greenwich Village and Little Italy. They'd ventured on the subway, window-shopped down Fifth Avenue and had tea at the Plaza. One night, Anna, Gerald and Marcus had been to the theatre and afterwards, they'd dined at The Players Club.

Anna had found it all thrilling and Gerald had proved the perfect companion. His knowledge of New York was considerable and he'd loved playing host. He'd been recognised everywhere they went, of course, and most people made a considerable fuss of him, which he adored. Only when Daniel Chase's name was mentioned or, indeed, if Daniel phoned, did he turn a little acid . . . but then, never for long. Despite their time together, though, Anna still felt she was walking a tightrope with him. There was such a lot going on in Gerald's mind which she felt she could not reach.

The previous day, Thursday, while Gerald was giving some interviews, Penny had come up from Scarsdale and she and Anna had spent most of the day shopping. They'd had a wonderful time and spent far too much money, but Anna was pleased with her purchases. Being in love, she discovered, created a whole new set of pressures concerning her appearance. She wanted to look her best for Daniel – whereas in the past, she'd never given much thought to how she looked, except on stage. She was wearing the first of her new clothes today – a cream jump suit which accentuated her long legs and slender figure, and was a perfect foil for her colouring. She knew she looked good, if only she could keep calm . . .

'Miss Wetherby, are you ready?' A young girl with a clipboard put her head round the door.

'Just about,' said Anna.

'Good. We're going into a news break right now, and then we'd like to put you on straight away.'

'Fine,' said Anna.

The interviewer, Jan Raban, was a typical smart, chic, tough New Yorker. As Anna stepped onto the set, Jan looked up, saw her and beckoned her over.

'Hi Anna, come and sit by me.' She smiled hugely, but not with her eyes, Anna noticed.

'Hello,' said Anna. 'Thank you for giving us air time.'

'My pleasure. Now, after the news, which is running at the moment, we'll go straight into the interview, OK? I'll just ask you three or four questions, then we'll take a break and then come back and do some more. It'll all be over in ten to fifteen minutes.'

'You make it sound like a visit to the dentist,' said Anna, nervous.

'Feels a bit like it, right?' Anna nodded. 'Don't worry, honey.'

Anna was reassured. A microphone was fitted round her neck. 'Watch that camera,' said a technician, 'you'll see when you're on.'

Lights blazed, and suddenly it was all happening. Anna was vaguely aware of the introduction – 'Anna Wetherby, the new British star of *Sometime . . . Never.*'

Jan turned her diamond-bright eyes on Anna. 'So, Anna, this is your first trip to Broadway?'

'Yes, it is,' said Anna, 'and I'm very excited about it.'

'You must be a very well-established actress in the UK to land a part like this.'

'No, not very,' Anna admitted. 'I have played the part in the West End, but before that, I spent years struggling in repertory companies.'

'Wow,' said Jan, 'then this really is the big break?'

'Hopefully, yes,' said Anna, smiling and feeling more relaxed by the second.

'Then it must be particularly daunting for you, playing opposite Gerald Kingdom?'

'It was in the beginning,' said Anna. 'His talent is so immense – but, of course, mine is only a small part and, somehow, I've managed to get over my initial terror. I think it's an enormous help to my own acting to have the opportunity to play opposite a master such as Gerald.'

'That's wasn't exactly what I meant,' said Jan sweetly. 'I was thinking more of his drinking.'

'H – how do you mean?' said Anna.

'Well, an experienced actress would be better able to cover up for him when he forgets his lines, or whatever.'

'He never forgets his lines,' said Anna, feeling her colour rise, 'and I don't know what you mean about his drinking. He's never drunk on stage.'

'That's not how I hear it,' said Jan. 'In fact, as I understand it, Walter Chase vetoed *Sometime* . . . *Never* because of Gerald Kingdom's drinking. I gather Walter's son is only pressing ahead with the production to try and prove some sort of point – a family feud of some kind.'

'I am an actress,' said Anna, with as much dignity as she could muster,' and the production side of the play is not my concern. All I can tell you, Miss Raban, is that I consider it to be an enormous pleasure and privilege to act opposite Gerald Kingdom, and I have the utmost respect and confidence in him, both as an actor and as a man.'

'Gee,' said Jan, 'that's some recommendation. OK, we'll take a break, but I'd love to talk to you some more, Anna.'

The cameras swung away and Anna turned angrily on Jan. 'I'm not prepared to answer any more questions on the subject of Gerald and his drinking. I thought I'd come here to promote the play.'

'Don't be naive, poppet. The punters don't want to hear about which days you're doing a matinée and the price of the seats. They want the muck raked, they want the story behind the glittering image.'

'I repeat, I'm not prepared to answer any more questions concerning Gerald,' Anna said.

'OK, OK, now stand by – we're on again in a moment . . . So Anna,' Jan continued, 'you've brought a touch of reality to many a young girl's dream. Here you are on Broadway, starring opposite one of the cinema's legendary lovers. How did it all happen? Did you always want to be an actress?'

'No, not always,' said Anna. 'It was something that kind of evolved when I was a teenager.'

'Did you go to drama school?'

'No, my parents weren't very enthusiastic about my going on the stage, so they didn't encourage it. When I'd finished my schooling, I simply joined a repertory company and began making tea, emptying the rubbish, that kind of thing.'

'Your parents didn't want you to be an actress . . . so, it's not something that runs in the family?'

'Well no, actually I was adopted.' Why on earth did I say that? Anna thought. It's something I never tell anyone, let alone this dreadful woman.

'Adopted? *Really?* That's fascinating. Do you know anything about your natural parents?'

'My mother was an actress,' Anna mumbled – the story was running away with her.

'Oh really! I say, that is something. Have you ever met her?'

Anna shook her head. 'No, I was adopted when I was a baby.'

Jan smiled a sickly smile. 'Now isn't that romantic? Little Anna, following her mother's footsteps onto the stage, although they've never met. Wherever she is, Anna, I'm sure if your Mommy knew what you'd achieved, she'd be real proud of you today. Well, that's all we've got time for. Thank you, Anna Wetherby . . .' her voice trailed on.

Damn, thought Anna. Why did I let my tongue run away with me, how did I do that? She murmured her goodbyes to Jan, who'd already lost interest in her, and stumbled off the stage.

Back in the make-up room, everyone was very enthusiastic. 'That was a knock-out, you really stood up to Jan, and that bit about your being adopted was great. Is it true?'

Anna stared in horror at the questioner, the short, fat girl, with carroty hair, who'd originally brought her down to Make-up.

'Of course it's true, why shouldn't it be?'

The girl shrugged. 'I guess I thought it might be a publicity stunt . . . you know,' she added lamely.

'No, it is not,' Anna replied angrily, 'and it's not normally something I discuss – it just sort of came out.'

'Jan has that effect on people,' the girl assured her.

Anna was still taking off her make-up when the telephone rang. 'It's for you, Anna,' the make-up girl called.

'Anna?'

'Daniel!' Anna collapsed with relief at the sound of his voice.

'Darling, you were great, fantastic. I was so proud. Mattie and I just sat here absolutely knocked out.'

'I wasn't good. I was awful,' said Anna. She was close to tears.

'Darling, what is it?' said Daniel, instantly catching her mood.

'Oh, the business about being adopted,' Anna said. 'As you know, I never tell anyone about it normally. Now because of that horrible woman, I told the whole of America. The girl here in the studio even thought it was a publicity stunt. Daniel, I feel sort of . . . sort of cheap, as though I've cashed in on my parentage in some way.'

'Anna, now you're being silly.' There was a pause while he consulted his watch. 'Hey, listen, I've got nearly an hour before I need to be down at the theatre. I'll come round to the studio in a cab and collect you. Stay where you are.'

'No, no, don't do that . . .' Anna began.

'Darling, you're upset, do as you're told. It will only take me about ten minutes.'

It felt so good in his arms. They sat in the back of the cab, kissing and cuddling like a couple of teenagers. Anna was crying.

'Darling, don't.' Daniel gently stroked the tears away from her cheeks. 'I love you,' he whispered.

'I love you too,' Anna said, between sobs, 'but why did I say those things, Daniel?'

'Jan Raban is a very experienced interviewer. She knows just how to drag information out of people in a very short space of time. She began by being tough and then, seemingly, became friendly and interested in you. It's a technique as old as time, and it works.' He kissed her. 'Honestly though darling, it doesn't matter.'

'It does to me,' said Anna, bitterly.

'Then don't let it. Oh God, I wish we had more time, I wish one of us had an apartment of our own. I want to take you somewhere and make love to you and drive all those demons out of your head.'

They kissed again, and for the rest of the journey Anna lay back in Daniel's arms.

'You've been crying,' Gerald said, accusingly, as Anna walked into the sitting room.

'Only a little,' she said defensively.

'Because of what you said about being adopted?'

His immediate understanding surprised and touched her. 'Yes,' she replied.

Gerald took her hand. 'That woman's an old cow,' he said. 'She interviewed me years ago and I must say, you managed far better than I did at the time. It's funny though – I didn't know you were adopted but, now that I do, it makes a lot of sense. I never could see you as the product of Stephen and May Wetherby, darling.' He smiled. 'I don't mean that disrespectfully, I think they're a splendid couple, but they're so staid and sensible, and you're so . . . well . . .'

'So what?' asked Anna, smiling too.

'Well, should we just say you're not very staid and sensible, darling.' He took both her hands in his. 'Now, listen, it's time you started behaving like a proper actress. I'm going to take you to Sardi's for lunch. It's where all proper actresses go, and we're going to be wildly extravagant and eat and drink far too much. No, don't argue, I have two very good reasons for making the suggestion.'

'What are they?' Anna asked.

'Firstly, you look simply delicious in that outfit and I simply have to be seen in public with you on my arm. Secondly, I'd like to thank you for your kind remarks about me just now. Your loyalty was much appreciated.'

Anna gave in gracefully. She cherished Gerald's words, which were all the more precious since she knew it was not normally part of his nature to express gratitude.

On Sunday afternoon, Marcus, Gerald and Anna were playing poker. A matchstick represented ten thousand dollars and when the telephone rang, Anna was only too pleased to answer it. She looked as though she was about to go down for quarter of a million. 'Hello,' she said, expectantly, hoping desperately it was Daniel.

'That has to be my darling Anna. I'd recognise those dulcet English tones anywhere.'

'Martin, oh Martin, is it really you?'

Gerald looked up from his game. 'Is he in New York?' he asked.

'Where are you, Martin?' Anna said.

'Right here in Fun City, darling.'

'Ask him to come round,' said Gerald.

'Martin, why don't you jump in a cab and come round to see us.'

'Where are you?' said Martin. 'Daniel has given me a list of telephone numbers, but no addresses.' Anna told him. 'OK,' said Martin, 'I'll be right with you.'

The evening was very useful from Martin's point of view since it gave him an opportunity to re-establish his relationship with both Gerald and Anna. He was agreeably surprised to see what a good state Gerald appeared to be in, and was altogether fascinated by the change in them both. Their relationship appeared to have altered enormously since he'd last seen them, and yet it was hard to pinpoint in what way exactly. He was sure that they weren't having an affair, yet in some strange way, their roles seemed to have reversed. Anna was the more confident and flamboyant of the two, while Gerald was quieter and less aggressive. Martin pondered the problem on his way back to the hotel that evening. He needed to understand what was going on, in order to get the best out of them both.

Rehearsals began the following morning, sharp at nine o'clock, and despite the fact that they were undertaken against a background of scenery construction, they went extremely well. Ralph had never had the chance to demonstrate his prowess before, but despite his apparent unsuitability, he proved an excellent butler.

The Barrymore Theatre was smaller than the Chase and therefore more suited to *Sometime . . . Never*. As the Chase Theatre was closed, pending Walter finding a new play to put there, Daniel had hired Amy and bought the costumes from his father, so there was a reassuring touch of familiarity around the Barrymore.

By lunchtime, Martin felt rehearsals had gone sufficiently well that they had done enough for one day. He followed Anna into her dressing room, armed with two mugs of coffee. 'That was very good Anna, darling,' he said.

'Oh Martin, you don't know what a relief it is having you back,' Anna said. 'It was such hell before – that awful American director and Gerald drunk all the time . . .'

'Don't think about it,' said Martin soothingly, 'it's all in the past.'

'Gerald's performance was absolutely stunning today, wasn't it?' Anna said.

'So was yours,' Martin assured her.

'Thanks to you.' She raised her coffee mug in salute.

'Not really, or should I say, not entirely.'

'What's the cause then?' Anna asked. 'If it's not all due to you, what is it due to?'

Martin stared at her for a moment. 'Anna, surely you've realised.'

Anna frowned, 'Realised what?'

'Robert's unrequited love for Sarah . . . you and Gerald are playing the parts for real.'

Chapter Nineteen

'I disagree, Daniel, it's entirely the wrong moment.' Anna's stubborn resistance was costing her dear. If her decision need only have been a personal one, she would have jumped at his suggestion.

'She's right, you know,' Martin said.

Daniel, Martin and Anna were sitting in Charlie's Burger Bar on Tuesday afternoon. Martin had suspended rehearsals. They were all perfect, he said. There was nothing more he could add and he didn't want them stale for the opening night on Wednesday.

'But there's no need to go on staying in that apartment, Anna.' Daniel was both angry and hurt. 'Thanks to the somewhat dubious publicity, tickets are entirely sold out for the first ten performances. Regardless of what the critics say, we have cash sitting in the bank now. OK, I agree, I can't afford to put you in the Algonquin with Martin, but at least I can put some distance between you and Gerald – at least have a place you can call your own.' Anna could sense the longing in his voice, and wondered whether Martin, too, had picked it up. Nonetheless, she was resolved.

'It's the wrong moment to move out so far as Gerald is concerned. Look Daniel, we're twenty-four hours away from opening. Once we've been running for a few days, once we have the critics' verdict and we're all a little more confident, I agree with you. But not now. Honestly, I just know it would be a dangerous thing to do.'

Anna looked pleadingly at Martin who instantly came to the rescue. 'Daniel, you've put a hell of a lot into this play, and you know, you must know what a gamble you've taken on with Gerald. Between us, Anna and I can keep him on the straight and narrow. If I hadn't thought that, I wouldn't have come to New York . . . but he's not easy, he's so unpredictable. Anna is right. Her moving out of the apartment at this moment is asking for trouble. He needs Anna there, Daniel, it's as simple as that.'

'Hell, Martin, I know you're right – it's just that Anna and I . . .' Daniel struggled for words and reaching out, took Anna's hand. 'Dammit, Martin, I love the girl and I just don't like the idea of her being alone in that apartment with those two old rogues, particularly Gerald.'

So that was the score, Martin thought. He had an eternal triangle on his hands now. 'I think Anna can look after herself,' he said reassuringly, but neither of them were listening to him. They sat gazing at one another, lost for a moment in their own private world. Of course, Martin thought, they've got nowhere to be on their own together – that must be tough. Still, perhaps at the moment it was just as well. Their feelings for each other were obviously too new to show the rest of the world as yet, but Martin was sure of one thing – Gerald knew. It accounted for his oddly subdued behaviour, for the added depth and poignancy of his performance. Martin didn't like it. His nerves were all on edge. He took a deep breath. 'Come on, you two,' he said in a falsely hearty voice, 'you're making me feel a gooseberry.'

'A gooseberry!' Daniel said, laughing. 'What in Christ's name is that, Martin?'

'It's a quaint old English expression meaning I feel left out.' The memory of Sophie suddenly flashed across his mind, and he winced involuntarily.

Anna caught his expression. 'Are you all right, Martin?' she asked anxiously.

'Yes,' he said, wearily, 'yes, sort of.'

It was Daniel who precipitated the panic by ringing Anna's apartment just after eight that same evening. 'Hello darling,' he said, 'is Gerald there?'

'No,' Anna replied. 'Can I give him a message?'

'I was just going to read him the article in this evening's

paper. It's really rather good – not the usual old, drunken stuff. The journalist really seems pleased to see Gerald back on Broadway.'

'That would have been a good idea,' said Anna. 'Actually I'm glad you've rung. I was just wondering whether I should be ringing you or Martin, since Gerald hasn't turned up yet. He said he'd be back early evening. It's probably nothing. He's probably just got delayed with some chums, but bearing in mind tomorrow is the big day, I couldn't help feeling nervous.'

'I agree with you,' said Daniel. 'Look, I tell you what, let's give it another hour. If there's still no sign of him by then, I guess we'd better think about sending out a search party.'

Daniel rang back quarter of an hour later. 'I think we have a problem,' he said. 'After speaking to you, I got nervous and rang Ralph. I remembered that he and Gerald had planned to have a drink after rehearsals this afternoon. Apparently they took to the booze in a fairly heavy way. Ralph left Gerald in the Rum House Bar about an hour ago – it's just opposite the Barrymore.' Daniel sighed. 'I sent Mattie round to see how he was but he'd already left, and the barman said he was in one hell of a state.'

'Oh, no!' said Anna.

'Look,' said Daniel, 'would you mind coming round here and I'll ring Martin too. I think we'd better split up into groups and start searching.'

'You think it's that serious?' said Anna.

'Yeah, I do.' Daniel's voice was flat and apprehensive.

A very sombre little group sat round the single table in Daniel's apartment. It was the first time Matilda and Anna had actually met, and they liked each other instantly.

Mattie looked at Martin. 'Hey, fella, I'm sure you and I could put a great act together. I know the city, you know the guy.' She smirked, and nodded towards Anna and Daniel. 'These two already seem to have some kind of partnership going, so it seems a pity to disturb it.'

Martin smiled. 'I agree.'

It was a strange few hours. By midnight, Matilda knew all about Robin; by one o'clock she knew all about Sophie. By two o'clock, Martin knew that Mattie was not the frustrated spinster he'd assumed her to be, but an intelligent, articulate, independent woman, who was a positive walking encyclopedia on the subject of Broadway, and its strange ways. Indeed, Martin was of the opinion that what Matilda Jackson didn't know about Broadway, wasn't worth knowing.

Daniel and Anna, by contrast, were not so compatible. As they roamed from bar to bar, in a seemingly fruitless search for Gerald, their irritation grew and they began blaming each other for what had happened. It was ten days since they had lain together in the bed in Scarsdale, ten days of incredibly hard work for Daniel, and mounting tension for them both. The pressure was starting to show.

Eventually, they found themselves back at the Barrymore. 'This is crazy,' Daniel burst out. All the words of warning he'd been given about Gerald and his drinking seemed to be doing a war dance in his head.

'Keep calm,' said Anna, laying a hand on his sleeve.

'Keep calm, keep calm. Is that all you can say?' Daniel turned on her, his face a blur of fatigue. 'I've given up everything for this guy. I've thrown up my job, put my best pal's business in jeopardy – hell, I've even had to stand by while you play nursemaid to the old shit – knowing how he feels about you, knowing he wants to get you into his bed again . . .'

'Stop it!' Anna screamed, putting her hands to her head. 'How do you think I feel? I'm the one who has to go on stage tomorrow night. What happens if we can't find him?' Tears began to pour down her face.

Daniel pulled her roughly into his arms. 'Oh, darling I'm sorry, I'm a brute. I just can't believe after all we've been through, he could do this to us.'

They stood in the circle of each other's arms, gaining strength from their closeness. At last Anna drew away and looked at her watch. 'I'd better call Marcus again,' she said wearily. 'You never know, Gerald might have found his way back there, or perhaps Mattie and Martin have had more success than us.' Her voice was flat and carried no conviction.

Daniel looked at her tired face. 'Roaring round the streets of New York isn't doing you any good. Here, I tell you what, there's a little restaurant round the corner from my place. Why don't we go there and have something to eat and drink – we can call Marcus from there, too?'

They saw him as soon as they walked into the restaurant. He was sitting up at the bar, half slumped across the counter.

'Thank Christ for that,' Daniel said.

They rushed up to him. 'Gerald,' said Anna, 'we've been looking for you everywhere.'

Gerald raised his head and looked at Anna with bleary eyes. 'Ah,' he said, slowly, 'it's Anna, it's darling little Anna. Anna my . . . my love, do you remember the black swans, *do you*?' Tears began running down his cheeks.

'What's he talking about?' Daniel asked anxiously.

'It's all right,' said Anna. 'Go and get a cab, I don't expect he can walk any distance.'

'Excuse me, lady,' the barman beckoned towards Anna in a conspiratorial manner. 'Is Mr Kingdom a friend of yours?'

'Yes,' said Anna.

'It's just that he's been talking to a reporter from the *New York Times*, and I reckon the guy's gone off to get a photographer. If you don't want him splashed all over the papers in this state, I guess you'd better be quick.'

'Thanks,' said Daniel. 'Do you think you can get him to the door, Anna, while I fetch the cab?' She nodded.

'Come on, Gerald,' said Anna, 'we're going home.'

'Home, darling, where's home? Where are we, for heaven's sake?'

'New York,' Anna said.

'Are we? I thought we were in Oxford, with the swans.'

'Don't be silly, Gerald.'

Anna managed to get his arm round her shoulders so she could take most of his weight.

'Do you want a hand?' said the barman.

Anna shook her head, looking the length of the crowded restaurant. 'No thanks, I want to get him out as quietly and as inconspicuously as I can,' she said.

'Get who out? What are you talking about, darling?' Gerald said.

'Shhh, you, of course,' said Anna, 'just concentrate on walking.'

Slowly, but without incident, they made it to the bar door. Once out in the street, Anna saw with relief that Daniel was standing in the middle of the road and had succeeded in hailing a taxi. Gerald's knees started to buckle under him.

'Quick, Daniel, give me a hand. Oh damn, *no!*' At the same moment as Gerald slipped unceremoniously out of her grasp on to the pavement, a light bulb flashed. The *New York Times* had their picture.

Marcus and Daniel got Gerald into bed, while Anna made coffee for them all. 'Do you realise,' said Daniel, coming through into the kitchen, 'that it's now past three o'clock. In less than seventeen hours' time, darling, you and Gerald have to be on stage. One of you is dead drunk, the other is dead beat.' Surprisingly, he grinned, 'And on you both hangs my reputation and future.'

Anna met his look squarely. 'We're not going to let you down, Daniel. I know right now it doesn't seem like it, but tomorrow night is going to be OK.'

'I agree,' said Marcus. 'The amazing thing about old boozers like Gerald and myself, is our phenomenal power of recovery.'

'Who's to say he won't go on a boozing trip tomorrow, as well?' Daniel said, somewhat desperately.

'Just don't worry about it,' said Anna. 'Leave him to me. Gerald and I will walk through the stage door of the Barrymore tomorrow evening at six o'clock precisely, and we'll both be sober.'

'Is there anything I can do?' said Daniel.

'Or me?' asked Marcus.

'No,' said Anna, 'just leave him to me. Now if you'll both excuse me, I think I'll go to bed.' She looked up at Daniel. 'Goodnight and don't worry.' She grinned suddenly, 'Hey, I wonder what's happened to Mattie and Martin – they're probably whooping it up in Greenwich Village by now.'

'I expect they'll ring in soon,' said Daniel. 'Good night, my love.'

At ten o'clock the following morning, Anna walked into

Gerald's bedroom, armed with a pot of coffee and a jug of grapefruit juice. She shook him, none too gently.

'What the hell are you doing?' he muttered grumpily. Anna raised the blind on the window. 'Stop letting in all that light, I can't stand it.'

'Shut up and sit up,' said Anna.

'Darling girl, that's no way to speak. What time is it anyway?'

'Ten o'clock.'

'Ten o'clock! Why are you waking me up so early, we haven't a rehearsal, have we?'

'No,' said Anna, 'but you have a lot of listening to do. Here, drink this first.'

She handed him the grapefruit juice, and he did as he was told, while she sat on the edge of the bed watching him. Marcus was right, Gerald's powers of recuperation were incredible. He sat in bed now, elegant in silk pyjamas, with barely a hair out of place – his colour was good, his eyes seemingly clear. He looks considerably better than I feel, Anna thought belligerently. He set down the glass. 'Now drink some coffee,' she ordered.

Silently, Gerald sipped the coffee. 'That's better,' he said. 'What is it you wanted to say, because I'd like to go back to sleep?'

'Firstly I want you to study this.' From under the tray, Anna pulled a copy of the *New York Times* open at the gossip page. There was the photograph of Gerald, sprawled out drunk on the pavement, with Anna desperately trying to support him. The caption read – 'Broadway's new star!' There then followed a fairly punchy article on the likelihood of Gerald making a fool of himself the following evening – but the editorial piece was immaterial, it was the photograph Anna wanted Gerald to see.

He stared at it for a long moment. 'That, I take it, was me last night?'

'Don't you remember?'

'I don't really remember anything after Ralph went home.'

'*Why*, Gerald?' Anna said.

'Oh don't ask bloody silly questions, darling,' Gerald said, irritably. 'Asking a man like me why I drink is like asking yourself why you breathe. I've always drunk too much, I always will drink too much, and before you start one of your moralistic lectures, I'd like you to know that I have no intention of ever reforming.'

'Gerald, a long time ago, or rather I should say, what seems a long time ago, I lost my temper with you – the day we opened in the West End. Do you remember?'

'Could I ever forget it,' said Gerald.

'At the time, I said that the person you would be letting down most would be yourself, and that if you wanted to make yourself a laughing stock, then that was up to you. That was true then, Gerald, but it's not true now. You've proved you can still act anyone else off the stage – you've proved that when you're on form, you are, without doubt, the world's greatest living stage actor.' Gerald started to speak. 'No, I'm not paying you compliments for the sake of it,' said Anna, ruthlessly. 'I'm saying what I'm saying for a purpose. It is because of your genius that a lot of people are walking the plank for you. Martin, you know, turned down the chance of directing a feature film, which could have earned him three or four times more money. Why? To come out here and see you through *Sometime . . . Never.*'

'I didn't know that,' said Gerald.

'There's a lot of things you don't know,' Anna replied. 'There's a little family in Scarsdale who've worked their guts out over the last few years to establish their own business, and who've now put most of everything they've ever earned into *Sometime . . . Never*. And then there's Daniel. He's given up his job, his home, his relationship with his father, and tied himself up in a debt which will take a lifetime to clear if the play goes wrong. He's done it all because he has faith in you and your talent. If you go on stage tonight and make a fool of yourself, it won't be Gerald Kingdom I'll cry for. I'll be crying for all the people, including myself, who've believed in you . . . wrongly.'

'You know, Anna, the way in which you delivered that speech, makes me seriously wonder whether you shouldn't consider becoming an actress.' Gerald's voice was cool, entirely without any sort of emotion. It was quite impossible to tell what he was thinking. Their eyes met. 'OK,' he said, 'I've listened, darling. Now would you please bugger off and let me have some sleep. Might I also suggest that you do the same yourself – you look bloody awful.'

'So would you, if you'd spent most of last night traipsing round the bars of Broadway.'

'If you remember, darling, I did.' They continued to stare at one another, and, miraculously, from nowhere, twin smiles suddenly lit their faces. 'I'll see you on stage then, darling,' Gerald said.

'No, you'll see me before that – at six thirty, with your whisky, as usual.'

Gerald inclined his head. 'I shall look forward to it.'

Daniel, it seemed, was the only person who remained in his seat. He sat, in shocked amazement, as the audience literally exploded around him. This was New York, he had to tell himself – hardbitten, sophisticated, cynical New York. The audience were shouting, laughing, clapping, crying, demanding to see Gerald and Anna back on stage, again and again. Daniel looked behind him up at the circle. There, too, everyone was standing, applauding without any restraint. It was the kind of reaction no critic could ignore.

Daniel turned round and slumped back into his seat. It had worked, despite everything, *it had worked*. He put his hand up to his face and felt the unfamiliar wetness of his own tears. The curtain lifted to reveal Gerald and Anna once more. Suddenly, Daniel was on his feet, shouting and clapping with the rest.

Anna wiped the last traces of tear-stained make-up from her face. She was more exhilarated, more excited than she'd ever been in her life. It had all been worth it. It seemed to her, at that moment, that everything that had happened to her to date had been a preparation for the moment when the audience had gone wild. She couldn't wait to find Daniel, to be in his arms again, to see the expression on his face.

There was a knock on the door and Amy waddled in to collect her dress.

'Well, child, how do you feel?'

Anna turned, her face flushed with excitement, 'Oh I don't know, Amy – thrilled, relieved – I can't find the words. Wasn't Gerald marvellous, wasn't the audience wonderful – I just couldn't believe it when . . .'

'Hush, child, you'll go off bang in a moment. I'll tell you this though, I've never seen nothing like it, not in all the years I've worked in the theatre.'

'Is that really true?'

'Upon my word, it's true, child. Now give your old Amy a kiss, and then you try and calm down some.'

A few moments after Amy had left, there was another knock, and Ralph popped his head round the door. 'Anna, darling!' They embraced, words quite unnecessary, tears in their eyes. 'Apart from having a sneaky cuddle,' he said, 'I am here for a reason. Two messages – the first-night party is at Sardi's and Dan said to come front of house as soon as you're ready. He said to tell you he'll drive you and Gerald round there in a cab – apparently there's a mob at the stage door. Also, there's a woman to see you, sweetheart. She says it's very important.'

'Who is she?'

'I don't know,' said Ralph, 'but she said it would only take a couple of minutes.'

'OK,' said Anna, 'tell her to come in.'

The woman who stepped, hesitantly, through her dressing-room door was instantly familiar, though Anna could not recall ever having met her before. In her youth, she must have been quite a beauty, and even now, in middle-age, though her looks had faded, she was still striking. She had bright red hair, obviously dyed, but her ginger eyebrows and big hazel eyes suggested she had been a natural redhead. She was tall and slender – well, but cheaply, dressed, and there was an air about her of having seen better times. She stared at Anna. 'Anna Wetherby.' Her voice was deep, with a trace of an American accent. It was a statement rather than a question.

'Yes,' said Anna, with a sudden, unaccountable prick of unease, 'yes, that's right. Who are you?'

The woman hesitated for a split second. 'I'm your mother, Anna,' she replied.

Chapter Twenty

The silence seemed to crackle backwards and forwards between the two women.

'I . . . is this some sort of joke?' Although she asked the question, Anna already knew the answer.

'No, it's not a joke, and before you ask, I'm not here to make trouble, nor do I want anything. I've probably done the wrong thing coming at all, but it was that television interview, you see.'

Anna leaned against the dressing table for support. She stared at the woman, looking for . . . she knew not what. Recognition, memory, something she could hold on to – there was a degree of familiarity, but why?

'The television interview?' Anna said faintly.

'Yes,' said the woman. 'Reading between the lines, you sounded uncertain, unsure as to whether you were doing the right thing, becoming an actress. Obviously, your . . . your parents haven't been very supportive – am I right?' Anna nodded. She seemed to be quite incapable of speech now. 'I just wanted to reassure you, to tell you you were doing the right thing. It's in your blood, you see. My father and mother, your grandparents, they were both on the boards – their parents were too. None of them, though, were ever in the big time, but *you* can be, Anna, you have the education. You're bright and you've got real talent. I saw that for myself this evening. You're the one who's going to make it. Don't deny your blood, Anna, don't turn your back on your talent.'

'But . . . but how do you know you're my mother?' Anna's voice was barely more than a whisper.

A ghost of a smile crossed the woman's face. 'I had a baby,

twenty-two years ago, in Torquay. She was born on 24th May. I couldn't keep her – I was only nineteen, with no husband and just starting out on my career. I was told that she could be offered for adoption to a couple from Oxford. He was a professor, I think. I asked that the child be named Anna – it was my mother's name, and they took her away from me within hours of her birth. I have the details right, don't I, but there's something else too. Come and look, Anna.'

Dazed, Anna straightened up, and shakily turned to stand beside the woman. Together they stared into the make-up mirror.

'As well as being younger, you're better looking than me, but look at our eyes. Yours are darker, but look at their shape . . . and our noses. Look at the way our hair grows, we both have widow's peaks, and look . . .'

'Stop,' said Anna, 'stop.' She turned away from the mirror and holding her head in her hands, she began to sob uncontrollably.

'I'm sorry,' the woman said. 'I'm sorry, this must be a terrible shock. Seeing you on television was a shock for me, too, but I've had a few days to get used to it.'

'I don't . . . I don't even know your name.'

'Georgina, Georgina Duncan.' Anna looked up, tears still streaming down her face. Even the name seemed familiar. Georgina immediately understood. 'You recognise the name, not because I'm your mother, but because I had quite a lot of early success in British films. It would have been around the time you first started going to the cinema. I use to think about that and wonder if you ever saw my movies.'

'Are . . . are you still an actress?' Anna asked.

Georgina shook her head. 'No. I got an offer to go to Hollywood and I did make a couple of movies, but after that the studio dropped me. Then I married, disastrously as it turned out. When my marriage was over, I tried to get back into the business, but I hadn't the contacts any more. I live and work in San Francisco still, but I'm what you'd call a hostess.'

'A hostess!' said Anna.

'No, I'm not a hooker.' Georgina's face was suddenly alive

227

with amusement. 'San Francisco has a stack of tourists. I take parties round the place, show them the sights. It's well paid, sufficiently well paid that I can afford a holiday now and again, which is why I'm in New York right now, visiting friends. Look, can I sit down for a moment or am I keeping you?'

'No, no, I'm sorry,' said Anna, regaining some of her composure, 'and I'm sorry to have made such a fool of myself just now. Would you . . . would you like a drink?'

'I think perhaps we'd better, don't you?'

'I only have wine,' said Anna. 'Will that do?'

'Fine.'

With a trembling hand, Anna poured two glasses of wine and handed one to her mother. 'There must be an appropriate toast,' she said.

'Let's just drink to your future, Anna.'

Anna sipped the wine. As she began to calm down, a million questions seemed to spring to her mind. 'Did you . . . did you have any other children?'

Georgina Duncan shook her head. 'No. I'm not really a very maternal sort of person, I haven't the staying power.' She grinned, 'One of the few advantages of getting older is one sees oneself so much more clearly. All my life I've flitted from one thing to the other. It's why my marriage didn't last. For some reason heavy relationships never work for me. Hey, tell me about your mother and father, Anna. Have you been happy?'

'Yes, they're very good, kind people. Ironically, just before leaving to come out to the States, I felt a lot closer to them, closer than I've felt in a long time. You see, when I was a teenager, I tried to find you and that hurt them very much.'

Georgina's eyes grew wide with shock. 'You tried to find *me*?'

Anna nodded, tears coming into her eyes again. 'Apparently it's a fairly normal teenage phenomenon among the adopted – the need to find out one's real roots. I got as far as Torquay and then a social worker talked me out of looking any further. She said you'd probably have a new family.'

'Were you very upset?'

'At the time, yes,' said Anna. 'But, worse than that, I upset my mother . . . I mean, my . . .'

228

'Your mother,' said Georgina, firmly. 'They're your parents, I was simply the vessel which brought you into the world.' She hesitated, apparently unsatisfied. 'So, despite your recent troubles, you had a happy childhood?'

'Yes, yes I did.'

'And what made you decide to become an actress?'

'As you say, I think it must be in the blood. I decided it was what I wanted to do, and then, when I found out that you were one too, it sort of clinched the matter.' Anna hesitated. She looked down at her hands which she was twisting nervously. 'About . . . about my father.'

'Yes, I wondered how long it would be before you asked me that. He's an actor too, Anna, British and quite a lot older than me. At the time he was engaged to someone else. It wasn't his fault it happened, poor lamb. I was a terrible flighty piece and he just didn't know what had hit him. We were on tour together. It's ironic, really, but Gerald Kingdom was starring in the play at the time.'

Anna started, momentarily appalled. 'You're not saying that Gerald Kingdom is my father?' She felt sickness rising in the pit of her stomach, a roaring in her ears.

'No, of course not. We all adored Gerald, naturally. He's an attractive man now, but then . . . he was really something. No, your father was never a star, though he's always been in work. You may have heard of him – his name is Richard Manning.'

Anna gave an involuntary gasp. 'Richard Manning! Oh no, Richard Manning, are you sure?' Again, there was the sensation of already knowing the answer.

Georgina looked startled. 'I may have been a bit of a rover, but not so much that I'd have not known a thing like that. Anna, are you saying you know Richard?'

'He – he played the butler in *Sometime . . . Never* when we were in the West End. I knew him . . . know him, very well indeed.'

'Oh my dear, I've gone too far, haven't I? I should never have told you so much. I should never have come here at all.'

'No, no,' said Anna, 'you have done the right thing – it's just all such a shock.'

229

'Do you like Richard?' Georgina asked gently, after a moment.

'Yes, yes, very much. He was very kind to me.'

'He is a kind man,' Georgina agreed. 'He was mortified when he found out I was pregnant. He tried to persuade me to marry him, but I couldn't let him do that. He was engaged to a very nice girl. I can't remember her name now, but they were dead right for one another.'

'Margaret, was it Margaret?'

'Yes, I think so.'

'He's still married to her,' Anna said.

'There you are, you see! Anyway, he looked after me really well. I don't know how he managed financially, but as soon as you were born, he sent me off on a holiday. We kept in touch for a year or two and then I went out to the States and that was that.'

Anna sat in silence. Richard – her father, the words kept going round and round in her head. Georgina was still talking and she had to concentrate hard in order not to lose the thread. '. . . Yes, it upset him dreadfully, our having to give away the child,' Georgina smiled, 'and it would never have happened but for the Yorkshire winter.'

'How do you mean?' Anna asked.

'It's to that you owe your existence, Anna. Have you ever played in Leeds?' Anna nodded. 'That theatre, those digs!'

Anna smiled through her tears. 'I know what you mean,' she admitted.

'The beds were so cold and damp – you went to bed cold, you woke up cold, but with two in the bed . . .' Georgina winked, tossed back her drink and stood up. 'I'm going now, Anna.'

'Going, but when can I see you again?'

'Never.'

Panic gripped Anna. '*Never*, what do you mean never? We've only just met.' She was on her feet too, trembling, her face ashen.

'Look, Anna, when you've had a chance to calm down, you'll know I'm right. There's no place for me in your life, or for you in mine.'

230

'You gave me my life.' Anna cried out the words, her voice desperate, urgent.

'But that's all I did give you, love. You know where you come from now, you know that the pursuit of your career isn't just a whim. You owe it to yourself and your parents to stick with the family you've got. Raise the odd glass to me now and again, by all means, but leave it at that, OK?'

'But can't I at least have your address?'

Georgina shook her head. 'There'd be no point. It would confuse you, confuse us both.'

'But what other family have you?' Anna asked. 'What happens if you're ill, and when you get old? Who'll look after you?'

For the first time, Georgina seemed visibly moved. 'Anna, I abandoned you when you were a few hours old. Why the hell should you worry about what happens to me?'

'I don't know,' Anna replied simply.

Georgina smiled. 'I can see now what you've inherited from Richard. Look, I'll make you a promise, if it will help you feel better. If I am ever in trouble, I'll call you.'

'But you may not know where I am,' Anna said, desperately.

'Yes, I will. This play will put you on the road to success – we both know that. I expect I'll only have to open the pages of my newspaper to find out where you are. But even if you don't hit the big time, you're a member of the Union, aren't you? They'll always put me in touch with you.' She smiled. 'Just keep paying your subs.'

'Oh, I will,' said Anna fervently, 'I will.'

Georgina stood awkwardly by the door, 'Well, goodbye then, Anna.'

Suddenly they were in each other's arms, and for the first and only time in her life, Georgina Duncan hugged her daughter. 'I must go,' she said, her voice hoarse. 'I'm sorry, Anna. I'm sorry we never knew each other, but I did the right thing, I'm *sure* I did, and . . . I'm very proud of you.' Without another word, she was gone, running down the corridor and out into the street.

The air was cold and crisp. Georgina squared her shoulders

and began to walk fast, away from the theatre, away from her daughter. Unbidden, the memory came into her mind of that other time when, still weak from the birth, she'd taken one last look in the nursery and then walked down the corridor, out of the hospital, and out of Anna's life for ever. She had been right – looking at Anna now, she knew she'd been right. So then, why the terrible ache in her heart, and why did she have this feeling that she kept denying the one aspect of her life that held any real meaning?

Several passers-by noticed the tall, striking woman, striding purposefully along the sidewalk. Her good looks, her positive step stood out in stark contrast to the tears rolling down her face.

Daniel found Anna a few moment later, standing in the spot where her mother had left her, staring into space. 'Anna, darling, what is it?'

Anna looked up at him as though he was a stranger. 'Daniel, could you find Gerald for me and ask him to come here right away.'

'Why, what do you want him for?'

'Don't ask questions, Daniel, just do it.'

Anna's obvious irritation quickly fired Daniel's own. 'There's no need to speak like that – Jesus, Anna, what's wrong with you? We made it – this is our moment of triumph – hey, come here.' He made a move to take her in his arms, but she shrank away from him.

'*Please*, Daniel, just get Gerald.'

'Oh, so that's the way things are, is it?' he said.

'Daniel, *please*, I can't explain now. I just can't.'

She'd been crying, he could see that. Her face was very pale and there was an odd expression in her eyes he couldn't identify. 'OK, I'll fetch him, but perhaps when you've finished with him, you might be good enough to spare me a few minutes, if it's not too much trouble.' His voice was bitter, his eyes hurt and bewildered, but Anna saw none of it. As soon as Daniel had left her, she sat down on the chair to wait for Gerald, and found herself giving way to tears again.

It was how Gerald found her a few moments later. 'Darling Anna,' he said, 'what on earth is it? You're in an awful state.

What's happened to my gorgeous girl – you look like a little drowned rat?'

'Oh Gerald, Gerald.' Anna stood up, threw herself into his arms and began sobbing uncontrollably.

He had the sense just to hold her, to let her cry, and when the sobs had begun to ease, he led her gently to the bed and made her lie down on it. Then he sat beside her, holding her hand. 'You've made my jacket very wet and uncomfortable, darling, so I'm going to need to know the full story of what's making you so unhappy, or I'll be forced to be angry – very angry indeed.'

'Do you . . . do you remember being in a play in Leeds, about twenty-three years ago?'

'Good heavens,' said Gerald, 'that's rather a tall order. I have difficulty enough remembering what happened last week, never mind twenty-three years ago. As for Leeds, I have a tendency to obliterate it from my mind, wherever possible.'

'Gerald, this is serious,' said Anna.

'I'm sorry, darling, I can see it is. Tell me a little more.'

'I don't know what play it was, but Richard Manning was in it and a girl . . . a girl called Georgina Duncan.'

'Ah,' said Gerald, 'you're talking about Richard's great indiscretion.'

'Go on,' said Anna.

'Well, I'm not sure I should. Richard and Margaret are friends.'

'I *do* know about it,' Anna said, 'I just want to hear you tell it.'

'We were playing in *Charley's Aunt*, Richard and I,' Gerald began. 'He was engaged to Margaret then, but she worked in London. In those impecunious days, there was no way Richard could afford anything as exotic as the train fare to see her. What spare cash he had I think went in the purchase of suitably large quantities of Newcastle Brown. My career was starting to take off. I'd made a couple of films which had been well received and my agent was busy negotiating my transfer to Hollywood. Towards the end of the run I was away a lot and without a drinking companion, Richard started to chum up with our co-star.'

'Georgina Duncan,' Anna said.

'That's right. She was a nice kid, but a bit fast and loose, and poor Richard was such an innocent.' Gerald smiled. 'Anyway he got the girl pregnant. She came from Devon somewhere I think.'

'Torquay,' Anna prompted.

Gerald looked at her curiously. 'Yes, that's right. She had the baby, but she couldn't keep it, of course. For a while Richard tried desperately to persuade her to marry him, but it was crazy – they were quite unsuited. In the end, he paid for her to take a holiday after the baby was born, and then they went their separate ways. Actually, I lent him the money to give her a really good break and, of course, being Richard, he was meticulous about paying me back every penny. It took him years, poor old thing.'

'You paid for the holiday!' Anna began to laugh. It was a dangerous laugh, close to hysteria.

'Yes, I did. Why, what's so funny?'

Anna sobered abruptly. 'I was that baby, Gerald.'

'You!' Gerald stared at her. 'Are you sure?'

'Quite sure,' said Anna. 'Georgina Duncan left here about ten minutes ago. She told me everything – only I feel so confused, and since you were there at the time, I . . . I felt, I needed . . . you, Gerald.'

'Poor little Anna.' Gerald slipped his arms round her and kissed her gently on the lips. Then he laid her back on the pillows, pushing the curls away from her face. 'Of course, I can see it now. You're very like her, only better looking.' He smiled. 'I can't see any likeness to old Richard though, except perhaps your grim determination to keep me off the whisky.' Gerald was suddenly serious. 'What about Richard? Are you going to tell him?'

'No, never,' said Anna vehemently. 'I'll keep in touch with him, always. Funnily enough, I was going to write to him tomorrow anyway and send him the reviews. He . . . he's always felt somehow like a special friend to me, even before this, but I'll never tell him, never tell him who I am. It wouldn't be fair to him or Margaret.'

'You're amazing,' Gerald said softly. 'Are you sure you're strong enough to handle it?'

Anna nodded. 'Yes, I think so.'

Gerald sat up and felt in his jacket pocket. 'I have something for you here. I was going to give it to you tonight at the party, but I think you could do with a diversion now.'

Anna sat up in bed and took the little velvet box Gerald handed her. She opened it and gasped out loud with pleasure. The box contained a gold chain and on it hung a beautifully carved black swan. The swan itself was made from jet, its laconic eyes were two tiny seed pearls.

'Oh Gerald, it's beautiful.' Anna looked up at him. 'Thank you. Oh thank you, I shall wear it always.'

'Will you?' asked Gerald. 'Will you, really?'

'Yes, I promise. Put it on for me, will you?'

With hands trembling slightly, Gerald took the chain from its box and hung it round Anna's neck. He wanted to leave his hands on her shoulders, to run them down her bare skin, but he knew that that was something he would never do again. Instead, he kissed her once more and pushed her gently, unprotesting, back onto the pillows. 'Lie there, just for ten minutes, darling,' he said.

'But the party . . .' Anna began.

'I'll go and make our excuses and explain to Daniel that we'll be a little late. Then I'll come back and collect you. Don't rush, there's no hurry. Try and sleep. It's always a good thing after a shock.'

Obediently, Anna shut her eyes. Gerald walked across the room, and then glanced back. She lay very still on the pillows, the black swan resting in the soft hollow of her neck. For a split second, Gerald hesitated. Then, resolutely, he turned away and walked out of the door.

Daniel sat hunched over his whisky at a table some distance from the rest of the company. At Sardi's – the traditional restaurant for first-night parties – the celebrations would go on until the early editions of the newspapers were delivered, and the fate of the play would be sealed, one way or the other.

'Dan?' Daniel looked up to see Matilda standing in front of him. 'What is it?' she said. 'What's wrong?'

'Nothing's wrong, Mattie. Go and join the party.'

'I don't understand it. Are you nervous about the critics?' Daniel shook his head. 'Well what's eating you then? The

235

play's a wow, you know it is. We've got one of the biggest smash hits in the history of Broadway. You have your own business now, cash in the bank . . .'

'Just leave it, would you Mattie, please.' Hurt, Matilda turned away. 'Hey, I'm sorry, I'm a louse,' he called after her. She waved and smiled at him. There, at least, was one woman he understood, Daniel thought morosely.

Everything Mattie had said was true. He'd done it, but his victory was a hollow one – for he knew now, if he had not known it before, that whatever happened in his life, it would be incomplete unless he could share it with Anna. He sighed and took another gulp of his drink. Of all the women he'd known, why in God's name had he fallen for the one who didn't seem to want him. What had upset her at this very moment of triumph, and why was it Gerald she wanted? Damn and blast all women.

'Mr Chase?'

Daniel looked up to see a waiter hovering over him. 'Yeah, what is it?'

'This message was left for you a few minutes ago.'

Daniel picked up the plain white envelope on which was inscribed his name. He recognised the writing instantly and tore open the envelope – 'Well done, son, I knew you had it in you – Walter B Chase' – it read.

Daniel stared at the simple message. So far as he could remember, it was the first time his father had ever called him *son*.

He was still sitting, staring at the note, when Gerald found him a few moments later. 'Daniel.'

Daniel stood up. 'How is she?' He couldn't disguise the hostility in his voice.

'She'll be all right,' said Gerald, 'but only if you follow my advice, precisely.'

'Look, Gerald, I really don't need you telling me how to handle Anna. You're a great actor but . . .'

'Shut up,' said Gerald, 'and listen. She's resting in her dressing room at the moment and she's in a state of shock. Make a call and book a sumptuous suite in the best hotel you can find. Then get a cab, collect her and take her straight

236

there. Pour a bottle of champagne down her and then make love to her all night. If she tries to talk, tries to explain, shut her up and make love to her again. Tomorrow morning she'll tell you all about it. Then, take her out to lunch and ask her to marry you, and you'll find she'll say yes.' Daniel was too surprised to speak. Gerald's piercing blue eyes sparkled dangerously. 'God damn it man, will you do it, because I tell you this – if you don't, I bloody well will.'

The pain in his eyes, the emotion in his voice left Daniel in no doubt that Gerald meant what he said, and it galvanised him into action. 'Yes, sir, I'm on my way.'

Gerald watched him go in an agony of spirit, unaware that he'd just performed the first truly unselfish action of his life.

Chapter Twenty-One

In Oxford, Stephen Wetherby stretched, yawned and looked at his watch. 'It's nearly six, dear. Fancy a sherry?'

May glanced up from the book she was reading, squinting at her husband over the top of her glasses. 'Yes, I would, thanks.'

Stephen walked over to the decanter and poured two glasses. He liked this time of the day best – the curtains drawn, the fire crackling in the grate, he and May reading or working, content and relaxed in each other's company. 'Have you read the letter from Anna yet?' he asked, handing May her glass.

'Yes, yes I have.'

'How do you think she sounded?'

'A little fraught, but otherwise all right. What did you think?'

Stephen took up his favourite position, standing in front of the fire, leaning against the fender. 'Well, this change of producer quite clearly has been very disruptive, but as she said, the good thing that has come out of it is that they now have Martin Peters to direct them again. I must say, I liked that young man. You know, May . . .' Stephen glanced quickly at his wife, 'I have a feeling that this really is going to be the breakthrough for Anna. I know you've always been against her becoming an actress – I know you thought it was a decision aimed to spite you, but you know, I believe she's done the right thing. I really do.'

May set down her book. 'I know you do, and I think you're probably right.'

'You do?' Stephen was surprised by her ready acceptance.

'Yes. I've thought a lot about Anna since she went away, and I just wish I'd been more supportive earlier on in her career.'

'Do you have regrets?' Stephen asked. 'I don't mean regrets about not being supportive with the stage career but about the whole question of adoption? She's caused you a lot of heartache one way and another. Do you sometimes wish we'd never done it?'

'Never for a moment,' May said firmly. 'I do have regrets though. I wish I'd spent more time with her during her childhood and I wish I'd handled the subject of her adoption better.'

Stephen smiled. 'You know, my dear, you're sounding like every caring parent since the beginning of time – never satisfied with the job they've done. You and I have made some mistakes – of course we have – but I think she's had a better start in life with us than she would have done without us.'

'Do you really think so?' May asked anxiously.

'I'm sure of it.'

'I . . . I do love her, you know, Stephen. I just find it so difficult . . .'

Stephen smiled. 'I know,' he said, 'you don't have to explain.'

'Not to you, but perhaps to her.'

'She understands,' said Stephen. 'Now, stop getting morbid. Have you started supper?'

'Heavens! No, I haven't.' May jumped to her feet.

'Well, don't. Let's go and have supper at Browns – it's still early, they should have a table. We'll take our diaries with us and, over the meal, we'll work out when we can take a few days off. We're going to America, my dear, to see that daughter of ours take Broadway by storm.'

In London, Richard Manning stepped through the stage door. He sighed and looked ruefully at the sky. It was dark, cold, and just starting to spit with rain. He had spent all day in rehearsal. He was exhausted, and the prospect of a long tube journey home was far from attractive.

'Ooooh, it's Mr Manning. Can I have your autograph, please?'

Richard stared at the figure looming out of the darkness.

'Margaret,' he said, with a laugh. 'What on earth are you doing here?'

She slipped her arm through his. 'It's a horrid evening and you've been working so hard, I thought I'd come and fetch you in the car.'

'That was kind of you, thank you,' Richard said, kissing her cheek.

'Actually,' said Margaret, as they walked along, 'I have an ulterior motive.'

'Oh dear,' said Richard.

'It's not very dreadful, darling, I promise,' said Margaret. 'It's just that I thought, on the way home, we might stop off somewhere and have some dinner.'

'That's a lovely idea.'

'Well, I know our wedding anniversary is tomorrow, and it is kind of the boys to have arranged a party for us, but somehow I felt it would be nice to celebrate it quietly on our own, as well. Is that awful of me?'

'What a wise and wonderful woman you are,' said Richard. 'How about Magnos? We can walk from here.'

'Done,' said Margaret.

'Twenty-two years!' Richard shook his head in disbelief.

'Have you been happy?' Margaret asked.

'You know I have,' he said, squeezing her arm.

In San Francisco, Georgina Duncan stepped into the airport terminal, still blinking from the sudden impact of the Californian sun. She looked around her and then hurried straight to a bookstall. She bought a paper and, dropping her luggage there in the middle of the busy terminal, she began thumbing through the pages until she came to the arts column. 'The Smash Hit of the Decade', it read, 'Gerald Kingdom's triumphant return to Broadway'. Her eyes zipped down the column – 'Anna Wetherby, a force to be reckoned with; Anna Wetherby, a startling new talent from the UK; Anna Wetherby, a match even for Kingdom's mighty talent'. Georgina smiled, a smile of pure maternal pleasure and pride. She'd go out right now and buy a scrap book for all Anna's cuttings. OK, maybe she was trying to realise her own lost ambitions through her daughter – so what? She knew that following every detail of Anna's career was going to be one of the greatest pleasures of her life.

In the apartment on United Nations Plaza, New York City, Gerald and Marcus sat by the window drinking champagne. All round them were spread the morning newspapers.

'With reviews like these, dear boy, *Sometime . . . Never* can run for ever, if you so wish.'

'Yes,' Gerald agreed, 'but I don't want to stay in it for more than six, perhaps eight months at the most. It would be good for Anna to stick with the play that long. It would demonstrate she's got some staying power. She shouldn't remain any longer though, and of course a lot depends on what offers come her way in the meantime.'

'Why is that relevant?' Marcus asked.

'I couldn't stay in the play if there was anyone else in Sarah's role,' Gerald replied dismissively.

Marcus glanced at his friend, and from the expression on his face, decided not to pursue the matter.

'Anyway,' said Gerald, after a pause, 'now young Chase can afford to pay us, I'd better find myself an apartment and let you have some peace.'

'Do you really want to?' Marcus asked. 'There's plenty of room here and you're very welcome to stay.'

Gerald looked up at him for a moment. 'That's awfully decent of you, dear boy but, reluctantly, I'll have to decline your kind offer.'

Marcus was intrigued. 'But why? It doesn't make any sense having a place of your own, particularly if you're only going to be in New York for a few months.'

Gerald smiled. 'Bless you, Marcus, but I don't think there's enough Gentleman's Relish in New York to pay my rent for so long.'

Marcus stared at him, shrewdly, for a moment. 'I could, of course, take your reluctance as a personal insult, but actually I don't think it has anything to do with me, does it? You're plotting something, Gerald. Is it by any chance connected with the delectable Miss Wetherby – I assume she'll be moving out now, will she?'

'Oh, yes, she'll be moving out.' Gerald hesitated. 'She's going to marry Daniel Chase.'

'Good Lord, is she? When did they announce that?'

'They haven't yet,' said Gerald, 'but they will.'

Again, Marcus felt instinctively he was treading on dangerous ground, and hurriedly backed off. 'Well, if it's not anything to do with Anna, what *is* it all about?'

'Marcus, you're turning into a real old woman by demonstrating this insatiable desire to meddle,' Gerald said irritably. 'If you must know, and it appears you must, I'm hoping someone will be coming to stay with me for a few weeks, or even a month or two perhaps, while I'm here in New York – certainly one person, if not two.'

'I'm hopelessly hooked now,' said Marcus. 'You'll simply have to tell me more. Who are these mysterious guests?'

'My daughters,' Gerald said, quietly.

'Good heavens! I'd forgotten all about them.'

'So had I,' said Gerald. He took a sip of champagne. 'As a matter of fact, I telephoned them last night.' He studied his glass, carefully avoiding Marcus's eye. 'It occurred to me that I had been somewhat remiss, being out of touch for so long.' He shrugged his shoulders and sighed. 'Anyway, I suggested they might like to come to New York and stay with me for a while. Thanks to *Sometime . . . Never*, I can at least afford to pay their air fare.'

'How did they react?' Marcus asked.

'They were shocked, naturally. I spoke to Juliet, the elder one, mostly. Actually, once she was over her surprise, we got on rather well. She sounded fun. I think she'll definitely come and, hopefully, bring her sister as well. I'm certainly not prepared to go to Australia – I just couldn't stand the thought of seeing their mother again.'

'How old are they now?' Marcus asked.

Gerald considered the question. 'Fifteen, sixteen, something like that.'

'And what brought this on?' Marcus asked. 'Why suddenly telephone them out of the blue like that?'

Gerald shrugged his shoulders. 'The male of the species is always so anxious to create in his own image – hence this obsession men have for siring sons. But, you know, I think perhaps daughters need their fathers just as much, if not more so. Don't get me wrong, I'm not trying to interfere with their lives. I just suddenly thought they'd reached an age where it might be helpful if I let them know I was around, let them know they could come to me if ever they needed anything.'

'I'm still a little mystified but I think it's a perfectly splendid notion,' said Marcus generously, 'and if I may, I would very much like to extend my invitation to include not only you, but your two young fillies, should they deign to set foot on American soil.'

Gerald looked at Marcus and frowned. 'Are you sure?'

'Of course I'm sure, dear boy. They'd be far better off here than in an hotel. Hotels are so restricting, and expensive too.'

'It's very good of you, Marcus.'

'My pleasure, and I'll go so far as to say you needn't even bother about the Gentleman's Relish. This fetish you have for showering me with young girls is quite delightful, and infinitely preferable. That's settled then?'

'Splendid,' said Gerald. 'Now tell me candidly, Marcus, do you think another bottle of champagne will impair my performance this evening?'

'Certainly not,' Marcus replied, 'provided I drink the larger half.'

In a suite in the St Regis Hotel, 5th Avenue, Anna lay in Daniel's arms. It was eleven o'clock in the morning and she'd just finished telling him the story of her birth.

'So how do you feel about it now, darling?' Daniel asked.

'Well, that's the odd thing,' said Anna. 'I feel good about it. I feel sad that I'm not going to see my mother again, but I respect her decision, and it's great to know where I come from. I've always felt sort of incomplete, up until now. Does any of that make sense to you?'

'It certainly does. I understand how you feel about Richard too, but are you going to tell your parents what happened?'

'I don't know,' said Anna.

'I think you probably should,' Daniel said. 'I guess they'd

find it reassuring, too. Hey, come here. All this talking means I haven't kissed you for at least twenty minutes.'

The diversion lasted some time.

'What time is it?' Anna asked lazily, a while later.

'Just after twelve.'

'Heavens, it's nearly lunchtime!' she said, appalled.

'And do you realise we don't even know what the critics said about *Sometime . . . Never?*'

Anna sat up. 'Oh my God, Daniel, how could we have forgotten that, how *could* we?'

'I guess it might have something to do with being in love,' Daniel suggested. 'I'll put a call in to Martin now. He'll tell us the verdict and then we'll collect some papers on our way out to lunch. Why don't you take first crack at the bathroom?'

Just over an hour later, Daniel ushered Anna through the doors of the Tavern on the Green in Central Park. 'We'd better watch out – you might be mobbed by adoring fans,' he said, grinning.

She turned and smiled at him. Her eyes had a soft dreamy quality about them as they gazed into his. Their night together had changed her again, softened her.

They ordered lunch and chattered happily enough. Anna, Daniel observed, seemed quite relaxed, whilst he was becoming increasingly nervous. Supposing she said no – but surely, after the night they'd spent together she loved him enough. He picked at his food while Anna talked excitedly about the reviews, about the famous people she could spot in the restaurant, about how long the run would be, about how much money Daniel would make . . .

Finally, over their desert, his mood got through to her. 'Daniel, is something wrong?' She was tucking into a plate of damsons and ice-cream, while Daniel made a lame attempt to do justice to the cheeseboard.

'Yes,' said Daniel.

'What is it?' Anna's voice faltered, her eyes suddenly wide with apprehension.

'I'm trying to get up the courage to ask you to marry me and I'm as nervous as a kitten.' They stared at one another.

'Was that it?' Anna asked, with a trace of a smile.

244

'It?'

'The proposal.'

Daniel grimaced. 'I guess it was. Darling,' he leaned across the table and took her hand, 'last night, when I thought you wanted Gerald instead of me, I realised that my life was meaningless without you. There would be no point to anything. But together, *together* Anna, we can build a future – a future for us and maybe, one day, our children. We can do anything, everything. I know it sounds corny, but I want it so much . . .'

'It doesn't sound corny,' Anna interrupted, her eyes suddenly bright with unshed tears.

'I haven't much to offer you,' said Daniel. 'I haven't a secure job any more. *Sometime . . . Never* is a success, but my next production might fail. I guess we'll both have to work hard for a while, and our apartment will have to be pretty modest, nothing fancy like the one I had.'

'Those things don't interest me,' said Anna. 'What matters are things like love and trust.'

Daniel nodded, and squeezed her hand. 'You have my love, all my love, always. Hell, I know I'm asking a lot, Anna, but for the time being at any rate, I guess we'd need to live in the States.' He shrugged his shoulders. 'Mind you, who knows where we might end up? I love England and, if you're homesick, we can always make our life there.'

'Do you trust me now?' Anna asked suddenly. 'I mean with regard to Gerald?' Daniel nodded. 'Are you sure?'

'Yes,' said Daniel, 'quite sure.' He wasn't ready to tell her what Gerald had said the previous evening. Perhaps he never would.

Anna smiled. 'And what about you? You're used to having an actress in every port. Isn't coming home to the same woman every night going to be boring?'

'It's what I've wanted all my life,' said Daniel, 'only I didn't know it until I met you.'

'I'm a little frightened,' said Anna.

'So am I,' said Daniel, 'but we can make it. Say yes, Anna.'

She looked into his anxious face and saw all the love there she would ever need. She stretched out her hand and took his again. 'Yes, please.'

'You mean it? Oh darling, you mean it?' Anna nodded. 'So when?' The urge now to make her his wife overshadowed everything. 'When, darling? How soon?'

Anna glanced down at her empty place. Slowly, deliberately, she picked up her fork and began counting the damson stones . . . 'This year, next year, sometime, never, this year, next year, sometime, never, this year . . .' She looked up. 'This year?'

Daniel grinned, 'Would you consider the Sunday after next to be indecent haste?'

'Unquestionably,' said Anna, 'but then decency isn't one of our strong points, is it?'

'Jesus,' said Daniel, 'thank Christ you had the right number of damson stones.'

Anna smiled at him, her eyes full of love. One day she'd tell him she'd had to swallow two to make it come out right.